THE RADCLIFFES

JAMES PATTERSON
PRESENTS....

THE
RADCLIFFES

THREE ROMANCES BY

T.J. Kline

GRAND CENTRAL
PUBLISHING

NEW YORK   BOSTON

Copyright © 2017 JBP Business, LLC

Grand Central Publishing
Hachette Book Group
1290 Avenue of the Americas, New York, NY 10104
grandcentralpublishing.com
twitter.com/grandcentralpub

First Mass Market Edition: October 2017

Grand Central Publishing is a division of Hachette Book Group, Inc. The Grand Central Publishing name and logo are trademarks of Hachette Book Group, Inc.

The publisher is not responsible for websites (or their content) that are not owned by the publisher.

The Hachette Speakers Bureau provides a wide range of authors for speaking events. To find out more, go to www.hachettespeakersbureau.com or call (866) 376-6591.

ISBN 978-1-538-71140-8

Printed in the United States of America

OPM

10 9 8 7 6 5 4 3 2 1

Dear Reader,

There's nothing more heartbreaking than being in love with someone you can't have—especially when that person wants to love you back. In this book, you'll find three of those love stories, where the characters would give anything to be together, even though the world keeps getting in their way.

Welcome to the world of the Radcliffes, San Francisco's most elite family. Their name has been synonymous with old money ever since they made a killing during the boom of the shipping industry. You'll understand their pedigree the moment you read about their mansion on the cliffs and their interactions with their staff.

But Gabe, Fallon, and Alexandra don't always keep a proper distance from the people who work for them. How can they, when they find their soul mates in such unlikely and impossible places? This is a collection of stories about challenging and breaking all the rules, all in the name of love.

I had a lot of fun reading about these characters, who weren't afraid to be bold and daring as they went after their passions. I hope that you love wrapping yourself up in their world as much as I did.

—James Patterson

CONTENTS

THE WEDDING FLORIST

Chapter 1

"THAT SON OF a bitch," Anna Nolan muttered to herself as she sat, fuming, in the standstill traffic along the
California 101. She was heading home after her boss had
humiliated her by giving *her* promotion to his unqualified
niece, cutting Anna's job in the process. "That ass could
have at least sent me home early enough to avoid this
mess."

She eyed the long line of brake lights flashing red ahead
of her, wondering why the fast lane was the only one *not*
moving. Maybe it was a metaphor for her career. How was
she going to come up with her rent now? Her landlord was
already breathing down her neck, and the warning notices
he'd tacked on her door two weeks ago made one thing
clear—there was a good chance she'd have to downsize
apartments soon.

Anna twisted to adjust the massive jewel-toned floral
centerpiece in the backseat. She'd taken it with her—okay,
stolen it—from the shop's refrigeration unit. Lifting it
straighter, she felt a small sense of satisfaction. *Her* designs
had earned her boss—ex-boss, she corrected—his high-end
clientele and, since no one else had seen this one design, she
wasn't about to let him keep it and take credit for it. Or try

to copy it, again. Not after kicking her to the curb without any warning. Technically—

She gasped as a flash of movement in the side-view mirror caught her attention. A speeding sports car cut through the creeping traffic, the sleek lines slipping between cars, coming closer and closer until she realized...it wasn't slowing. Anna let go of the flower arrangement, faced forward, and stiffened as she braced herself for impact. She gripped the steering wheel and pressed her foot on the brake even harder as the sports car smashed into the rear passenger side of her car, jolting her sideways. It pushed her old Ford onto the shoulder.

Anna took a deep breath, mentally taking inventory of her situation. Nothing felt broken. Miraculously, she hadn't rammed into the car ahead of her and the car behind her had avoided the mess. Easing her foot to the gas, she moved her vehicle away from the sports car, cringing as she heard metal scraping. Anna prayed she would at least get a glimpse of the other driver's license plate before he bolted.

Parking on the shoulder, she looked backward in time to see a tall man slip out of the sports car. She unclipped her seat belt and shoved her door open. "What the hell were you doing? Do you have any idea—"

He held up a hand, then pointed at his cell phone to indicate she should wait until he finished his conversation. "Yeah, I just sideswiped a car on the 101. Go ahead and start without me. I won't be home in time for dinner."

Anna's mouth dropped open. This man had hit her car and he couldn't even be bothered to get off his damned phone?

"Okay, I'll see you tomorrow, love." He tapped the screen and tucked the phone into the pocket of his slacks. "Hey, sorry about this. I was late and I guess I wasn't paying attention." He shrugged and gave her a nonchalant smirk, as if that would remedy the entire situation, as if it was no big deal. "Don't worry, I've already called CHP and reported it."

"Excuse me?" Even in the dying light, with the sun sinking low and reflecting off the waters of the San Francisco Bay, something about this man caused a vague sense of recognition to tug at her mind. Anna narrowed her eyes. Perfect chiseled features, penetrating hazel eyes. But she couldn't quite place him. "Don't I know you?"

He held out his hand and gave her a dashing smile, as if he'd expected this to happen. "Gabriel Radcliffe. I'm—"

Her heart plummeted to her toes as she realized she was talking to "San Francisco's Most Eligible Bachelor."

"I know who you are. Everyone in San Francisco knows who the Radcliffes are."

The man's family had more money than Midas. No wonder he acted like she was nothing more than a minor aggravation. Ignoring his outstretched hand, Anna slipped between the two vehicles to get a look at the damage he'd done to her car.

"Shit! Really?" She threw her hands up in the air. "Could this day get any worse?"

After hurrying back to the driver's side, she pulled the insurance card from her glove box. Then she turned to the backseat for the cell phone in her purse. Toppled on one side, with its array of colorful roses, carnations, and lilies crumpled and scattered, was her arrangement.

Oh, no! No, no, no! Forget the phone.

Water pooled around the side of her purse and over the pictures that had come loose from inside her portfolio—the one and only thing she had left to help her land another job since she'd told her ex-boss exactly where he could stick his letter of reference. One day, she'd learn to curb her tendency to burn bridges. Anna quickly yanked the photographs from the water. Shaking them off while droplets reflected the dying light, she prayed they weren't ruined, but didn't hold out much hope.

"Why do these things always happen to me?" she muttered to herself.

"Look, lady, why don't I just write you a check for the damages?"

Anna looked over her shoulder and saw Gabriel leaning over the dented hood of his Audi, scribbling quickly as she tried to dab the water from the pictures with the front of her T-shirt.

"What?"

"Here." He ripped a check from the register before tossing it back inside his car and walking toward her. "This should more than cover it."

She glanced down at the ruined pictures in her hands, then at the check in his. There were a lot of zeros on it.

Was that twenty thousand dollars?

The check was almost enough to buy a new car. It was certainly enough to cover the cost of the damages and the late rent she owed, with a little more to tide her over until she found another job. She eyed the man standing in front of her. His body language looked carefree, but even with his eyes partially shadowed by the sunset, the lift of his brows made it clear his patience was wearing thin.

There was no question she *should* take the money. She should call a tow truck, get her car fixed, and deem this entire disaster a blessing in disguise, but his complete disregard for her welfare and his sense of entitlement enraged her. She was tired of being overlooked and cast aside. First by her boss and now by this guy. In San Francisco, you either had to be "old money" or know someone to get ahead, and, unfortunately, she was failing on both counts.

All she wanted was to design beautiful flower arrangements, but the universe didn't seem inclined to give her a break. Every time she seemed to get ahead, to start saving to open her own shop, karma seemed to kick her in the ass and knock her back three steps.

He shook his hand slightly, the check fluttering as he encouraged her to take it, breaking her from her thoughts. Anna held the pictures against her chest with one hand and plucked the paper from between his fingers with the other, staring at his flowing script. This might not solve her problems, but it could sure go a long way toward helping with them. If she was willing to be satisfied by a temporary fix.

As much as she might be tempted, she couldn't accept it. *Damn my stubborn pride.*

"You didn't seem too worried that I could have been injured, or concerned that you might have ruined my chances at getting another job. You're probably not worried about much, are you, Mr. Radcliffe? I seriously doubt you're worried about what your insurance costs, so I can only assume that you're trying to pay me off."

"Excuse me?"

Anna's hands shook and her mind screamed at her to stop. Her fingers moved quickly as she tore the check in half, then in half again. Her hands didn't stop moving until the check had been shredded into tiny pieces.

"No, no way. You're not buying your way out of this."

Chapter 2

AS THE TORN pieces of check rained down at his feet, Gabe had no doubt his shock was apparent on his face. He'd seen a lot in his thirty-two years, both in life and business, so it took a lot to render him speechless, but this scrappy redhead had just managed it. He'd assumed that she'd be impressed once she realized who he was *and* saw the amount of the check, especially since it was likely more money than her car had cost brand-new.

The top of her ponytail barely reached his chin, but she planted her fists on slim hips and stepped up to battle him. "I'm sick and tired of people thinking they can just toss me out like last night's garbage. I'm a person, too." She stormed back to her car.

Gabe ran after her. "I didn't say—"

"You didn't have to!" She glared at him before bending over into her backseat, giving him a view of her worn jeans that were hugging some pretty dangerous curves. "You think I haven't met enough of you to know? Money doesn't make you more important."

Eyes in your head, Gabe. You're engaged, even if you don't want to be. Stay away from this one.

"Look," he said, trying to soothe her again. "I'm sorry you seem to think—"

"I don't think—"

His patience snapped. "Well, that's obvious."

She stood up and pierced him with her anger. "Do you see this mess?" She pointed at the backseat of her car.

Gabe glanced into the backseat to see multicolored flowers strewn all over, water spilling from a toppled vase onto more pictures of what appeared to be more floral arrangements.

"This is what was left of my career and you've just flushed it down the toilet." She shook her head and hit the palm of the hand that wasn't holding pictures against the top of her car. "Do you have any idea how difficult it is to survive in this city *with* a job? Now try to imagine living without one." Her gaze slid over him before she dismissed him with a scoff. "What am I thinking? *You* have no clue what it's like to want for anything, do you, Mr. Radcliffe?"

"I'm sorry. I'll buy you more flowers, okay? Settle down and I'm sure we can get this worked out."

"Oh, you are, are you? You still think you can just throw money at this and make it go away." She jerked several more pictures from the pile, sighing at the damage. "The flowers aren't the problem. These are."

She shoved several wet pictures at his chest. Gabe jumped backward, clutching them so they didn't fall to the ground, but keeping them at arm's length so they didn't drip on his Armani suit. "The pictures?"

"Yes, this is—*was*—my portfolio."

"I'll pay to have the pictures reprinted."

"Which would be great if I still had the photographers' names, or the arrangements from the shoots." The woman glared at him again, but this time he saw more than anger in her face. Frustration and doubt clouded her eyes. "This is nearly ten years of my career, gone to hell. All because you were in too much of a hurry to watch where you were going."

"Now, wait a minute—"

"No, *you* wait a minute." She flipped her long auburn hair back over her shoulder and jabbed a finger into his chest. Gabe forced himself not to smile at the cliché. "We're going to exchange insurance information and you're going to accept full responsibility for this accident. This was your fault."

"I never said I wouldn't." Red and blue lights flashed as they wove between the slow-moving traffic.

Great. Of course the officer arrives when she is in a full meltdown.

Women and agitation made for a toxic combination. Gabe had no idea what she might say to a cop in her current state. He should probably consider himself lucky there wasn't already a news crew out here. The last thing he needed right now was his grandmother breathing down his neck about embarrassing the family. It was difficult enough keeping her happy while trying to deal with her demands about his upcoming wedding.

Wait! The wedding.

Gabe looked back at the pictures in his hands. Stephanie Maurier, his fiancée, and his grandmother *had* been telling him they wanted him to be more involved. He knew nothing about floral arrangements, but even he could see that this woman was talented. The arrangements in the photographs looked more like artwork. He could imagine seeing them displayed in a magazine. She'd put them together in a way that used every part of the plant to make a statement. They weren't like most arrangements he'd seen that merely looked like flowers in a vase.

He looked back at the woman muttering unintelligibly from the back of her car, tossing handfuls of blood-red roses onto the side of the highway in the middle of rush hour. There was a good chance he was going to regret this.

"What if I were to offer you a job?"

Chapter 3

"ARE YOU KIDDING?" Anna couldn't have heard him correctly. He didn't even know her name.

"Look, you said you needed a job. I need a florist for my wedding. And I'm still willing to pay for the damages to your car, so it'll be a win for everyone."

She cocked her head to one side and eyed him suspiciously. "You? Getting married?"

"We haven't made the announcement yet, but yes."

A California Highway Patrol vehicle slowed and pulled behind the Audi, lights flashing as the sun melted into the horizon. She squinted as she watched the police officer climb out of his car. "Is everyone okay?" he called out to them.

"See? That should have been the first question out of your mouth." Anna glowered at this man in his expensive designer suit and shiny shoes. She thought she saw guilt flash across his eyes but dismissed it as a trick of the fading light.

"I'm offering you an opportunity to work as the florist for what will be the most talked-about wedding in San Francisco's recent history. It could make your career. The same one you just accused me of flushing down the toilet." He glanced quickly over his shoulder at the officer and back at her, lowering his voice as the cop approached. "I'm trying to make this right. That's what you wanted, isn't it?"

Anna looked into Gabriel Radcliffe's face, trying to read his expression. This was a once-in-a-lifetime opportunity, the kind of chance people who'd been in the business for years would kill for. Too good to be true. And that was exactly why she shouldn't trust him.

"What do we have here?" The officer walked up and stopped between them before she could answer Gabriel's question. "Do we need to call an ambulance?"

"No, we're both fine," he answered for her. "I was the one who called and we were just getting ready to call a tow truck, Officer. This was completely my fault."

The officer looked to Anna for confirmation but she pinched her lips together, reserving comment until she could figure out what Gabriel Radcliffe had up his sleeve.

"Why don't you tell me what happened, sir?"

Gabriel proceeded to tell the officer exactly what had occurred, not even leaving out the fact that he'd been using his phone, which would earn him a bigger fine. "If you follow me back to my car, I'll get you my insurance information, Officer."

The cop nodded in Anna's direction, promising to return for her documentation and her side of the story. As she watched them walk away, Anna realized that Gabriel Radcliffe had manipulated even the police officer into compliance, and was, likely, expecting the same from her. He'd anticipated that she'd take his check and when that didn't work, he'd upped the ante with a job. It was pretty clear he was a man accustomed to achieving success in all things and wouldn't settle until he did.

She didn't want to roll over and be another person who

bent to his will, but this was the break she'd been waiting for. There wasn't going to be any function in San Francisco more high-profile than a Radcliffe wedding. The referrals alone would open doors she couldn't dream of reaching any other way. This was a job that would elevate her reputation as a florist through the stratosphere. Not to mention, she needed to pay her bills.

The officer headed back toward her while Gabriel leaned a hip against the hood of his car. He was suddenly relaxed and patient. Confident. Once again, he became the man who'd first arrived at her car door.

"His information checks out, ma'am," the officer stated as he scribbled down some information. "Can you get your license, registration, and proof of insurance for me, please?" Anna retrieved the information from her car, passing it over. "Are you sure you're not injured?"

"I'm fine. Just a bit shaken up."

The officer leaned his head to one side, speaking into his radio to request a tow truck before turning the volume down. "It'll be here in a few minutes. Want to tell me your side of what happened?"

Anna told the officer about the crash as he took notes. He stopped and looked up at her dubiously. "You know who he is, right?" She nodded. "Then I'm sure you also realize you're getting off pretty easily since Mr. Radcliffe is admitting all fault."

She stared at the officer, dumbfounded. "That *is* what happened," she insisted. Was this officer suggesting that she might be to blame?

"I'm sure it is." He didn't sound convinced as he wrote on the back of a business card. "Call this number later in the week to get a copy of the report for yourself. Be sure to let your insurance company know." He waved Gabriel over and handed them both back their licenses. "If either of you have any questions, call this number," he said, tapping the business card Anna held. "Thank you for your cooperation, Miss Nolan, Mr. Radcliffe," he added, handing Gabriel a card, before heading back to his car.

Anna watched as the officer edged his patrol car back into traffic.

"I'll wait with you for the tow truck," Gabriel said as he looked at her expectantly.

"Okay."

He nodded, looking slightly sheepish as he leaned against the side of her damaged car. "So," he said, drawing out the word.

"I mean, okay, I'll take the job," she clarified.

"Of course."

She bristled at the arrogance in his tone, as if he'd never doubted she would accept the offer.

Was the cost of elevating her reputation really worth the cost of her pride?

Chapter 4

GABRIEL WATCHED THE woman in front of him as she signed the documentation for the tow company. In spite of the fact that she'd just accepted his job offer, he could see how wary she was of him. He shuffled through the still-damp pictures from her portfolio while he waited for her to finish with the driver.

These really were beautiful. Some of the arrangements were obviously from weddings, but there were others from different types of events. He didn't think Stephanie would be upset with his choice when he told her.

"Thank you for this opportunity, Mr. Radcliffe. I promise you won't be sorry." He looked up, caught looking at her pictures, and she held out her hand. Gabe passed the photographs over to her. As she took them, her fingers brushed his and he was surprised by the rush of heat that shot up his arm. "I guess I'll catch a ride with the driver."

It didn't take a genius to read the trepidation in her eyes at the thought of climbing into a truck at night with the burly stranger. The driver didn't exactly instill Gabriel with confidence for her safety, either.

"Why don't I take you home?" he offered. "It's the least I can do."

She chewed at the corner of her lip and looked back at the man waiting beside the tow truck, cringing as he spat at his feet.

"Oh, come on," Gabe said with a laugh. "I'm a better option than *that*, right?"

She rolled her eyes in response, but he saw her relief. "I *should* be able to trust my new boss, right?"

"Absolutely."

Gabe led her back to the car and opened the passenger door, pretending that he couldn't feel the heat emanating beneath his hand at her lower back. Shutting the door, he scolded himself the entire way to his seat. She was beautiful, but he and Stephanie were about to announce their engagement. It didn't matter if it was a media ploy, or a way to satisfy his grandmother's need for social advancement. His family needed him. Stephanie needed him. He was going to keep his promise to both of them. It was incentive enough to squash any attraction he felt.

Anna punched her address into the navigation system, and Gabe merged his dented car back into traffic. "So, Miss Nolan, do you have a first name?"

She eyed him from across the car. "Anna."

"Anna," he repeated. It suited her—simple yet elegant, pretty but not ostentatious. "Family name?"

"It was my grandmother's."

She studied him from the passenger seat. He could practically see the questions forming in her mind but she looked too hesitant to ask them. "Go ahead."

"What?" She slid closer to the door.

"You look like you have things you want to know."

She chewed nervously at her thumbnail. "Why'd you offer me a job? I mean, don't get me wrong," she added quickly. "I appreciate it, but I seriously doubt it's typical for you to select your employees based on a roadside interaction."

He bit back a grin. "Not usually. Most of the time, there aren't cops involved and I'm the one putting someone in the hot seat, not the other way around."

"Yeah. I'm sorry for that." She grew animated, twisting in the seat to face him as she defended her actions. "But you have to understand, I've been busting my ass for the last ten years to get the promotion I was promised, only to get passed over because of nepotism. Then some guy comes out of nowhere and hits my car."

Damn, that *was* a bad day. It did make him wonder why she hadn't just accepted his check from the start, however. She obviously needed the money.

"The fact is, Mr. Radcliffe," she went on, "I really want this job. I know I can come up with something great for your wedding. But I don't want you to think it's a way to buy me off."

"Buy you off?" He felt himself bristle at the suggestion. "You mean, like a bribe?"

"You've already accepted fault for the accident and you're willing to take care of my car. That's really all you owe me, regardless of what I might have said during my meltdown." She ducked her chin, avoiding his gaze. "I want this job, but I want it because I'm a good florist, not because you think it will keep me from suing you."

"I don't think you're going to sue," Gabriel said with a chuckle.

"Well, I'm not going to the press, or tabloids, or whatever, either."

"Ah." He nodded, staring out at the road ahead of him. "You think I'm hiring you because I'm worried you'll leak the story?"

"Aren't you?"

"Not really." He glanced across the car at her and saw the surprise flicker over her dainty features. "Anna, I'm good at reading people. I wouldn't have come as far as I have, even with my family's money, if I wasn't. Someone who tears up a twenty-thousand-dollar check when they need the money has far too much character to do something that underhanded."

"How do you know I need the money?"

He shrugged, avoiding her question. The truth was he didn't want to point out her worn clothing, beat-up car, or unemployment. Nor did he want to start second-guessing his decision. Gabriel prayed his gut instinct about her was right. If it wasn't, his grandmother was never going to let him hear the end of it.

Chapter 5

ANNA WASN'T PLEASED by Gabriel's dismissive shrug, but supposed she shouldn't expect more from someone who had never had to work a day in his life. She turned toward the window. "We can't all drive fancy cars and wear designer clothing, Mr. Radcliffe," she said.

She was surprised when he laughed. "It wasn't just your car or your clothing, Anna. I don't mean to sound like a snob."

She shot him a dubious glance. "You do pretty well for not trying. Even if I had your money, I wouldn't blow it on things I don't need to impress people I don't care about."

His smile instantly faded and he dropped his hand to the gearshift, running his long fingers over the top thoughtfully. "You'd be surprised. Money has a way of making even the best of us do things we don't want to believe we would."

Anna felt a sliver of guilt that her thoughtless comment had caused his sudden change of demeanor. She found herself wanting to ask him about it, to offer to listen, but they didn't know each other well enough for that. Instead, she watched his hand playing over the leather of the gearshift. Long, tapered fingers with a broad palm. She could easily imagine his fingers dancing over piano keys, playing classical music. As he gripped the stick, she was surprised to see that although his nails were clipped and neat, his hands were rough and calloused.

"Sorry," he muttered. Following her gaze, he rubbed his hand over his thigh. "I was actually heading home from my vineyard and I still haven't gotten all of the dirt from my hands. It kind of embeds itself in your skin."

"Vineyard?" she asked.

He nodded and the smile returned. "I own a vineyard in Sonoma. I'll take you on a tour when we head up there for the wedding," he offered.

Damn, he was handsome. Attraction snaked through her at the thought of him working outdoors. Anna stared at his hands again with a newfound respect for the man beside her. Just the thought of him wandering through grapevines and digging his hands into the soil made liquid heat rush through her. There was nothing sexier than a man who didn't mind working hard with his hands.

"So, you were playing in the dirt?"

"Testing soil," he corrected with a lopsided grin. "I like to be involved in every aspect from planting and harvesting, all the way down to designing the label."

Maybe she'd been too quick to jump to conclusions about him. She rubbed a clammy palm over the denim of the side of her thigh, nearly knocking several of her pictures loose from the ruined portfolio in the process. Being around him was dangerous. She could feel the alarms sounding in her body.

"Mr. Radcliffe?"

"Will you please call me Gabriel?" He glanced away from the road to meet her gaze. "Or Gabe, like the rest of my friends."

"Gabriel." She couldn't help the way his name fell from her lips, with a sigh as her heartbeat seemed to pick up speed. "I'm not sure—"

"Gabe." He frowned as he turned into the run-down apartment complex that would be her home for only a few more weeks. "This is where you live?"

"Just pull into that open spot under the canopy," she said, pointing ahead.

"Here?"

She heard the revulsion in his voice, but she wasn't going to stay in the car long enough to discuss her living situation with him. She needed to put some distance between them before she ended up making a fool out of herself in front of him, again. Being alone with him in such close quarters was making her realize it had been a long time since she'd been attracted to a man, and never one like him. And she couldn't be attracted to Gabriel Radcliffe; he was her boss. And he was getting married.

He put the car into Park and turned toward her, opening his mouth to speak.

She pushed open the car door, slung her purse over her arm, and pressed her portfolio against her chest before he could stop her.

"Anna?" She looked back toward him, just as she reached the stairs. "I'll look forward to seeing you at the Radcliffe Mansion at nine."

His gaze slid slowly over the length of her, making her feel as though every butterfly in the Bay Area had just taken up residence in her stomach. Anna's brain seemed to shut down, unable to do anything more than nod as she spun, tripping at the first stair and catching herself on the railing, nearly spilling her photographs. She ignored the pain in her shin as she bolted up the rest of the stairs without looking back.

Chapter 6

THE NEXT MORNING, Anna woke up to her alarm before the light even began to filter through her butter-yellow curtains. She reached over and slapped at her phone, knocking it to the floor, as punishment for waking her from the very erotic dream she'd been having. Her body still hummed with desire as an image of Gabriel Radcliffe's face emerged from her memories. Anna groaned as the events of the previous evening crept into her mind.

Just the memory of Gabriel was enough to conjure up sensations she wasn't sure she should even admit to. The man was gorgeous. He looked more like a fashion model than the vintner he was. Anna knew better than to let herself think about him too much. Even if he wasn't already engaged, he was so far out of her league, she couldn't kiss the soles of whatever designer shoes he wore.

She sighed, throwing back the blankets. "You know mixing business with pleasure is a bad idea," she said out loud as she sat up on the edge of the bed and rubbed her eyes. "Especially when that *business* is already engaged."

It didn't matter how charming Gabriel—Gabe, she corrected herself—had been when he drove her home. She couldn't think about how his gaze might have lingered on her several moments too long, or how it had enough heat in it that she'd felt her stomach tumbling and twirling. While he exuded quiet elegance and strength, she had all the grace of a three-legged rhino in a dancing contest. It was pitiful for her to even acknowledge the way her heart rate sped up when he'd said her name, slow and breathy, like he was tasting it.

Anna picked up the phone from the shabby carpet, glancing at the time. "Ugh, it's too early for…crap, my car."

The backup alarm she'd set on her phone began to sound and she swiped a finger over the screen, slumping her shoulders in defeat. She was going to need to get out early to catch public transportation in order to arrive at her new position with the very man who'd tormented her dreams.

She flipped on the shower and, while waiting for the water to heat, made her way to her closet, trying to decide what to wear to meet with her new boss and his bride-to-be. Settling on an ivory, cowl-necked sheath dress and a pair of cream-colored faux suede boots, she laid the outfit on her bed. Steam poured from the shower and fogged up the mirror as she stripped down and jumped inside. Letting the water beat down on her tense shoulders, relaxing the muscles of her back, she dropped her neck forward, her damp hair falling into her face as she tried to concentrate on her day ahead.

Instead, images of Gabriel's hands filled her head. Visions of her dream last night broke past the barrier of her consciousness and she could almost feel them on her body. Touching, caressing.

Anna quickly stood upright and poured body soap onto a loofah, determined to scrub away any inappropriate thoughts of the man, forcing herself to mentally form a checklist for her day. It was going to be a busy day at the Radcliffe Mansion.

Her cell phone rang from the bedroom and Anna tried to rinse her hair quickly. Yanking open the door and wrapping a towel around her, she hurried into the room, but the phone had already stopped ringing. Anna rushed through her morning rituals, the anxiety in her stomach knotting, making it impossible to eat. Instead, she poured a large cup of coffee into a travel mug and tucked the remains of her portfolio under her arm before heading out the door to catch the Muni.

Anna stopped at the foot of the stairs where a limousine idled on the street. The driver stepped out of the car and moved around to open the back passenger door for her. "Oh! Um…"

"You *are* Miss Nolan, aren't you?" The driver's voice held a slightly haughty tone. At Anna's nod, he continued. "Mr. Radcliffe sent me to pick you up for your meeting with him, his grandmother, and Miss Maurier this morning."

"Who?" She held her portfolio to her chest, her purse hanging from her arm.

The driver pinched his mouth together. "His grandmother is Mrs. Wilhelmina Radcliffe, and Miss Stephanie Maurier is Mr. Radcliffe's fiancée," he clarified. "We really should get going, ma'am, before we hit the morning commuter traffic. Mrs. Radcliffe doesn't tolerate tardiness."

Anna slid into the backseat of the plush car, clutching her coffee and portfolio.

The driver bent into the car and said, "I am Mr. Remington, ma'am, and I am at your disposal whenever you need me."

"But why…"

"Mr. Radcliffe has instructed it."

Mr. Remington stood and made his way around to the driver's side of the car. Anna sat in the back as he eased the car onto Guerrero Street, feeling awkward and uncomfortable in spite of the smooth leather seats. The limo was too big, too elaborate, and too pretentious for her liking. She unbuckled her seat belt and moved closer to the window partition, tapping the glass to get Mr. Remington's attention.

"Yes, ma'am?"

"Would you mind prepping me a bit? Maybe on what to expect?"

From his profile, Anna could see Mr. Remington smile slightly. "I'd be glad to, ma'am. What would you like to know?"

"Mr. Radcliffe seems rather generous," she hinted. "I mean, I would have been fine taking the bus."

"Nonsense, ma'am. He insisted that if not for him, you'd have a car to drive, and I'm happy to do it." He glanced at her in the rearview mirror with a conspiratorial smirk. "To tell the truth, most days I sit in the driveway buffing the car, waiting for someone to need my services. It's a welcome treat, ma'am."

Anna chewed at her thumbnail nervously. What if Gabriel decided this was a mistake? What if his fiancée overruled his decision? After all, it was her wedding, too.

"Don't be worried, ma'am," Mr. Remington said, looking at her reflection in the rearview mirror. "The Radcliffes are good people, regardless of what some people might say."

Anna felt her stomach drop to her toes before it knotted up again. Instead of instilling confidence, the driver's words only made her more stressed about this upcoming meeting. What did other people say?

Chapter 7

ANNA SUCKED IN a breath as a security guard opened a gate at the curb, and the car drove through and pulled up a long, U-shaped driveway. The Radcliffe Mansion looked more like a modern-day castle than a house, complete with what looked like a butler out of a movie, standing and waiting for her, apparently.

Mr. Remington jumped out and opened her door. "Mr. Graves will take you up to the house, ma'am." He bowed his head slightly. "I'll be waiting here to take you home when you finish."

Anna took the portfolio he held out to her. "Thank you, Mr. Remington." She glanced up at the massive house. "Wish me luck."

He smiled at her. "You'll do fine, ma'am. Just keep your head high and don't let them smell any fear."

Easy for you to say.

"Follow me, ma'am."

Anna hadn't been called *ma'am* so many times in her entire life. She followed the butler as he led her up the marble staircase at the front of the house where it ended at a large terrace, looming and statuesque. Mr. Graves escorted her through giant front doors, into a magnificent rotunda with dark marble walls and satiny, cream-colored marble flooring. From the door on her right, an austere gentleman emerged wearing a long black coat, slacks, and a straight tie. His posture was ramrod straight, and his every step precise. He stopped in front of Anna and nodded his head sharply once.

"Miss Nolan, it is a pleasure to meet you. I am Mr. Lowell, the manager of the Radcliffe household. If you'll follow me, I'd be happy to take you to where Mrs. Dillard, the head of our housekeeping staff, is waiting for you." He glanced down at the portfolio and the travel mug of coffee that she'd been too nervous to drink. "Would you like me to take that cup, Miss? I'd be happy to have it washed for you."

Anna blushed, unsure how she was expected to act in a place this fancy. She was a small-town girl from a Podunk town in the Midwest. She'd only seen houses like this on HGTV.

"It's okay," she muttered, clipping the lid closed on her travel mug and tucking it into her knockoff Coach purse.

"Very well," he said with another nod. "This way, please."

Anna held her breath as they made their way through the grand rotunda to an atrium flanked with marble statues and pillars, crowned with a beautiful arched glass ceiling to let in the light. She looked up at it, rising several stories above her, in awe of the Grecian architecture.

"This place is amazing," she whispered.

"Yes, Miss. It's a lovely house. It was built by Mr. Lawrence Radcliffe in 1902 for his bride. Since then, it has remained in the family." They walked through the atrium to a door at the back of the house. Mr. Lowell led her inside, announcing her as if she were royalty. "Miss Nolan has arrived, Mrs. Stowe."

A woman looked up from a wing chair in the center of

the room. "Good morning, Miss Nolan. I'm Mrs. Stowe, the wedding planner for Miss Maurier's wedding. Please have a seat. We have little time to get acquainted before Miss Maurier and Mrs. Radcliffe arrive. Would you like a drink?"

"No, thank you."

"You may leave, Mrs. Dillard."

Mrs. Stowe looked like she'd just swallowed the world's most sour lemon as she waved away the woman Anna assumed was Mrs. Dillard, who had been waiting silently nearby with a serving tray. On the table in front of Mrs. Stowe were color swatches that lay in coordinated piles, an open calendar, and a list of contacts in what looked like a Tiffany binder. Even the pen she used to write with seemed to be plated in gold. The woman pinched her thin lips together and sat, crossing her legs at the ankle and folding her hands in her lap. She couldn't be much older than Anna, but she was definitely more comfortable in these surroundings than Anna was.

"I'm thrilled to have this opportunity, Mrs. Stowe. I—"

"I'm sure you are." She narrowed her eyes, her gaze sliding over Anna as if she were a disgusting specimen of vermin. "You do realize that I've looked you up. I know you were fired from your last position, and that you are hardly qualified for an undertaking such as this."

"Excuse me?" Anna saw a shadow moving in the open doorway and knew someone was eavesdropping on their conversation. "I'm sorry you feel that way, but—"

Mrs. Stowe held up a hand. "Don't even bother. I may not be able to change this situation, but I just want us to be clear from the beginning. I don't like you and I don't trust people who sneak into a position without earning it."

Anna stiffened, ready to defend herself. "What, exactly, are you implying?"

"I'm not implying anything." Mrs. Stowe inspected her flawless manicure. "People who sleep their way to the top, especially within these very small social circles, are usually ousted quickly and lose all credibility, Miss Nolan." She pinned Anna with a withering glare. "You'd do well to remember that because, I'm sorry to say, word spreads fast."

Impotent rage built up within Anna and she knew there was nothing she could say without jeopardizing this position she needed so desperately...but her pride wouldn't let her remain silent. "Are you suggesting that I slept with "

"Good morning, ladies." A thin, perfectly tailored woman swept past Anna. "Mrs. Radcliffe will be in shortly, but I want to warn you both that she cannot stay long this morning. Miss Maurier is caught in traffic so we will begin without her."

Begin without the bride-to-be?

"I am Mrs. Meyers, Wilhelmina Radcliffe's personal assistant." She made her way to one of the love seats and slid her notepad on the table, passing each woman a sheet of paper. "Here are the points Mrs. Radcliffe wishes to discuss today. Of course, we've added the floral arrangements now, Miss Nolan, since you've been hired to the planning staff. Thanks to Mr. Radcliffe."

Anna's gaze quickly scanned the agenda, seeing her name, and not *floral arrangements* listed at the bottom. Dread crept through her as she eyed the notepad on the table, seeing her name hastily scribbled several times. Mrs. Meyers flipped the cover of the portfolio pad closed and Anna saw the two women exchange a conspiratorial glance.

There was little doubt rumors about Anna had already spread throughout the house, and Anna knew exactly who had started them.

Chapter 8

SAN FRANCISCO WAS filled with cutthroat professionals, but Anna had never felt more helpless than she did sitting in front of these two women. They presented a formidable wall of distaste. Holding her portfolio against her chest like armor, Anna realized these she-wolves were ready to tear her heart out.

Mrs. Stowe arched an icy brow. "Are you unwell, Miss Nolan? You suddenly seem a bit pale."

Her words mimicked concern, but the undercurrent of contempt hung in the room like a storm cloud. The same ire Anna had felt at Gabriel's entitlement simmered in her chest, but she tempered it. Last night, she'd been frustrated at her circumstances; today, the opportunity of a lifetime was laid out in front of her. She had everything to lose if she didn't control herself. She had to tread carefully. Whether she liked it or not, these two women held the power to destroy her future in their hands.

Squaring her shoulders, Anna took a deep breath and closed her eyes, willing her voice to remain steady and emotionless. "I need to use the restroom."

Mrs. Meyers smirked, her thin lips almost disappearing

behind pearly white teeth. "Of course. It's to the left of the door behind you."

Unwilling to turn her back on the pair of vampires just yet, Anna slid her portfolio with the few pictures of samples she'd been able to salvage from the car onto the chair. "Thank you. I'll only be a moment."

She took a step backward, feeling like she was escaping a lion's den, when the heel of her boot crumpled beneath her and her back collided with a hard wall of muscle.

"Ow!"

Anna wanted to slip away but the hands that kept her from tumbling to the floor had a firm grasp on her upper arms, sending heat swirling through her to rest low in her belly.

"I suppose I deserve that after ruining your car last night, but I thought we'd come to a truce." Gabriel's chuckle surrounded her, soothing her raw emotions and sweeping away the harsh judgment of the women seated across the room. "Are you all right?"

Anna nodded, trying to recover her equilibrium as the two women watched with shrewd attention. "Thank you, Mr. Radcliffe."

Gabriel arched a brow at her, obviously surprised by her sudden meekness after the way she'd ripped into him the night before, but Anna wasn't about to give either of these harpies fuel for more rumors. Gabriel released her arms, leaving her skin chilled where his hands had been warm and comforting.

"Anna, I'd like you to meet my fiancée, Stephanie Maurier." Gabriel moved aside as an exquisite woman stepped out from behind him. Her golden-blond hair was swept back in an elaborate braided hairdo that cascaded over one shoulder. Large blue eyes twinkled with excitement and a genuine smile spread over her lips as she reached out to shake Anna's hand.

"Anna, it's wonderful to meet you. Gabe has been going on about your work since he saw your pictures last night." She turned back toward her fiancé, nudging his ribs. "If I'd known a fender bender would get him involved in the wedding plans, I'd have arranged it sooner."

Stephanie was not what Anna had expected, especially after the frigid greeting she'd received from the pair seated before her. Gabe's fiancée was warm and gracious, with absolutely none of the condescending superiority Anna had been subjected to so far. Stephanie reached for Anna's arm, leading her back toward the sofa to sit at her right side.

"So? Let me see these pictures." She cast a sympathetic gaze toward Anna. "I know Gabe said that most of them got ruined, but we'll fix that. We'll have the wedding photographer take extra pictures of our arrangements for you, Anna. You can let him know, right, Mrs. Stowe?"

The woman fixed Anna with a plastic smile. "Of course, Miss Maurier."

Stephanie let loose an exasperated sigh. "How many times do I have to ask you to call me Stephanie?"

Mrs. Stowe cocked her head to one side and nodded in submission. Gabriel chuckled quietly and Anna felt a shiver trickle down her spine at the intimacy of the sound. His hands landed lightly on the back of the couch, those long, tapered fingers caressing the top of Stephanie's shoulders as he leaned toward her. Anna caught the scent of his woodsy cologne and tried not to inhale it, but holding her breath made it even harder to keep her pulse from racing. Or maybe that was just his nearness.

Of course you're attracted to him. He's not San Francisco's Most Eligible Bachelor for nothing. But he's not the guy for you.

Anna refused to indulge in any fantasies about Gabriel Radcliffe. This man was her boss, and engaged to someone who seemed very nice. She wasn't about to give any more credence to the rumors already floating around.

Anna glanced up to see Mrs. Stowe and Mrs. Meyers watching her closely. She scooted to one side, putting space between her and the happy couple.

"I'll leave you ladies to your wedding planning. Grandmother should be in here shortly and I have a few calls to make."

Stephanie smiled at Gabe, adoration evident in her face as he pressed a chaste kiss to her cheek. "I'll see you for lunch." Gabriel stood, addressing the others in the room. "Ladies, it was lovely to see you again."

Once he'd taken a few steps toward the door, Anna began to relax. She'd remained completely professional with Gabriel, in spite of the goose bumps rising on her arms and her heart beating a million miles per hour.

"Oh, Anna, I forgot. Mr. Remington knows he's to be at your disposal until your car is repaired. Just call me anytime and I'll send him for your use."

So much for maintaining a professional appearance.

Chapter 9

IT HADN'T TAKEN more than a few minutes for Stephanie to look through the few pictures Anna had left in her portfolio. Relief coursed through her when Stephanie loved each one she saw. Unfortunately, Wilhelmina Radcliffe still hadn't shown up by the time Mrs. Stowe announced that she had to leave for another appointment, and unable to make any real decisions, Stephanie begged Anna to reschedule for the next day. Then she'd rushed off to lunch with her fiancé.

Adding the descriptive tag to Gabriel's name made Anna feel guiltier for the vivid dreams she'd had about him last night. She resolved to keep plenty of distance between her and Gabe because she was a professional, damn it. Not to mention, she actually liked Stephanie. While the two of them might seem to have little in common, they had similar taste and ideas when it came to wedding decorations. Anna wasn't about to jeopardize her career because of a sexy guy who smelled like wood. And laundry soap. And a hint of leather.

He smelled all male.

*   *   *

The next day, Anna was once again escorted through the atrium by Mr. Lowell. This time, he led her to the door on the left, into a dining room. A crystal chandelier hung over a round table with several place settings, but this room was far more simplistic than the living room she'd been in yesterday. The dark wood beams contrasted with pale apricot walls. The entire room was bright and cheery due to the wall of windows lining one entire side of the room.

"Miss Maurier and Mrs. Radcliffe will be in shortly, ma'am. Please, make yourself comfortable."

Anna had barely set her purse on one of the dining room chairs when Mr. Lowell exited the room. All alone, she tried to ignore the uneasy anticipation that fell over her. After her meeting with Mrs. Stowe and Mrs. Meyers, she wasn't sure what to expect from Wilhelmina Radcliffe. She'd heard stories of the woman. She was a legend in San Francisco, taking over her husband's failing business after his death and salvaging the family fortune. But respecting her business acumen and enjoying working for her might prove to be two very different things.

Anna looked out the window and took in the view of the garden at the back of the house. Most of the landscape beyond the property was blocked by tall Brisbane Box and sycamore trees, meant to keep out the prying eyes of neighbors. A gardener was busy trimming several low box hedges encircling a gazebo. Several birds flew past the windows in an attempt to land on the edge of the feeder, scattering seeds on the ground for the more intelligent few who pranced like dancers below.

Anna inhaled slowly, trying to let the beautiful early afternoon sun brighten her outlook on this meeting. Maybe Mrs. Radcliffe would be like Stephanie. It wasn't fair for Anna to judge a stranger based on her assistant. The sound of women's laughter came from one of the doors to her left. If the staff here had fun while they worked, Mrs. Radcliffe couldn't be all bad.

"I don't know. All I heard was that she deliberately sideswiped him."

Anna felt a sudden chill settle over her. She eased closer to the door, hating herself for eavesdropping, but almost certain the staff was talking about her car accident. Pretending to inspect a painting over the fireplace, Anna leaned closer to the door.

"I heard she was crying and asked for a boatload of money, but instead, Mr. Radcliffe took her home. I can only imagine what happened once he got there."

"I'll hit his car on my way home tonight if he'll take *me* home."

Giggles followed but Anna couldn't listen to any more. She threw open the door to the dining room and stepped into the hallway. There had to be a way to put a stop to the gossip before Stephanie or Mrs. Radcliffe heard about it, but she had to do it without arousing any more suspicion.

One of the maids came to the door with a pitcher of ice water for the table. "Oh! I didn't realize anyone was in here." She glanced furtively into the room Anna had exited.

"I…" Anna looked around her for an excuse, her eyes falling on the wide expanse of inviting greenery outside. She had to find a little privacy, just for a moment, to try to figure everything out. She needed fresh air, to be surrounded by flowers, so she could regain her composure. "I'm going to wait in the garden."

Brushing past the maid before she could reply, Anna raced through the back door. The last thing she expected to do was trip on the threshold and fall right into Gabriel Radcliffe's lap.

Chapter 10

"I DON'T CARE what he said—whoa!" Gabe's phone clattered to the ground as soft curves landed in his lap and long, red hair draped over his arm in waves of glorious fire.

Anna squirmed until she nearly fell to the marble patio as well. "Oh! I'm so sorry. I—" She suddenly stilled and it didn't take a neurosurgeon to figure out why.

Whether from the feel of her wiggling in his lap, or her soft breasts pressed up against his chest as he caught her, Gabe's body responded with bold ardor. The sweet scent of her shampoo—some sort of fruity vanilla scent—enveloped him and made him want to drag her closer. He fought the urge to drink her in.

"What are you doing out here?"

"I needed a second."

She reached for the arms of the chair, but instead, her hands braced on his forearms. The muscles twitched beneath her fingers and he felt the jolt of her electricity travel up his arms.

"Don't move," he ordered, his voice thick and gravelly. If she continued, he was going to embarrass both of them. He could still hear his vineyard manager talking through the cell phone that was lying on the ground.

Gabe slid one arm under her knees and the other around her back, standing to return her to her feet. "There. Hold on for one second." He picked up his cell phone, informing his manager he'd call back later before tossing the phone onto the chair. "We have to stop meeting this way, Anna. People are going to talk."

He saw her cheeks flush. It had been a joke, but apparently, he'd hit a nerve. Anna hurried down the stairs, away from him, toward the gazebo. He followed and reached for her hand, tugging her to a stop. When she turned, her eyes were misty with unshed tears.

"What the hell?"

This same woman had given him a verbal lashing two nights ago for an error in judgment. She had the courage of a lioness, so he couldn't imagine what would reduce her to tears.

"Hey, Anna, talk to me. What happened?" Suspicion crept over him. He tipped her chin up so that he could see her face. Hesitation flickered in her eyes but was gone so quickly he almost thought he'd imagined it. "Did my grandmother say something?"

Gabe stared down into her face, his gaze caressing her, wanting to read her mind. He was unable to fathom what lay behind those emerald eyes. Her mouth parted slightly, as if she was about to say something, but then she closed it. Her eyes seemed to lighten and he noticed gold flecks in them for the first time. Gabe felt her breath against his neck as she stared up at him, and it was taking every ounce of self-control to keep from dipping his head to kiss her, to see if she tasted as sweet as she smelled.

"Nothing happened." She took a step back from him, away from his touch, and cocked her head slightly. "Wait, should I be worried about your grandmother?"

He should have been relieved that she'd kept him from

making a very stupid mistake. Instead, disappointment crashed through him. He shoved his hands into his pockets to keep from reaching out to her again and shrugged his shoulders nonchalantly. "Who knows? I guess it really depends on her mood today."

A wry smile slipped over her full lips. "Wow. You really know how to instill confidence, don't you?" She walked across the yard.

"Would you rather I blow sunshine up your ass?" *Her perfect, apple-shaped ass…*

Anna stopped midstride, her head snapping back to look at him. "Not exactly something I'd expect San Francisco's Most Eligible Bachelor to say."

"Maybe I'm trying to shock you," Gabe suggested. He wasn't sure why he was playing this game, but there was something about Anna Nolan that made him want to take giant leaps away from his comfort zone.

"Then you'll have to do better than that." Her eyes gleamed with mischief as she stopped in front of his grandmother's orchids. "These are lovely."

Gabe heard the awe in her voice. "My grandmother has a great gardener. He manages to keep this entire property up on his own."

Anna looked around them at the floral oasis that rivaled the city's botanical garden. "Alone?" She tipped her head to one side. "He must be a magician. He has orchids in the same area as blue flax but they grow in completely different soils and environments."

Gabe didn't care about the landscape of the yard. He was more interested in the woman in front of him. But her fascination with the flowers and their habits made him want to impress her with his knowledge. "Jian not only cares for the yard, but landscaped every inch of it." Gabe pointed toward the Chinese man shaping a topiary bush. "Do you want to talk with him?"

Anna glanced back at the house.

He followed her gaze and saw the shadow that passed near one of the curtains in the dining room. He knew she was supposed to have lunch with Stephanie and his grandmother and, if that's who he'd seen watching them, it was best not to keep them waiting.

"I'd love to, but I really should get back inside."

"Ah yes, where the guillotine likely awaits." He bowed slightly. Gabe looked up at her with a wink. "It's been nice knowing you, Anna."

She arched a brow and pursed her lips. "You're not helping me feel any better about this lunch, you know."

"She's really not so bad. Just remember to treat Grandmother like the royalty she thinks she is, and you'll get along fine." Anna narrowed her eyes, trying to decipher whether he was serious. "Come on, I'll walk you back inside." He tucked her hand into the crook of his elbow. Anna's fingers tensed on his forearm so he curled his other hand over hers. "Relax, Anna. You were ready to go toe-to-toe with me on the side of the freeway. I think you can manage lunch with an old woman."

As they reached the patio, his grandmother met them at the doorway, her chin held high and her arms crossed. Her gaze scanned Anna quickly, taking in every inch of her new florist, before her lips thinned to a harsh line. He felt Anna's hand tremble slightly on his arm so he squeezed her fingers reassuringly. Before anyone could speak, Gabe released Anna and leaned forward to kiss his grandmother's cheek.

"Thank you, darling." The smile she gave Gabe died quickly as she looked at Anna once again.

"Grandmother, I'd like to introduce you to Anna Nolan. Anna, this is my grandmother, Wilhelmina Radcliffe."

Chapter 11

ANNA CLASPED HER hands in front of her body. She certainly didn't want this woman to mistake her nervous agitation as fear. Mrs. Radcliffe pursed her lips and wrinkled her nose as she took in Anna's clothing, not even offering to shake hands in greeting.

"Tessa," she called, waving her fingers into the air, making her large amethyst and diamond ring wink in the sunlight. "Please escort Miss Nolan to the dining room where Miss Maurier is waiting."

Anna understood why Gabriel joked that his grandmother saw herself as royalty. She certainly carried herself like a queen. This pompous show of authority was almost humorous. One side of her upper lip lifted as she smiled to hide her disapproval. Anna wasn't fooled.

Tessa motioned Anna toward the hallway. "This way, ma'am."

"I'll take her," Gabriel offered.

"I need to speak with you a moment." Mrs. Radcliffe placed a well-manicured hand on his arm. "Privately." Turning her venomous gaze back toward Anna, she smiled patronizingly. "You'll be fine, won't you, dear?"

Anna swallowed the scathing words attempting to spill

from her lips. Self-preservation was a higher priority than her pride, and Anna needed a paycheck now that she'd lost her job. It wasn't the first time she'd put on an act of subservience for a client. Feeling a bit like she'd sold her soul to the devil himself, she smiled broadly at Wilhelmina Radcliffe.

"Of course. It was a pleasure to meet you, Mrs. Radcliffe."

Before she could stop herself, Anna dipped into a perfect curtsy, fit for the Queen of England, and followed the maid who pinched her lips together tightly, her eyes wide with disbelief. The maid might be able to stifle her response but Gabriel didn't bother. His deep, rich laughter followed Anna into the house as she hurried past Mrs. Radcliffe, whose eyes were mere slits of blue rage.

Anna prayed that she hadn't just burned yet another bridge.

"I don't like her, Gabriel. She's cheeky."

Gabe grinned as his gaze followed Anna into the house. "Yes, she is."

The woman who curtsied was the one he'd seen on the side of the highway, the same fiery woman he hadn't been able to quit thinking about since he'd left her at her apartment. When she'd fallen into his lap, it'd felt like a dream come true.

"You should be more careful," his grandmother scolded. "The staff is already talking about her and why she's here. What were you thinking? If you must have a dalliance, keep it private, and wait until *after* your wedding."

"Anna isn't a 'dalliance.' She's the florist for the wedding *you* wanted me to take more interest in. Or have you forgotten?"

"My intention wasn't for you to hire some urchin off the street. I assumed that your 'interest' would be to find a suitable home for you and your new bride." She dipped her chin, giving him a pointed look.

"I'd be happy to stay in Sonoma, Grandmother, if you'd rather not have me here." He preferred working his vineyard instead of playing Schmooze the Millionaire with her obnoxious, snobby peers anyway.

"That's not what I meant. We are Radcliffes. Our name is synonymous with San Francisco. Your home is here." She brushed a lock of hair back from her forehead. "And there are several very nice homes in Pacific Heights, even if that's where the nouveau riche technology riffraff are moving in."

Gabe knew exactly where this discussion was going and he didn't want to have it again. It was a never-ending battle with his grandmother to have control over his own life. Even now, she had too much influence. He'd seen his grandmother control his parents, giving and taking in turn, using her fortune to force people to follow her will. He'd sworn not to live this way, yet here he was, ready to give in because she deemed it necessary. She might hold the purse strings of the Radcliffe fortune, but it didn't give her the right to dictate every aspect of his future.

"I have to call my manager back and you have a luncheon to host."

His grandmother gave him a cold laugh. "Like either of those women want me in there." Gabe moved past her and she reached for his arm, stopping him. "You *do* recall there is far more at stake with your marriage to Stephanie than your desires, correct? Right now, your only concern should be keeping Stephanie satisfied. This marriage benefits us all."

"I know, Grandmother. Trust me. Neither of us is likely to forget that our happiness doesn't have the slightest bearing on this wedding. We are merely chess pieces in the pursuit of status."

"Oh, stop being so dramatic. It's not like you and Stephanie aren't compatible. You've grown up together, and you care about each other."

Gabe crossed his arms over his chest. "It's my understanding that marriage requires more than friendship as a foundation."

"Exactly. It requires similar backgrounds and goals. It requires commonalities, which you and Stephanie have."

He shook his head as he retrieved his phone from the chair. "Call me crazy, but I thought love might have something to do with it."

"Love?" she scoffed. "Love has no place in marriage for people like us, Gabriel. Emotions are fickle. Love is exactly why Stephanie's father is in the position he is now. He married a gold-digger because he thought he loved her, then she took off with his friend. Now half of everything his family built is lost. He's in the middle of a scandal, trying to recover from financial ruin. Louis Maurier has been too good to us and we're not going to let him fall to ruin simply because he made the mistake of marrying for *love*."

She made love sound worse than a fatal disease. "I'll keep that in mind," he said.

"You do that, Gabriel. Keep your eyes on the prize, and leave that *girl* alone. We owe Louis Maurier, and I'll do everything in my power to make sure our debt to him is paid."

"Even if that means sacrificing everyone else's happiness, right?"

"Don't fool yourself. I've sacrificed more for this family than you'll ever know."

Chapter 12

ANNA TOOK A bite of the apple–pear salad, closing her eyes as the goat cheese practically melted in her mouth. The sweet pear and tart apples complemented one another, while roasted pecans gave just a hint of earthiness. Normally rabbit food didn't do anything for her, but Anna had to admit, this was a delicious deviation from the ramen noodles she'd boiled for herself last night.

"You really think we can figure out an elegant centerpiece that would tie in Gabe's vineyard?" Stephanie asked. "He loves that place."

"Absolutely." Anna paused between bites. "We could bring in some grapevines and find grape leaves to use as an accent. You could have urns on the tables with hydrangeas for a rustic Tuscan theme."

Stephanie's eyes lit up with delight. "I love that idea."

"Nonsense."

Both women turned as Wilhelmina Radcliffe appeared, striding to the table and taking her seat. A maid appeared in the doorway with her lunch in hand as the regal woman settled herself. "A Radcliffe wedding will be the talk of all of San Francisco, an elegant affair. Grape leaves and hydrangeas, honestly, how very banal," she scoffed, rolling her eyes at Anna. "Have you ever been to Tuscany, Miss Nolan?"

Stephanie laid her hand on Mrs. Radcliffe's forearm, saving Anna from admitting she hadn't. "Wilhelmina, Gabe and I decided that we want a small, simple ceremony." Anna could see the look of wistful dreaminess in Stephanie's eyes. Stephanie poked her fork at her salad. "We were hoping for something private, at the vineyard in Sonoma, with only family present."

"Out of the question." Mrs. Radcliffe replied with finality, reaching for her crystal goblet of sparkling water. "If you want simple and private, my dear, you are marrying into the wrong family." Mrs. Radcliffe laughed, practically snapping her starched cloth napkin before laying it over her lap. "No. The wedding will be held here, at the mansion. Just like his parents' wedding was and his sisters' weddings will be. It's tradition."

Anna looked from one woman to the other. She could see the disappointment in Stephanie's expression, but couldn't understand why the bride-to-be would willingly give up on her wishes. Anna wouldn't, if it were *her* wedding.

But it's not, so keep your mouth shut.

Her mind's warning couldn't still the outrage Anna felt. "Excuse me, Mrs. Radcliffe, but if Stephanie and Gabriel have their hearts set on the vineyard, would it be so bad for them to have the wedding they want?"

Ice-blue eyes glared at her from across the table as Wilhelmina Radcliffe dabbed her mouth delicately. "I wouldn't expect *you* to understand, my dear."

"Because I'm not rich?"

"Oh, how uncouth," Mrs. Radcliffe said as she set her napkin aside. "I don't have time for this sort of nonsense."

"Anna, please," Stephanie whispered. "Mrs. Radcliffe, of

course we'll have the wedding here at the mansion. I hadn't understood that it meant so much to you."

"Well, if you're certain you don't mind my input, I think it would be a wonderful way to honor Gabriel's grandfather." The older woman sniffed slightly, covering her mouth with her hand.

Anna suspected Wilhelmina Radcliffe was hiding a victorious smirk behind those elegantly manicured fingers, but she didn't say anything. Stephanie would be the one dealing with the woman after her marriage to Gabriel. A sick, twisting feeling suddenly churned in Anna's belly at the thought of Stephanie as Gabriel's wife.

But Anna quickly shoved it aside. She had no right feeling jealous.

Three maids entered to clear the table before returning with steaming cups of coffee and a decadent-looking cake. Stephanie took a dainty bite of hers, and Mrs. Radcliffe met Anna's gaze, daring her to test her insubordination further. Anna pushed the cake away, unable to stomach any more peacocking today. Mrs. Radcliffe might as well have tied a sign around Anna's neck proclaiming she didn't belong.

"Anna, why don't we take a tour of the house," Stephanie suggested. "We can decide which arrangements would look best in the rooms." Anna nodded silently, her gaze remaining focused on that of the steely-eyed woman across from her. Stephanie clapped her hands slightly in excitement. "I'll let Mrs. Dillard know."

Mrs. Radcliffe nodded her approval, smiling at Stephanie as she left. Once the dining room door closed, her gaze snapped back to Anna. With careful deliberation, Mrs. Radcliffe folded her hands and laid them in her lap. She peered down her nose at Anna. Finally, Mrs.

Radcliffe smiled, but there was no pleasantness in her expression. "It seems Stephanie and Gabriel both like you very much."

Anna didn't trust Wilhelmina Radcliffe in the slightest and was careful choosing how to word her response. "The feeling is mutual. I'm very appreciative—"

"I'm sure you are." Mrs. Radcliffe arched a disdainful brow. "I'd hate for you to mistake my grandson's kindness as any sort of…" She paused, as if searching for the right term. Anna had no doubt this woman *always* had the exact word on the tip of her tongue. "*Affection.* You are from very different worlds and I'm afraid you have misconstrued his actions concerning you."

"Of course not, ma'am."

"Aren't you just the smart girl? Saying all the right things."

Anna felt the disdain rising in her chest, threatening to choke her. "I'm sure I don't know what you mean."

Mrs. Radcliffe rose from the table. "I'll be frank with you since there's no sense in wasting each other's time. I'm sure my grandson would love to have one last bit of fun before his wedding to Miss Maurier, but his fortune is well-protected. A *florist* such as yourself is no match for the likes of my lawyers."

"Mrs. Radcliffe, I hardly think—"

Anna stopped as Stephanie rushed back into the room, her excitement evident in her pink cheeks and twinkling eyes. "Mrs. Dillard says she only has a few minutes, but that should be enough for us to know what we're looking for at the flower market tomorrow, right?"

"Run along, ladies." Mrs. Radcliffe's smile brightened as she turned her attention to Stephanie. "I'm meeting with my ladies' group tomorrow, so I apologize, but I can't join you."

"What a pity." Stephanie leaned forward to press a quick kiss to the woman's cheek.

Anna clenched her jaw. It wasn't a pity at all. Anna couldn't wait to get away from the beast of a woman.

Chapter 13

ANNA RAN A brush through her auburn waves in an attempt to tame them but then gave up, letting them fall loose over her shoulders. Glancing at her reflection, she couldn't help but wonder what Wilhelmina Radcliffe would think about her now, dressed casually in a dark maxi skirt, camisole, and denim jacket. She probably wouldn't *say* anything, but she'd give Anna that look she had yesterday.

Anna pushed thoughts of the miserable woman out of her mind. Today, she and Stephanie were venturing into Anna's neck of the woods, to her favorite place in San Francisco, the Flower Mart. Hurrying into her kitchen, Anna filled a travel mug with coffee as she glanced at the clock on her stove. Mr. Remington should be arriving any second. Snatching a muffin, she slid her tote over her arm and ran out the door to find the car already idling in front of her building. Several of her neighbors peered from behind their blinds, curious about a limousine. When he saw her on the stairs, Mr. Remington slid from the driver's seat to open the passenger door. Embarrassed by the attention, Anna ducked down and jogged toward the car.

Coffee spilled from the mug onto her hand, scalding her. "Ow, shit!" She slid into the backseat, trying to wipe the liquid off her hand without getting it on her skirt. "Sorry, Mr. Rem—oh!" Gabriel sat across from her, an amused smile on his face. "What are you doing here?"

"Stephanie is ill so she sent me in her place." He reached for several napkins from the console beside him and handed them to her. "Are you all right?"

"Yes, thank you." She stared at him, hating the way her heart immediately began to flutter at his grin. This was a bad idea. Her brow furrowed as she asked Mr. Remington to let her out. She turned back to Gabe and said, "We should just wait until Stephanie is well. This is really something the bride should do."

"I assure you, Anna, I am fully capable of selecting flowers for the wedding, but if it would make you more comfortable..." Gabriel pulled his cell phone out, dialed, and then explained the situation to someone who could only be Stephanie on the other end.

"Yes, she's right here." He held the phone out to Anna.

Anna reached for it, careful not to let her fingers touch his. She didn't want to subject herself to that sizzle of heat from his touch. Putting the phone to her cheek, she could feel the warmth from his body still lingering, as did his scent—clean, crisp, and slightly musky—making her think of dangerous seductions and sinfully delicious temptations.

"Anna?" Stephanie's voice sounded weak through the receiver, and guilt swept over Anna. "Gabe knows what I'm looking for. Please, go shopping today." She coughed slightly. "I'll make the final decisions tomorrow so you can place the orders."

Anna's gaze slid to Gabriel, looking smug and far too attractive. "Okay," she agreed hesitantly. "We'll send you pictures of his selections."

"Perfect. And, Anna?" The bride-to-be sighed into the receiver. "Try to have some fun today."

Fat chance, Anna thought.

She'd be too busy reminding herself that this was business, not pleasure. It felt good to be this close to Gabriel. Way too good.

Gabe's gaze slid over Anna as she disconnected the call with Stephanie. She still looked reluctant as she handed him the phone. He didn't blame her for her hesitation. After his reaction to her in the backyard, being alone with her seemed a bit too dangerous to be prudent, but Stephanie wanted them to take this one thing off her shoulders. He had to help her. Besides, it wasn't like he could tell her his reasons for not wanting to go. So he motioned for Remington to drive.

"I told you." Gabe smiled, trying to lessen the electric tension between them. "At least now I won't end up with a bunch of pansy-ass girlie flowers at my wedding."

Anna didn't quite hide her grin behind her coffee mug. "Actually, pansies were the one flower Stephanie insisted on," she countered.

Gabe played along, his mouth curving into a half-smile, relieved. "Figures."

"You're lucky Stephanie warned you to wear comfortable clothing," Anna pointed out. "We're going to be walking—a lot."

"I thought we might be."

He glanced down at Anna's painted toes, peeking out from ivory-colored sandals, and felt the wash of desire at that bit of femininity. Gabe swiped a hand down the side of his denim-encased thigh, forcing himself to look away. He had to fight the urge to brush back the lock of her hair that had fallen against her cheek. She didn't seem to notice, but he couldn't stop staring at the way it caressed her smooth skin.

"You do realize most people down at the Market aren't going to be wearing two-hundred-dollar jeans, right?"

He hated that she immediately assumed he only wore designer clothing. It made him seem pretentious and he realized he didn't want Anna to think of him that way. It was precisely the reason he'd asked Remington to drive him to a department store to find some "regular" jeans when he found out he was taking Stephanie's place.

"For your information, these are Levi's."

Her brows raised. "Oh, well, excuse me," she teased. "I stand corrected." She took a sip of her coffee and eyed him from across the car. "You do realize that your *Levi's* still cost more than this entire thrift store outfit, right?"

He wrinkled his nose, conjuring up images of dirty piles of clothing stored in garbage bags. "Thrift store?"

"So sorry to offend your delicate sensibilities, Mr. Radcliffe, but San Francisco is expensive. We weren't all born into trust funds, you know," she scolded.

"Says the woman carrying a Michael Kors purse."

"Macy's clearance, nineteen dollars." She shot him a triumphant smile. "And I only bought it to impress clients like your grandmother."

"Ah, a savvy yet shrewd businesswoman."

The car came to a stop at the corner of the Market and Remington held the door open, helping Anna out. Gabe tried not to notice the way her skirt hugged the curves of her perfect bottom. Taking a deep breath, he reminded himself that he was here to pick out flowers for his *wedding*, regardless of the fact that he didn't want to go through with it.

Gabe climbed out of the car, looking around at the large warehouse building in the industrial section of town. It wasn't what he'd been expecting. "This is it?"

Anna looked back over her shoulder. "This building houses some of the best suppliers in the state. Don't knock it 'til you try it, Mr. Radcliffe."

"Will you call me Gabe, already?" he growled, following her to the door.

"I don't think that's a good idea."

"Why not?" He hurried in front of her, holding open the door for her to enter. Gabe settled his hand at her lower back as he guided her inside.

She moved away from his hand. Anna's bright-green eyes shuttered. "Because you are my employer and, as your grandmother so adamantly reminded me, we come from very different worlds. I know my place."

Gabe tried to read her expression, but he couldn't mistake the caution in the depths. He stopped, waiting for her to turn toward him. "Anna, I don't care what my grandmother said. She and I don't see eye to eye on many issues. I'm asking you, again, to call me Gabe. Just because I've hired you doesn't mean we can't be friends."

She tightened her jaw, looking ready to argue with him again. "Yes, it does."

"Well then, I'd better let my personal trainer know," Gabe said with a chuckle. "Because he's been my best friend for the last twelve years, since we met in college." She pursed her lips, trying not to return his grin. "Go ahead," he teased. "Say it."

Anna rolled her eyes, giving in to the grin tugging the corners of her perfect pink lips. "You are the *most* exasperating man."

"You're not the first person to say that."

Anna nodded and strode away, heading toward the first aisle of flowers, leaving him to watch her go. Gabe suddenly realized that, in spite of her acquiescence, she still hadn't used his name.

Chapter 14

"THESE ARE THE pansies we were talking about." Anna reached forward and plucked a pot filled with blue, yellow, and white flowers from a wire rack.

"I thought we agreed not to use pansies." Gabe stuffed his hands into his pockets as she spun to face him, her long hair twirling around her. He held his breath as her scent assaulted him, making his body ache.

"But they would look perfect in the atrium with the stained glass," she argued.

"But they're called 'pansies.'"

She slid the pot back on the shelf with a sigh, thanking the short Latino man who offered her assistance. "Are you really so insecure in your manhood that you won't use a flower symbolizing love and admiration because of its name?"

"What about these?" Gabe pointed toward a long-stemmed brush-like flower at another booth, across the aisle. "They're the same sort of bluish-purple."

"Those are hyssop." She laughed, plucking one from the bucket holding several. "Traditionally used for sacrifice. I mean, I could see your grandmother wanting to put this flower all around me, but I doubt Stephanie would like it in her wedding."

Gabe couldn't help seeing the irony of his selection. It was exactly how he felt about this wedding—like the sacrificial lamb sent in to maintain his family's standing in society. "You might be surprised," he muttered.

Anna frowned. "Do you mind if I ask a personal question?"

Normally, Gabe would have refused. He'd learned the hard way that it was always better to keep personal matters close to his chest.

When he didn't answer right away, Anna bit her bottom lip. "Never mind, it's none of my business."

Something in the unassuming way Anna dismissed the matter made Gabe want to agree. "Go ahead."

"Stephanie wanted to have the wedding at your vineyard, but your grandmother refused to even entertain the idea. I've seen a lot of brides make demands, but Stephanie backed off immediately, even though I know it's what she wanted. Would you consider talking to your grandmother? Convince her to change her mind. Stephanie really seemed to have her heart set on it."

Gabe took a deep breath, surprised by Anna's intuition. He was unsure how best to respond. The explanation was complex, calling into question the relationship dynamic between his grandmother, Stephanie, and him. "You have to understand that my grandmother is accustomed to power, practically drunk on it, after years of building an empire. People don't question her. What she wants, she gets. Stephanie wouldn't be happy if I said anything."

Gabe felt himself feeding into his grandmother's zeal for power, allowing her to demand more. As long as he continued to allow her to dictate his life, he was nothing more than another player in her game. The realization weighed heavily on him.

"Yet you hired me, against her wishes."

"What makes you say that? I doubt she cares."

Anna tipped her head to one side. "Gabe, we both know she doesn't approve of me."

She'd finally called him by his name and at the sound of it falling from her lips, lust kicked him in the gut. He sucked in a breath, focusing on their conversation instead of the heat pulsing through his body. "It doesn't matter. I'll ask Stephanie if she wants me to push the issue."

Reality crashed in. He was about to marry a woman he didn't love and one who didn't love him in return. Being with Anna was forcing him to face that fact head-on. He wanted to believe that he could ignore this attraction sparking between them.

Gabe wandered down the aisle, leaving her to follow. He had to keep some distance between them but he found himself continually drawn to her.

"What?" Anna asked.

Damn, she'd caught him watching her. In for a penny…

"What is it you want, Anna?" he asked. It was a ridiculous question. One that was too deep and philosophical for a flower market, but he wanted to know everything about her.

"What do you mean? I don't want anything from…"

"I mean, what do you want from life?"

She paused at a booth filled with a rainbow array of flowers, from roses and carnations in the front to more exotic plants lining the back. "See these?" She slid a bright-yellow, daisy-like flower out from a large bunch, as her eyes lit up with some fire from within. He couldn't help but grin. "See, that right there. They make you smile. You can't help but feel joy. Flowers make people feel. I just want to be able to make people experience emotion."

He didn't have the heart to tell her it hadn't been the

flowers that made him smile. He didn't bother to remind her that flowers also expressed sympathy. Not every emotion was pleasant. Life didn't always bloom the way it was intended. The weight of his decisions bore down on him, making him feel morose.

"I know what you're thinking. But even the flowers people send to funerals and hospitals cheer people up. I want my own shop where I can spend my days surrounded with flowers, using them to make people see beauty and happiness. It's all I've ever wanted."

Gabe couldn't argue with her logic and took the flower from her, twirling it between his fingers. He looked around at the wild array of color. They faded beside Anna, the wildest bloom of them all. Her mossy green eyes seemed to glow. He could loan her the start-up costs. He'd done it for friends before. Taking a step closer to her, he reached for her hand.

"I could help you, Anna."

"You have." She smiled at him, grateful. "This wedding is a career-maker."

Her words were innocently honest, devoid of the heated desire swirling through his veins, hot and heavy. Anna was reaching into his soul with no clue how she was affecting him. His gaze fell on her mouth. Her breath caught, as if she had suddenly read his thoughts.

"A flower for your sweetheart?" An old man hurried toward them from the back of the booth, bearing a bundle of roses, shaking Gabe from fantasies he shouldn't be having about this woman.

Anna tore her gaze from Gabe's. "Oh, I'm not—"

"Give me all of the purple ones." Anna tipped her head to one side, confused, and narrowed her eyes as Gabe pulled some bills from his pocket. She couldn't understand his reasons; he didn't even understand them.

The old man's smile split his face. "Let me just wrap those for you." He shuffled back to where an elderly woman worked at a table.

"Those are beautiful." Anna's voice was soft, her smile tender. "Stephanie will love them."

Gabe almost laughed at her assumption. These flowers weren't for Stephanie. That hadn't even been a consideration when the man mentioned Gabe's "sweetheart." He'd bought them with every intention of giving them to Anna, just to see joy fill her eyes. When the man returned with the flowers, Gabe passed him several bills.

"Let's go get lunch."

"But we still have booths to hit, and I promised Stephanie we'd take pictures," she argued.

Gabe pulled out his phone and snapped several photos of various flowers immediately surrounding them. "There," he said, tucking it back into his pocket. His gaze slid over Anna, taking in her bewilderment. "Didn't I see a café when we came in?"

"It's this way." She turned to lead the way and he heard the disappointment in her voice.

"And, Anna, these are for you." He held the bouquet of lavender roses out to her.

Anna spun around, taking a step to her left and yelping as her ankle buckled beneath her. Her fingers reached out, grasping for him, but she missed and toppled to the ground.

"Anna?" Gabe squatted down, setting the flowers to one side, and reached for her. "Are you okay? Did you hit your head?"

"Ugh! I'm fine," she grumbled, her cheeks turning nearly the same color as her hair. "I just tripped." She plucked at the skirt that was now shredded over her knee. "Damn it!" Her knee was scraped and blood welled over the scratches.

"Can you walk?"

She rolled her eyes, allowing him to help her stand. "Yes. In case you haven't noticed, I'm a klutz. Not the chick-flick, isn't-it-cute-how-clumsy-I-am kind, either. I'm the ends-up-in-the-ER-with-broken-ankles kind."

"Apparently." He slid his other arm around her waist, drawing her close and cursing his body's immediate response as he inhaled the sweet scent of her, grabbing the bouquet as he stood. "I'll have Remington meet us at the café with the first aid kit."

"First aid kit?"

"From the car."

She looked at him like he'd grown another head.

"We have one in every car. You never know when—"

She laughed at him.

"What?"

"You're just a regular Boy Scout, aren't you, Mr. Radcliffe?"

"And it's a good thing for you, Miss Nolan," he said, pulling out his phone and texting his driver to meet him at one of the tables outside. "This is the second time I've rescued you."

"Or have been the cause of my accident."

In spite of Gabe's offer to carry her, Anna insisted on hobbling by herself, stopping occasionally to dab at the blood on her knee. "I can't believe you made poor Mr. Remington walk this far to bring a Band-Aid," she moaned.

Gabe ignored her comment as Remington arrived, taking the first aid kit from his hands. "Thank you. We'll be at least another thirty minutes for lunch." With a nod, Remington left and headed back to the car to wait. Laying the flowers on the table, Gabe knelt in front of Anna, opening a packet of antiseptic and a gauze pad from the kit. "Okay, let's see it."

"It's fine. I can do it."

"Anna, don't be ridiculous."

Gabe reached out a hand as she scooted her chair backward, capturing her ankle. Her gaze met his and he saw the fire his touch had ignited. Her breath caught as he slid his hand up the back of her calf.

Maybe she isn't as unaffected by me as she appears.

Flames of yearning licked at him, testing his self-control as he folded the torn skirt up over her knee. Carefully brushing away tiny pieces of dirt caught in the scraped skin, he clenched his jaw tight in order to maintain a thread-grip on his sanity. He shouldn't be touching her, shouldn't be *wanting* to touch her.

He held the antiseptic pad over her knee. "This might sting," he said, his voice thick with desire.

She flinched, but remained silent as he cleaned and bandaged the wound. When his fingers brushed over the back of her knees, she gasped. The sweet sound was almost enough to undo him. Even as his body burned from within, self-loathing consumed him. He let his hand fall away from her silken skin. He had to.

"I think that should take care of it."

"Thank you." Her voice was barely a whisper.

Chapter 15

"WHAT'S YOUR FAVORITE food?" Gabe asked. Anna had been acting oddly since he'd bandaged her knee and Remington was making good time through the afternoon traffic. He didn't want their day to end this way. Maybe a few harmless questions would get them back to the amicable ground they'd been on before.

"What?" She turned to face him. "What brought that up?"

"You're being too quiet. It's making me worry. Just answer the question."

"Pizza."

"Really? I sort of figured you for a corned beef and cabbage kind of girl."

She wrinkled her nose. "Just because I have red hair doesn't mean I like Irish cuisine. For your information, I'm Irish *and* Scottish. And I hate cooked vegetables. Slap that corned beef between two toasted pieces of rye and we're talking. What about you?"

"Pizza."

"Like you eat pizza," she scoffed.

"There's a lot you don't know about me." She rolled her eyes in disbelief. "Try me."

Her eyes gleamed with mischief as she accepted his challenge. "Favorite drink?"

"Merlot."

"I should have guessed it'd be wine. Favorite book?"

"*To Kill a Mockingbird.* You?"

"Charlotte's Web."

"Really?"

"What can I say? I loved animals growing up." Anna shrugged. "Favorite school subject?"

"PE. But that's true for every boy."

"What about in college?"

"Finance." Her eyes widened and he laughed. "It sounds more impressive than it was, but I was good at it. What about you?"

"I didn't go. Favorite color?" she asked before Gabe could follow up on her response.

"Green," he said, staring directly into her emerald eyes, unable to stop himself. He was grateful that she didn't seem to realize the reason for his choice.

"Favorite place in the world?" She smiled when he paused, looking confident that she'd finally stumped him. Remington turned down her road and stopped the car in front of her building.

"Sonoma, at my vineyard," he said. "You'd love it."

Her smile disappeared and her gaze met his. Gabe could see the warring emotions there. He was feeling the same way.

"Gabe," she whispered. Remington opened her door before Gabe could do something he'd regret.

"I'll walk you to your door."

Gabe exited the car first, holding his hand out, waiting for her. After what felt like an eternity, she slid her hand into his palm. He wished he didn't feel the sizzle of heat traveling up his arm or the pleasure coursing through his body, reawakening the hungry emotion he'd given up at his grandmother's insistence of his engagement. He felt the warmth of her body and longed for more. Settling his hand at her lower back, he walked with her up the stairs in silence, even as his mind spun with fantasies, every single one involving the redhead beside him.

Anna searched for her key in the bottom of her tote, juggling the bouquet. Finally, after she pulled it out and slid it home, she faced him, biting her lower lip as she stared at the flowers. "I…I think it might be better if I only deal with Stephanie from now on."

Gabriel took a step closer to her, the distance between them disappearing. Her hand immediately settled on his arm, branding his skin. Her fingertips clenched his forearm slightly and her eyes darkened. Anna moistened her lips.

"We shouldn't," she whispered.

"You're right, but I can't help it."

Dipping his head, Gabe brushed his lips against hers. The caress was barely a kiss, but it scorched him. Her breath mingled with his and the sweetness of her nearly drove him mad. She tasted like strawberries, sweet and tart, like the woman herself, and he wanted more. He parted her lips with a sweep of his tongue and she sighed, rocking into him, answering his yearning with her own. Longing slammed through his veins in time with his pulse.

"No!"

Anna jerked away quickly, spinning on her heel and pushing her way through her door, slamming it shut behind her without any explanation.

Gabe leaned his forehead against the metal frame for a moment, gathering his wits. He had no right to feel the way he did about Anna. If spending the day with her proved anything, it showed him that he couldn't go through with this wedding. No matter what he'd promised. Gabe wanted Anna.

Anna leaned back against the closed door, struggling to catch her breath, pressing a hand to her racing heart. She'd just kissed her boss. Okay, so technically, her boss had kissed *her*, but she had been willing to be kissed. Yearning burned through her, igniting her core, racing through her limbs, turning them liquid and making her weak. The flowers and tote dropped from her arm as she slid down the door to the floor, drawing her knees to her chest.

What were you thinking?

She wasn't thinking. She had been *feeling*. The way his hand had cupped her jaw, and the way his fingertips had brushed over her earlobe. The scent of him surrounded her. She could almost feel the moist heat of his mouth against hers again. Anna pressed her fingers against her lips. The taste of him lingered, so sinfully forbidden yet so welcome.

How was she going to face him? She couldn't possibly work with Stephanie any longer, nor would Stephanie want Anna to after Gabe told her what happened. *If* he told her what happened. There was a good chance Gabe would never tell anyone. Wilhelmina Radcliffe's words haunted Anna.

One last bit of fun before his wedding.

Anna picked up the roses and rubbed the velvety petals with her fingertips, wondering if she had been played by a playboy. She stood and made her way to the garbage can with the flowers. She was no one's "last bit of fun." Lifting the lid, her hand hovered with the bouquet.

What if he wasn't toying with you?

It was impossible. Stephanie was perfect—kind, beautiful, from the same world as Gabe—but Anna had seen something in his eyes today. It was different than the way he looked at Stephanie. Maybe it was a foolish fantasy, but no one else had to know. Anna carried the flowers into her kitchen and filled a vase with warm sugar water. Carefully clipping the ends of the flowers, she arranged them, setting the vase on the counter.

For only a few days, she'd let the flowers be a reminder of a beautiful mistake she could never repeat.

Chapter 16

ANNA BOLTED UPRIGHT, awakened by the shrill tone of her cell phone. She reached for it, swiping her finger over the screen. "Hello?"

"Anna, I hope I didn't wake you."

Stephanie.

Light broke through the crack in her curtains, piercing her like an interrogation spotlight. Shame flooded through her. She'd kissed Gabe, her boss, Stephanie's fiancé. How could she have done something so stupid?

Anna glanced at the time. It was almost ten.

Shit, I've wasted the entire morning dreaming about him.

Anna cleared her throat as she rose from the bed. "Good morning, Stephanie." Anna headed for her coffeepot, praying the caffeine would jolt her brain into functioning properly and keep her from saying something she'd regret.

"Gabe said yesterday went well."

Fear settled in the pit of Anna's stomach as her eyes fell on the bouquet of roses. They stared back accusingly, reminding her of what she'd done. She managed to grunt a reply.

"Join me at the house today. Most of the wedding party will be here and I'd like to introduce you to my sorority sister. Her wedding is a few months after ours. Would you be interested?"

Hell yes!

Anna's gaze fell on the lavender roses again. They were usually known as the symbol of love at first sight, but now they reminded her of betrayal and stupid mistakes. This opportunity was too important to risk because she was attracted to the groom. She had to find a way to stay away from Gabe Radcliffe.

"Of course."

"Good." Stephanie sounded as excited as Anna should have felt. "I'll have Mrs. Dillard set a place for you. See you at one!"

No more mistakes, Anna vowed. She needed to forget about last night altogether.

"Damn, I don't know what's gotten into you today, but harness it more often. That's a personal best, man." Every muscle in Gabe's chest quaked as he pressed the barbell up for his final rep as his best friend and personal trainer, Brandon Demasi, spotted him. "You want to talk about it?"

Gabe dropped the barbell into the rack and scooted out from under it, taking the bottle of water Brandon held out to him and chugging half of it. He wiped the sweat from his face with a towel, and then draped it over his thigh. "No, thanks."

"Ah, so woman trouble." Brandon nodded with a slight laugh.

Gabe scowled at him. "I didn't say that."

"You didn't have to." Brandon crossed his arms, leaning over the barbell. "I've known you too long not to recognize that look. So, what's up with Stephanie?"

Gabe had known Brandon since his second year at Stanford. When the football player turned training coach informed him of his business plan upon graduation, Gabe seized the opportunity to help a friend and step away from his family's "old money" obligations. Instead of spending his trust fund on kegs and cars, he invested it, starting with Brandon. He began building a fortune outside his grandmother's reach. So far, Brandon's business had been mutually beneficial and solidified both their friendship and their finances.

"Nothing's up with her."

"If that were the case, you wouldn't be working this hard. You've upped your weight and reps." Brandon stood up, changing out the weights for Gabe's next series of exercises. "Spill it."

"Remember how my grandmother wanted me more involved in the wedding?" Brandon nodded, rolling his eyes. "Well, I hired a florist."

Brandon laughed out loud. "What the hell do *you* know about flowers?"

Gabe shrugged. "Nothing. I sideswiped her with my car. And when I found out what she did for a living, I figured it was a good way to get my grandmother off my back and make up for the damages I'd caused."

"You have insurance for that." Brandon slid the last plate onto the barbell and tightened the clip on the end. "Okay," he said with a wave of his hand. "Get on with the story. You have a few more sets."

"Stephanie was sick yesterday so she sent me out with the new florist." Gabe lowered his voice, knowing it wouldn't be the first time his grandmother had one of her staff spying on him. "I kissed her."

"Damn, dude," Brandon muttered. "Did you tell Stephanie?"

"What do you think?"

"Damn," Brandon repeated as he inhaled slowly before letting out a low whistle. "Look, I know you care about Stephanie, but, Gabe, you obviously don't want to go through with this wedding. You've gotta talk to her."

"What I have to do is marry Stephanie Maurier. You know I don't have a choice."

"Stephanie's father will manage. He'll take a hit, but people have recovered from far worse than a messy divorce. If you're falling for someone else—"

"I'm not." Gabe slid his hands around the barbell, hoping his curt reply would end the conversation. Stress bunched the muscles of his chest and back as he thought of Anna, leaning into him last night at her door. The sweet taste of her still lingered on his lips. "Besides, we both know that I can't call off this engagement. I'll be disowned. The family fortune and name…"

"Yeah, yeah, being a Radcliffe opens doors," Brandon said as he lifted the bar and helped Gabe settle it over his chest. "I've heard that bullshit for years. But you're doing fine on your own without your grandmother's pull or your family's money. Our gym is opening its third location here in San Francisco and two in LA next summer. You have the vineyard and winery. Look how great those investments have turned out." He let go of the bar as Gabe started his first set of incline presses.

"You don't know what you're talking about," Gabe growled, pressing the barbell upward.

"Sure, I don't," Brandon said with a chuckle, letting Gabe finish the set before he pushed the matter further. "You need to quit letting your grandmother steamroll you."

"You don't understand." Gabe grunted as he caught his breath, prepping for his next set.

"Oh right. I forgot. We lowly hired help have no clue about the troubles you trust fund babies face, right?" Brandon shook his head. "Then tell me what you're going to do."

The weights clinked loudly as Gabe pressed them up, using every bit of his frustration to do it. "No clue."

"My advice: call off the engagement."

Gabe dropped the barbell into the rack midset. "And what am I supposed to do when I'm disowned and can't afford to open the other three gyms? Or the winery goes under?"

Brandon arched a dubious brow. "*If* that were to actually happen, we'd build our business slowly, like regular people without millions of dollars of family money backing them. We could start by only opening one new location. Or find another investor and open all three. It does happen, you know."

Gabe sighed and ran a hand through his hair, pulling at the back of his neck to loosen the muscles. Last night with Anna, he'd simply reacted in the moment, a needy, undisciplined moment. But today, in the harsh light of reality, Gabe knew there was far more at stake than just his love life. He wasn't sure he could walk away so easily and hurt people who cared about him.

Chapter 17

THE TENTATIVE KNOCK on his door made Gabe pause, midshave. "Come in." Stephanie entered, looking flawless and regal in her linen pantsuit. "Ready for the vultures to descend, huh?"

"Stop, Gabe. I hate this as much as you do, but it's what has to be done." She watched his reflection as he turned back to the mirror to finish shaving. "I don't know why your grandmother is pushing this union, but now, after what my mother did..." She shook her head, regret tinging her blue eyes.

"Is this *really* what you want?" He reached for the washcloth, wiping away the leftover shaving cream, and then followed her out into the bedroom. "We're friends, Stephanie, but we're not in love. Do you want to give up on that to save your father's reputation? Or to further whatever plan my grandmother is hatching?"

He could see the indecision in her eyes. He cared about Stephanie, he always had. They were good friends and she'd fit in with his family—she got along with his sisters, and had social status and money—but he didn't want to end up like his parents, who barely tolerated each other.

"I don't see where either of us has a choice." She dropped

to the corner of the bed and shrugged. "They're making the engagement announcement public soon. I've tried to convince your grandmother to keep it a small affair, but you know how she is."

Gabe nodded and sat down beside her, reaching for her hand. "We could walk away."

She rolled her eyes at him. "Easy for you to say—you have a vineyard and the gyms. I have a degree in design, and there aren't too many openings for designers with no practical experience. I live off my trust fund, Gabe. I never thought my mother would run off with everything Dad built." She laid her head against his shoulder with a sigh. "I like you, but the thought of being your wife doesn't send me over the moon with excitement, either. We're in this together, for better or worse, unless you figure something out."

Gabe felt the weight of responsibility grow even heavier. He wanted to promise he would find a way to release them both from being forced down the aisle by their families, but Stephanie was right. She had nothing else to fall back on and he wouldn't cast her aside. He wouldn't turn his back on his friends.

"It's Anna, isn't it?" Stephanie looked up at him through her dark lashes. "I'm sorry, Gabe. I think you two would've been good together. It just seems too late." Gabe heard the defeat in her voice.

He slid his arm around her and squeezed gently. "Don't give up just yet."

"Anna!" Stephanie rose from the love seat and hurried to greet her as she entered the living room, where several women waited for lunch to be served. Looking around her, Anna felt immediately out of place, especially with her knockoff clothing. Usually she had a healthy dose of self-confidence, but amid the perfect women surrounding her, her morale took a nosedive.

"This is the floral magician I was telling you about. She can make anything look beautiful." Stephanie's praise made Anna feel a little better.

"She should have tried harder with that dress and those shoes." A brunette seated in a wing chair laughed, glancing to another woman for confirmation.

Several of the women tittered quietly and Anna clenched her jaw. It was going to be a long, trying lunch. If these first few minutes were any indication of how many times she'd bite her tongue, she was in trouble.

"Personally, I love the combination of black and tan, Anna," Stephanie said as she shot a warning look at her friend. She might be trying to help Anna feel more at ease, but it was going to take more than a compliment to make Anna feel like she wasn't trapped in a room filled with prissy debutantes ready to pick her apart.

Stephanie tugged at her arm. "Come with me. I want to introduce you to Fallon and Alexandra, Gabe's sisters."

Anna felt worry skitter down her spine. If either of them were half as bad as their grandmother, she might as well jump in front of a firing squad and get it over with. But as soon as she met them, she realized she needn't have been concerned. They were both bubbly and kind, and she instantly liked them.

Anna had only said a few words to them when Mrs. Dillard announced lunch and led everyone into the dining room. The bridal party was split between two large round tables. Anna was grateful to be seated to Stephanie's left, until she saw Wilhelmina Radcliffe arrive in time to take the seat on Stephanie's right.

"Good afternoon, ladies. I apologize for my tardiness, but I had a prior engagement." Her smile was genuine as she looked around the table at Stephanie's friends until her gaze fell on Anna. Mrs. Radcliffe's eyes narrowed to slits. "Why, Miss Nolan, I'm surprised to see you here."

"I invited her. With Krista's wedding just a few months after mine—"

Mrs. Radcliffe laid a hand on Stephanie's shoulder, making her pause. "Your kindness to others never fails to astonish me." Lifting her chin, Mrs. Radcliffe looked down her nose at Anna. "It's a...*pleasure* to see you again, Miss Nolan."

"Anna, please." Anna hid her satisfied smile at Mrs. Radcliffe's obvious displeasure.

The old woman lifted a glass of water to her lips. "How droll," she murmured.

Anna slowly inhaled, counting backward from one hundred to keep from saying something she'd regret. The conversation rallied around clubs and charity events, subjects Anna had little experience with. She was grateful that, for most of the meal, she was ignored. The few times her input was requested, she was able to nod and fake her way through the conversation. Anna congratulated herself on keeping her temper and surviving unscathed when Mrs. Radcliffe suggested they take their coffee and dessert in the living room.

As the ladies rose with cups in hand, the woman beside Anna roughly bumped her elbow, spilling Anna's coffee down the front of her dress. "Oh, Anna, I'm so sorry, but you bumped my arm," she gushed, setting her own cup down. Her words were apologetic, but her tone definitely wasn't. Wilhelmina Radcliffe's eyes gleamed with catlike sadism, pleased with Anna's misfortune.

Stephanie turned with a napkin, trying to dab at the hot

coffee soaking through the thin material. "Oh! Are you all right?"

"I'm fine," Anna muttered, blotting at the dress.

"I'll have Tessa find you something else to wear," Stephanie offered.

"I'm sure I've left something in one of the rooms," Alexandra chimed in, looking at her grandmother for confirmation.

"If not, I'm sure one of the maids has something that would suit her while they launder her dress," Wilhelmina said with mock concern.

Alexandra scowled at her grandmother and one of the ladies gasped in shock but several others laughed quietly at the suggestion. Anna lifted her chin, her pride flaring brightly. She was unwilling to be shamed by the pettiness of these haughty women. She might not be rich, but she deserved as much respect as anyone else in this room.

"Actually, Stephanie, I have to run. I have an appointment this afternoon, and now it looks like I'm going to have to change," Anna lied before meeting Wilhelmina's gaze. "I believe it's rude to be late, regardless of prior engagements."

Wilhelmina was waving for the maid. "Tessa, please show Miss Nolan out."

The women followed Wilhelmina out of the room as Stephanie hugged her. "Anna, I'm so sorry. I didn't expect them to act that way."

"Don't worry about it. I've been around catty women before. It doesn't bother me." Anna gave her a confident smile, even though she wasn't feeling confident at all. She wondered when it had become so easy for her to lie. Working with the Radcliffes was becoming a nightmare.

Chapter 18

"ANNA?" FROM THE office in his sitting room, Gabe caught a glimpse of her running down the back patio stairs, heading toward the garage.

What was she doing here?

Honestly, he didn't care *why* she was there, he was just happy to see her. Gabe hurried down the stairs to the exit from the back of the atrium. "Anna," he called as he stepped outside.

She looked back at him, wiping her face, but not before the sun reflected off her tear-stained cheeks. His heart clenched and he felt his stomach knot at the thought of anyone making her cry. Rage surged within him.

"What happened?"

"Nothing. It was nothing," she insisted. "Just me being clumsy again," she amended with a forced smile.

He tipped his head to one side. He didn't believe her for a second. Glancing back at the house, he saw Mrs. Meyers watching them from the window of the music room, her lips pursed sourly. This had something to do with his grandmother; he'd bet money on it.

"Come on." Gabe reached for her hand.

"I'm going home, Gabe. I don't—"

"Fine. Then we'll get Remington." He started toward the garage when Anna jerked her hand from his.

"No. Don't you see?" She threw her hands into the air. "I don't want a chauffeur taking me home. I don't want to worry about people looking down their noses at me. I'm going *home*. I'm tired of trying to measure up to this." She waved a hand back at the house.

Anger built in her eyes, even as tears beaded. He understood her agonized frustration at being constantly judged. He'd faced it for years in reverse—forced to succeed and live up to the Radcliffe name. It was a facade, all of it, and he'd thrust her into the middle of this social minefield he hated so much.

And he *did* hate it.

He hadn't even realized how much until he'd met Anna. She'd awakened him to the reality of freedom outside the demands of his social circles. When he was with her, he forgot about being Gabriel Radcliffe, heir to the Radcliffe fortune, and was simply Gabe. Anna treated him like she did everyone else, especially when she teased him. She made him feel grounded. Around her, it was like he could be more than another Radcliffe in a long line. She made him feel like he could create his own legacy.

Gabe closed the distance between them. He cupped her cheek, wanting to be a rock for her. "I'll get my car and drive you home."

"Really?" Her hands slid over his forearms and, for a moment, no one else mattered. "You'd leave to take me?"

"Of course I would."

Anna narrowed her eyes and doubt flickered in the depths as she glanced back toward the house. "I should probably have Mr. Remington take me."

"Because the rumors have already started." Gabe's

shoulders slumped. He knew there would be talk; there always was.

Anna didn't deny it and avoided meeting his gaze.

"So what?" he said. "I'll squash them when we get back. Come on."

Gabe reached for her hand and pulled her into the garage. Hitting his key fob, he started the car before holding her door open. After he jumped in, he revved the engine, letting the rumble fill him with excitement as he watched her laugh nervously.

"You realize this isn't helping anything, right?"

"Anna, there are always rumors. If it's not staff, it's paparazzi. Hell, my second cousin once started one about herself."

"Doesn't sound like your life is as great as it seems." She turned toward the window.

"Trust me, it's not."

She looked back at him, surprised by his admission.

"It's really not."

"This isn't the way to my apartment," she pointed out. "Where are we going?"

"Away from the prying eyes, rumors, and bullshit."

"Gabe?" A note of warning colored her tone, but he ignored it, pressing his foot down on the pedal. "You're not going to throw me off the bridge, are you?" she asked.

"Nope, but we're going somewhere near the bridge." He smiled at her across the car.

"Not instilling confidence. How do I know you're not a serial killer?"

Gabe chuckled. "Just going to have to trust me, I guess."

"Not the answer I was looking for."

Gabe wove through the afternoon traffic, second-guessing his destination. It wasn't a place he'd normally take a woman he was interested in, but that was precisely why he wanted to take Anna there. To prove that she was different, that she made *him* different. Gabe turned into the parking structure.

"The Embarcadero?" she asked, and he could hear the confusion in her voice.

"Yes, ma'am."

"But why?"

"You'll see." Gabe helped her from the car and led her down to the pier, twining his fingers through hers. The movement was completely natural. He remained silent until they reached the end of the pier, where massive ships had docked alongside it. Gabe let go of her hand to grip the metal railing. "I practically lived here when I was a kid. Did you know that my family originally made their fortune in shipping?"

"I didn't know that." She moved closer, her shoulder brushing his. Her sweet scent enveloped him, more potent than the salty air that lifted her auburn tresses to kiss her cheeks. Tucking the lock behind her ear, she watched him rather than the scenery.

"Once I was old enough to work with him, this was the only time I ever saw my dad. He taught me the value of hard work and sacrificing in order to get ahead. I never knew the cost until I was grown, when I realized I never knew my father. And the man I know now…" Gabe shook his head, turning to face her. "Now I'm supposed to fall in line and make sacrifices for the family. I'm not sure it's worth what I'm giving up."

"You can't let someone else dictate your decisions, Gabe. You're the one who's going to live with your choices."

Gabe let his gaze glide over her. She was so beautiful. And not the same way Stephanie was. She didn't need primping to enhance her beauty; it was natural. There was nothing manufactured—Anna's loveliness simply was. Like the woman herself, she didn't try to pretend to be something she wasn't. While most women he knew fought to maintain stick-thin figures, Anna embraced the curves, valleys, and dips of her body that begged to be explored. They were her perfections.

"What is it about you, Anna?" he asked.

She frowned and took a step back.

"How is it possible," he said, "that someone I met by accident only a few days ago has me reconsidering everything I've been raised to believe? You have me thinking about just walking away from it all."

"I…I didn't try—" She shook her head.

"I know you didn't," he said with a chuckle, reaching for her hand and tugging her into his arms. The moment she touched him his pulse kicked a notch higher. "You're just you, and that's what has me so bewildered. My father did everything my family demanded, yet he's miserable. My sisters and I never even considered challenging my grandmother's authority. It's how things are for us."

Gabe shook his head, recalling how insistent everyone had been that he and Stephanie get engaged immediately.

"You have me second-guessing everything. I now know what I want, Anna."

He wanted *her*, plain and simple.

He looked into her eyes, willing her to see the truth there. It wasn't the best step for his reputation, it wasn't the prudent step for his social standing, but it was the right step. Anna Nolan had stolen his heart, but in doing so, she'd given him the opportunity to regain his freedom.

Chapter 19

PRE-WEDDING JITTERS. *That's what this has to be.*

Anna could feel Gabe's heart pounding beneath her fingers. She inhaled deeply, closing her eyes, fighting back the desire to take advantage of his moment of weakness. Surely, he didn't have many. She knew she needed to move away from him. But before she could, Anna felt his lips cover hers.

She gave in, opening beneath him, and it felt so right. Their breath mingled with the cool salty air. Their tongues danced as his fingers burrowed into the tangled mass of her windblown hair. She tried to convince herself that she needed to stop, but her hands clung to his shoulders like the lifeline he'd become to her. Heated longing coursed through her veins, igniting her blood, making her want things that could never be for the two of them. She was a small-town girl scrimping to make ends meet; he was one of the wealthiest men in San Francisco. They were worlds apart. There were too many differences between them. This wasn't a fairy tale and there would be no happily ever after for them.

Anna pulled away. "Gabe, we can't."

His lips found the curve of her jaw, pressing a kiss to

the hollow of her throat. Liquid heat nearly melted her resolve, pooling low in her belly. A sigh of desperation fell from her lips as she realized how many people could be hurt. Anna splayed her hands over his chest. "Gabe, I can't. Stephanie."

He dropped his forehead to her collarbone and sighed, his breath fanning over her skin, making goose bumps rise. Anna bit back a groan as he pressed a quick kiss to her neck. "There's a lot you don't know about Stephanie and me."

"I know you're getting married." Her words were enough to strengthen her resolve. "I need to get home." Anna moved away from him, but the haunted expression in Gabe's eyes made her think twice.

He looked like a man on the verge of giving up.

Anna stopped in her tracks, looking shocked. "Wait, what? What happened between you two?"

He smiled at her. How could she not know? "You did."

"Me?" She paled. "Gabe, I'm so sorry. I didn't mean to cause any trouble."

It was so like Anna to immediately think of others first. He smiled and took a step, closing the distance between them, his fingers brushing her jaw. "You didn't. You opened my eyes and made me realize I couldn't go through with something that had been nothing more than a business arrangement."

He could see her confusion. This wasn't how most people lived, so she couldn't comprehend it. He twined his fingers in hers. "Come with me. I'll explain everything."

She didn't move. "Where?"

"We'll take a drive. I want you to see the *real* me, not Gabriel Radcliffe of the San Francisco Radcliffes. I want you to see Gabe."

She bit her lower lip, contemplating, and he worried she might refuse. "Please, Anna."

"I don't want to hurt Stephanie," she said.

"Stephanie and I are just friends. It's all we've ever been, since we were kids. Seriously. This trip was her idea."

Chapter 20

GABE TURNED OFF the main road and Anna could see the excitement building in him. His face grew animated as he talked to her about the vineyard and winery, explaining how his was one of the only biodynamic vineyards and how he'd spent years cultivating the perfect balance between the various plants, beneficial insects, and animal habitats. But even with his elaborate descriptions, she wasn't prepared for the beauty laid out before them as he turned into the drive leading up to the main house.

Through the cypress trees and crepe myrtles dotting the side of the road with color, Anna could see rolling hills covered with vines. A sea of green. Men working between the vines shouted and waved, and Gabe returned the greeting enthusiastically, calling each person by name. As they drew closer to the house, she could see the landscaping. It was impeccably well-kept, but seemed like a natural, flowing design of plants, each one specifically chosen to serve a purpose. The house itself wasn't nearly as large as she'd expected it to be. Nestled behind several black oak trees was a Tuscan-style villa, complete with pond set off to one side and several small ducks milling nearby.

"You have ducks?"

He laughed. "The ducks and geese are wild. But I keep a few chickens near the barn."

Anna's brows shot up on her forehead. "Barn? You have a barn?"

He nodded. "We have some cattle, sheep, and a few goats. I even keep a couple of horses, but they belong to my sister Fallon. I can have my livestock manager saddle them up if you want to go on a ride to tour the vineyard."

The surprises just kept coming. "Wait, you ride horses?"

Gabe simply looked over at her and smiled. "Come on." He hurried to hold her door open for her, his eyes glinting like a kid on Christmas morning. Reaching for her hand, he led her to the front door and unlocked it. The porch was covered in an assortment of colorful potted plants that were trimmed to accentuate the stone entry. He led her through the open-concept house and she instantly fell in love with every room. Stone tile covered the floor in the entryway until it gave way to hardwood in the family room.

The entire structure seemed hewn from the outdoors with its rustic wooden beams and stone masonry features. The space had a clean, classic tone that made it clear that it had cost him a fortune, but seemed so unpretentious she couldn't help but feel at home, even if the living room alone was the size of her entire apartment. In stark contrast with the Radcliffe Mansion in San Francisco, this place was warm and inviting.

"Gabe, it's beautiful," she whispered, still awestruck. "Nothing at all like your other house."

A frown creased his brow. "I hate that house. It's so—" He paused, looking toward the backyard. "Cold. There are some good memories there, but this is where I feel at home." His eyes shone with a playfulness she'd never seen before. "Come out back."

She followed him and gasped at the fairyland that greeted her. There was the large pond in the backyard instead of a pool, and he'd transformed the entire space into a woodland oasis. Over a wide stone patio were old-fashioned bulb lights, strung across the pergola. Star jasmine was woven throughout, perfuming the afternoon breeze.

Anna wandered to the edge of the water and kicked off her shoes, sitting on the miniature dock with her feet dangling into the water. Four ducks milled along the edge across from her, eyeing her speculatively. She leaned back on her hands, letting the afternoon sunshine caress her face, soaking in the moment, taking in the differences between the man who'd sideswiped her on the 101 and the man who was taking off his shoes to sit beside her.

He laid a hand over hers. "What do you think?"

There was so much emotion in his voice. Not pride, although she could hear that, but hope. A touch of anxiety. He wanted her to love this place as much as he did.

"You don't have staff here?"

"Not really. I have a housekeeper and gardener who come once a week. But, other than that, it's my livestock manager, Marco, and the vineyard staff who are here with me every day."

Anna turned to look at him.

"I know nothing about taking care of livestock and Marco's here to keep them healthy."

He was so matter-of-fact about it that it almost made her laugh, and she shook her head in disbelief.

"What's so funny?"

"You. You're so different here." She flipped at the end of the tie he'd loosened on the drive up. "More relaxed. More passionate about what you love to do. It's like you've left the person you're supposed to be behind and let the man you want to be out of his cage."

He returned her smile and she felt warmth radiate throughout her body, heating her, making her shiver with yearning. Gabe rose, holding a hand out to her, his eyes dark with hungry desire that matched what flowed through her veins.

"That's exactly how it feels." He seemed inordinately pleased by her observation. Gabe pulled her to her feet, wrapping one arm around her waist, and leaned toward her ear.

Her heart stopped for a moment before leaping into her throat. Her pulse pounded as his lips brushed over the outer shell. Anna shivered and a chuckle rumbled quietly against the hollow behind her ear. "Cold? Let's go inside and get a glass of wine."

Gabe watched as she raised the glass to her lips, longing kicking him square between the eyes. He might have thought it was the wine, if he'd actually had more than a sip. No, it was all Anna. She closed her eyes as she savored the tangy fruit and pepper flavors, emitting a sigh of pleasure as she settled her glass on the kitchen island. He shifted on the other side, his pants suddenly too constraining.

"How long ago did you buy this place?"

"About eight years ago. I decided this was what I wanted to do in college, but it took a while to find the right place. Then I had the grapes brought in. But it was only about five years ago that I had the house built."

"You don't waste any time, do you?"

Gabe leaned over the counter, covering her hand with his own. "Not when I see something I've always dreamed of having."

Anna sighed and slid her hand from his. "Gabe," she protested.

"Anna, you're the woman I've been wanting to find all my life. You don't care about my name, or my family's money. I want someone in my life who wants me for me. As Gabe. As this."

"We're just so different."

"Are we really, though?" He knew they weren't, and now he had to make her see it. They were both passionate and willing to work hard for what they loved. He moved around the island to get closer to her. Brushing her hair behind her ear and looking deeply into her eyes, he said, "San Francisco isn't me. It's my burden. I'm me when I'm with you."

Chapter 21

ANNA COULDN'T BELIEVE she'd heard him correctly. Staring at him, wide-eyed, she fought to keep her heart from bursting out of her chest. Her eyes misted as she met his gaze and nodded. It was all she could manage before Gabe pressed a kiss to her temple and her pulse picked up its pace. They stood like that for a moment, silently relishing the feeling of being together with no barriers, the sound of their hearts beating in unison. Gabe laid his cheek against the top of her head, exhaling slowly.

"I'll show you your room."

Her heart froze. She was suddenly surer of what she wanted with Gabe than she'd ever been in her life. Anna wrapped her arms around his waist. "Don't you mean our room?"

"Anna, if I stay with you, I can't promise to keep my hands off—"

"I don't want you to," she said as she wound her hands around his nape, dragging his mouth down to hers. She needed the heat of him—his mouth, his body. She needed to feel his skin against hers. Without registering the movement, her body arched into his. "Please," she whispered against his mouth.

Gabe's hands slid down her sides to cup her butt and,

grasping her thighs, he lifted her, pressing her heat against him. This was what her body had fantasized about from the first night she'd met him on the side of the road, what she'd convinced herself could never be. His body answered with a matching desire. Anna wrapped her legs around his waist, letting him carry her into the bedroom.

After toppling with him onto the bed, she rose to her knees, fumbling with the buttons of his shirt, eager to rid him of the garment as quickly as possible. Gabe shrugged it loose as he kicked off his shoes. Then he tugged her dress over her head and threw it aside. Anna practically melted into the bed. Gabe moved up the length of her, the spattering of hair on his chest tickling her skin deliciously and teasing her senses. His hardness pressed into her softer curves.

Brushing his hand over her flat abdomen, Gabe licked at her navel. "I've dreamed about this."

His breath was hot on her skin, burning her. It made her insides melt as passion ignited her blood, pooling beneath his lips. His tongue trailed upward, over the ridges of her ribcage, teasing the curve of her breast. He reached up to unclasp her bra, dragging the straps down her arms. His mouth replaced the material, his tongue twirling over the tight peak of her nipple, sending sparks exploding within her. Anna gasped, arching into the heat of his mouth as Gabe licked her, drawing out a soft moan from her throat.

His hands glided over her skin, tracing the curve of her hips. She could feel his arousal pressing against her heat. Her own body was throbbing and begging for release. Anna's fingers dug into his shoulders, drawing him closer. She needed more. As she reached for him, Gabe caught her hand.

"I don't want to rush this. I plan to enjoy every second teasing you."

He raised her hand, letting it fall against the tight muscles of his butt before his fingers trailed over her inner thigh. Anna couldn't help her body's reaction as it trembled, desperate for him to fill her. He found the center of her desire, ready for him. Gabe circled the nub of her pleasure with his thumb, driving her mad, and she cried out, her body bucking against him. His lips moved over her flesh, tasting, teasing, lifting her higher. His hands were magical as he caressed her, finding places on her body that made her quake. Anna felt the tightness coil in her.

"Gabe," she moaned. "Please."

He stroked her, stoking the fire in her. He growled with the effort of restraining himself. With that incoherent plea, Anna gave in to the pleasure coursing through her, riding it as her body trembled against him. Gabe held her to him, kissing her, soothing her, as her soul rejoined her body and both of them collapsed into the pillows.

She gazed up at him and laughed quietly, her limbs weak. "If that was foreplay, I'll never make it through the rest of the night."

Gabe gave her a confident, lopsided grin. "We'll see about that."

Sucking in several deep breaths, fighting to regain even a little of his self-control, Gabe rose and plucked his pants from the floor. After sliding his wallet out, he removed a condom. Her hands slid around his waist, her body pressing against him from behind, and then she took the package from his fingers.

"Let me." She pressed a kiss to his shoulder.

Watching their reflection in the mirror, Anna sheathed his straining erection. Gabe could barely focus as her hands gripped him. Spinning her so that her back was to the mirror, he lifted her onto the edge of his redwood dresser. Anna's heels dug into his hamstrings, forcing him closer.

"It wasn't supposed to be this fast."

Anna smiled at him. "This isn't nearly fast enough for me."

Anna clung to him as he buried himself into her heat. Gabe felt every part of her body surrounding him, clutching him. He'd known making love to Anna would be unlike anything he'd ever experienced, but he'd never expected it to be heaven itself.

Her body gripped him, meeting his every thrust, pulsing with his as he let go. Anna cried out his name, her face against his neck, as release found her.

Gabe couldn't breathe, couldn't move, for fear it would destroy the pure ecstasy of the moment. Her lips traced his neck and her breath whispered against his heated skin. "Gabe?"

His fingers trailed down the length of her back and she shivered against him. "Mmm?"

"As much as I've enjoyed this…" She reached for his hips, groaning softly as his body jerked in response. "I don't want to stay on the edge of this dresser all night."

"Think you could stand?"

"I'm sure I could manage." Her eyes gleamed with wicked mischief. "Why? What did you have planned for me?"

Gabe laughed, carrying her to the shower. He shook his head and turned on the water. "I'm planning to memorize your perfect body." His thumbs brushed over the delicate line of her shoulders, moving to trace the curve of her breasts. "But it might take a few tries for me to remember every inch." He stepped under the spray, their bodies slick against each other, and bent to lick the rivulet running between her breasts. "I have a very bad memory."

Chapter 22

THE SUNLIGHT BLAZED through the windows, falling across the bed and announcing the morning. Gabe felt Anna stirring against his chest, stretching, pressing her curves against him and making his libido kick into overdrive. He watched her wake, feeling more alive than he could remember. Every part of him felt light and free. But it wouldn't last long.

They needed to talk. About what would come next. Because they had to have a plan in place before they returned to San Francisco to tell his grandmother. He'd already decided, in the early morning hours, how he would help Stephanie and her father, even if he had to sell the vineyard and give them the money. He would still have the gyms and a few other small commercial property investments in San Francisco to rebuild his future on. In fact, he had one particular space in mind that would make a wonderful flower shop.

"Good morning," he said with his lips against the top of her head. "Did you sleep okay?"

She smiled up at him. "No. Someone refused to let me sleep," she teased, sliding up his body to lie atop him.

"Anna." He whispered her name like a prayer.

She pressed her lips to his briefly before trailing them over his jaw and neck.

Gabe's body instantly responded and he quickly rolled over, pinning her beneath him, wanting to bury himself inside her again. Her fingers trailed down his back, urging him on. He growled and playfully nipped at her shoulder. "You're distracting me. Stay here while I go make us coffee."

"Aw," she protested as he sat on the side of the bed and reached for the pants he'd cast aside last night.

Gabe turned toward her and winked. "Do not move from this bed," he ordered.

"Wouldn't dream of it," she assured him, spreading her arms out as the sheet fell to one side, exposing her breast.

Gabe closed his eyes as he made a quick exit. Anna would be the most glorious death of him.

Gabe came back into his bedroom carrying two steaming cups of coffee. As much as she wanted to stay here and enjoy having him all to herself, she knew they needed to head back to San Francisco. Gabe had already assured her that Stephanie knew about them, but she wanted to talk to her face to face, woman to woman.

"You look awfully serious for someone with no clothes on." He gave her a tentative smile as he sat on the edge of the bed and passed her the mug. When she didn't return his smile, he took a quick sip. "Okay, what's going on in that beautiful head of yours?"

"We need to go back. I need to talk with Stephanie."

"Okay," he agreed.

"And your grandmother."

"No, not without me." His tone didn't brook any argument. However, Anna had never been one to quit while she was ahead.

"Excuse me, but I'm a grown woman. I don't need your permission." She slid from the bed and tried to ignore the heated gaze that slid over her body, warming her and making her want to forget all about going home.

"I just don't think it's a good idea, Anna. She's…difficult to deal with at times."

That was the understatement of the century. She reached for her clothes, slipping into them quickly. "It's something I need to do, for my own peace of mind. I need her to understand that I love you, that I'm not just a gold-digger. If we are going to be together, I need to try to have a relationship with her as well. She's your grandmother and part of your life."

Gabe's hands fell gently on her shoulders and turned her to face him. She looked up, praying he could understand her desire to be on good terms with his family.

"Okay. I get it," he said as he pressed a kiss to her lips. She wasn't surprised when desire burst inside her, hot and heavy. "But we need to at least shower again before we go."

Anna leaned back slightly, giving him a dubious look. "Fine, but it'll be a *quick* shower."

Gabe smiled as he teased the tip of his nose over her neck, letting the scruff of his morning beard scrape her shoulder lightly. "Trust me, it will be quick."

Chapter 23

"I'M SO GLAD you suggested we have lunch. Since you seem so keen on inserting yourself into our family, I agree that we should get to know each other better."

Anna stared back at Wilhelmina Radcliffe from the opposite end of her dining table, refusing to let the other woman intimidate her. She watched as Tessa laid bowls of soup in front of them. "Your tone belies the sentiment."

"Well, well." The smile that slipped across the woman's face was almost authentic. "Honesty from you at last, Miss Nolan."

"I've been nothing but honest with you from the moment I met you, Mrs. Radcliffe."

"I see. Since you're being so transparent, I'm sure you wouldn't mind telling me the extent of your relationship with my grandson." She sipped the broth daintily from her spoon.

Anna was dumbfounded. Before she could answer, Wilhelmina nodded. "So it's as I suspected. Otherwise you would have denied it outright."

Anna realized she'd been trapped. She'd have to keep her wits unless she wanted her head on the next silver platter brought out. "I love your grandson," she stated, matter-of-factly. The words sounded heavenly falling from her lips.

Wilhelmina tipped her chin, looking down her nose at Anna. "I did tell you to stay away from him. But you ignored my warning. However, I suppose it's better if I tell you rather than you making a fool of yourself."

Anna remained silent as dread circled her heart.

"Most men about to experience fatherhood for the first time tend to panic." She gave Anna a pointed look. "It's only natural that he strayed."

Anna felt like her heart had just been ripped out. Gabe, a father? He'd told her it had been Stephanie's idea for them to go to the vineyard. She felt so naive for believing him and giving in to him so easily. When had she become that woman?

"Ah, I see. He didn't tell you any of that, I presume?" Wilhelmina set down her silverware, reached for her glass, and shook her head sadly, sipping her water. "Let me guess, he told you he loved you?"

Anna felt physically ill, holding a hand to her stomach.

"He said they aren't in love." Anna's voice sounded weak, even to her own ears.

"Of course they aren't." Wilhelmina's smile turned patronizing. "Only the naive few in our circles marry for love. But, Gabriel and Stephanie do care for each other. Stephanie is carrying his child, after all." When Anna didn't answer, Wilhelmina laughed. "Gabriel must be a far better actor than I ever gave him credit for."

Anna bit her lip and stared at the crystal goblet in front of her. Light refracted through it, making rainbows over the table. Suddenly she realized Gabe's feelings for her were mere illusions. He'd plied her the way the crystal refracted the light, painting dazzling colors over the mess of her life. And she'd completely believed him.

"My dear, I'm sorry to sound vulgar, but you were nothing more than a bit of a conquest for him. One last bit of fun, as I warned you would be, before his engagement was announced and he settled down. And now, you see why the engagement must be announced immediately."

Wilhelmina couldn't have driven her point home more deftly if she'd used a sledgehammer. She crushed every hope Anna might have had for her future, both in her relationship with Gabe and in her career. "I think it would be best for you to leave the employ before you do anything more to embarrass yourself. And I'm willing to help you. I have a lovely commercial lot in Santa Barbara, right near the ocean. Out of the goodness of my heart, I'd like to help you start your own shop there."

Chapter 24

ANNA'S CELL PHONE rang, overly loud in the stillness of the botanical garden. She'd come here to decide whether to accept Mrs. Radcliffe's offer to help her start her own shop. After digging the phone out from the bottom of her purse and seeing Gabe's number on the screen, she swiped her finger over it, sending his call to voice mail yet again. He'd already called at least six times in the past two hours. She thought he would have gotten the hint by now.

"You don't want to talk to me?"

She spun at the sound of Gabe's voice, shocked to see him walking toward her. "What are you doing here?"

He shrugged. "Tessa called and told me you'd left in the middle of lunch with my grandmother. I went to the flower market and two other parks before I came here."

"How did you find me on this bench? The park's fifty-five acres."

"I asked a docent where I could find the most colorful flowers in season right now." Anna was taken aback, surprised that he knew she would seek out color and life. She came to see the bright flowers in the exhibit to renew her spirit. "Anna, what happened at lunch?"

She turned away from him, unable to refuse the earnest appeal in his hazel eyes. "I had to. This can't work. There's you and Stephanie—"

"We're over," he finished. "I told you that."

She twisted around to face him. "No, not when the two of you are having a…"

Gabe frowned, his brows pinching together. "A what?"

"Your grandmother told me about the baby."

"What baby?" He closed the distance between them and reached for her cheek. "She told you Stephanie was pregnant?"

Anna bit her lower lip, nodding dumbly.

"There is no baby. Stephanie and I have never slept together."

Anna sighed as his grandmother's words slid like poison through her mind. *A conquest. One last bit of fun.* "I'm not just some fling. I deserve better than that."

"What are you talking about, Anna?"

She wasn't sure who she could believe anymore. She shook her head, walking away from him. "I don't like being toyed with, Gabe. I have feelings."

He reached out, grasping her wrist, and tugged her back into his arms. Anna's hands landed against the hard wall of his chest. Her heart pounded frantically as her body instantly responded to his touch, craving more. She caught her breath as the scent of him surrounded her, more intoxicating than the fragrance of the flowers in the garden. A shiver of desire trickled down her spine, almost making her knees buckle.

"Why would you think I lied to you?" Gabe stared into her face but she couldn't answer him, or tell him about his grandmother's accusations. "Whatever she said, it isn't true."

"How can I believe that?" she whispered, her heart breaking.

"I've never felt the way I do when I'm with you. Anna, I'll sell the winery if it means I get to be with you."

"You can't." She'd seen firsthand how much the vineyard meant to him, how alive it made him feel. She couldn't let him give it up.

His finger brushed a lock of hair behind her ear, caressing the line of her jaw, sending heat bursting through her core. A smile tugged at one side of his lips. "I was going to marry someone I didn't love because I'd given up hope of finding a woman like you. I'd gladly give up one hundred vineyards for you. Don't tell me you're willing to turn your back on what we have because of an old woman's crazy lies."

She was torn. Anna wanted to believe Gabe, to fall head-first into the longing that threatened to drown her. Logic warned her to turn her back on him, walk away and protect herself from being used, but her heart couldn't deny the waves of desire washing over her at his nearness. His hand fell to her waist, pulling her toward him slightly, and she couldn't convince herself not to be swept away.

She didn't want to deny her heart. She had been ready to give up based on the words of a bitter woman trying to maintain a grasp on her own agenda. But Gabe was sacrificing everything he loved to prove himself to her.

"Please," he said. "I love you, Anna."

Anna wouldn't look at him. Gabe slid his fingers along the side of her neck, his thumb tracing her jaw, tipping her face up so he could look into her eyes. She lifted her gaze to his and he could see the confusion and hesitation there. But he could also see the longing for what they could have.

"Tell me what you're thinking."

"There's no baby?"

Gabe jerked his cell phone from his pocket. "I'll call Stephanie right now and you can ask her yourself. I swear to you, Anna, there is no baby and there will be no wedding." A half-smile tugged the corner of his mouth. "Except, one day, ours." Her gaze leapt to his and she rolled her lips inward. He could see the moment she decided to believe him, when her eyes reflected every emotion he was feeling for her. "I love—"

Gabe couldn't wait any longer. His mouth covered hers, and immediately, her fingers traced a path into his hair as shock waves reverberated from her very touch. Every part of him seemed electrified, pulsing with need. Winding his arms around her back, he dragged her against him, pressing their bodies into full contact. This was what he'd been looking for. Anna filled a void in him that no other woman could.

"Hey." Anna pulled back from his kiss. "You don't get to steal this moment from me. You're going to be patient and wait for me to tell you that I love you, Gabriel Radcliffe. I love your dirt-stained hands, the kind way you treat the people who work for you, and, most of all, I love the passion you have."

He couldn't help the goofy grin that he was sure must be on his face. He bent down to kiss her again, his lips brushing hers briefly. "You're incredible. And now, we have to go."

"Where?"

"You'll see."

A smile spread over her face, lighting her eyes with emerald fire, making his heart ache with the beauty of it. This woman had changed his life, helped him find his true desires and had opened up a new world for him. Anna's palms cupped his stubble-covered jaw and he felt his body tighten at the desire coiling tight in his loins.

"Okay," Anna said as she stood on her toes and pressed her lips against his, her tongue sneaking into his mouth to seal her promise. And Gabe knew he was never letting this woman go.

Chapter 25

ANNA LOOKED AROUND the posh suite of the Palace Hotel in amazement. Every inch of the room exuded wealth and luxury. She heard the door to the main room close and turned away from the massive canopy bed and plush comforter, trying to ignore the butterflies taking flight in anticipation of sharing that bed with Gabe soon.

His hands slid up her arms, settling over her shoulders to coax the tense muscles. Anna dropped her head back against his shoulder, relaxing into his touch as sparks ignited, her body aching for his caress.

His lips found the curve of her ear. "Room service will deliver anything we want tonight. We'll face tomorrow and whatever it brings in the morning."

She spun in his arms at the worry she could hear in his voice. "What does that mean?"

"It means that tomorrow, we'll tell my family the truth. There's a good chance my grandmother will disown me. I won't be rich tomorrow, but tonight, I can offer you this." He waved a hand at the gaudy room.

Anna cupped his face in her palms, the rasp of his five-o'clock shadow tickling her palms deliciously. "I don't want this. I just want you."

His phone rang in his pocket, vibrating against her hip. She smiled playfully.

"Is that a phone in your pocket?" she teased.

He tugged it out and looked at the screen. "It's Stephanie. I'll call her later." He slid the phone onto the nightstand. "Where were we?"

"Right here."

Anna tugged her shirt over her head and cast it aside, stepping closer to unbutton his. Her fingers ached to touch him again while other parts of her burned for his caress. She slid his shirt over his shoulders and pressed kisses to his bare chest, loving the way she could feel his pulse beneath her lips. Gabe unbuttoned the shirt at the wrists and spread his hands over her tiny waist, sliding his palms up her back and igniting the fire in her into an inferno.

He cupped her breast, his thumb brushing the taut peak through the material, and she gasped. Gabe smiled. "Let's see if we can last a little longer this time."

His tongue found her breast, toying with her over the lace, before he removed the garment slowly, teasing her body into a response. When his mouth covered her, she cried out, her body arching into his touch.

"Don't you dare," she pleaded. "Please."

"I'll give you everything I can."

"Gabe, will you pick up? This is important. Call me back." Stephanie's tone was firm in her voice mail. Anna was asleep and Gabe didn't want to disturb her, so he tugged on his pants and went into the hall.

Stephanie answered on the first ring. "Where have you been?"

"Busy."

"Too busy to find out that we are off the hook?"

"What are you talking about?" Gabe couldn't help but feel leery at Stephanie's sudden pronouncement.

"I went to surprise my dad for lunch today and didn't realize he was meeting with the accountant. I heard them talking. Gabe, he's not broke." Her voice pitched up two octaves as she got more animated. "When I confronted him about it, he finally told me that your grandmother was the one with nothing. She needs *our* money. That's why she's pushing this marriage."

Gabe was floored, but he trusted Stephanie implicitly. She wouldn't lie to him. Plus, her news gave him the reason why his grandmother would stoop so low as to try to convince Anna that he was having a baby with Stephanie. But why would Stephanie's father go along with it?

"Do you realize what this means?" Stephanie screeched, excitedly. "We're free, Gabe. You need to go, find Anna, and tell her you love her."

Gabe chuckled into the phone. "Too late. I already have." He hadn't felt this unbelievably happy in a long time. Since they could cancel the wedding, he didn't have to sell the vineyard.

"Oh, Gabe. I'm so glad." Stephanie paused for a moment as if the full impact was just hitting her as well. "What are we going to do? We have to say something to your grandmother."

"I think it's better if I do this alone." There was another long pause on the other end of the line. "Stephanie?"

"Yeah?"

"Why would your father agree to this?"

"I was wondering the same thing, so I confronted him about it. He said that your grandmother threatened him— well, threatened me. Because even when she's broke, my father recognized that your grandmother is very influential in our social circles. She said she'd spread a rumor that I wasn't 'marriage material' and said it'd ruin me in a heartbeat. But my father knew she'd never tarnish my reputation if we were married."

"It feels medieval, like he was selling you off with a dowry."

Stephanie laughed quietly. "I guess he figured it was the lesser of two evils. He knew we were friends, and that you would never hurt me."

"And he knew you'd no longer be vulnerable to my grandmother's barbs. Sounds like your father had good intentions. I'm sorry my grandmother's weren't quite there," Gabe said with a sigh.

"*Pssh*. I've always known how she is and I could never fault you for it. It was really an ingenious form of blackmail on her part. There was absolutely no trail of evidence that would allow my father to go to the police. But, Gabe, do you really think she's as broke as my father says?" Stephanie sounded worried for him. Even after all his grandmother had done, she didn't hold it against Gabe.

"Broke for her and my parents? Probably. I'll have to look into it but I know they had a lot of money tied up in real estate, and with the market crashing a few years ago..."

Gabe had a sneaking suspicion it might be worse than Stephanie or her father thought. His grandmother had pushed this union hard. The loss had to be for at least several million dollars. Wilhelmina Radcliffe didn't do anything on a small scale and Gabe was afraid that this included her screw-ups. If they'd ignored Mr. Maurier's advice to diversify, they were likely bankrupt.

Gabe had never been more grateful for trusting the man. He'd done all he could to protect Gabe and his sisters' investments, making sure each was kept in their own names rather than the family's parent company. No one could touch the vineyard or winery any more than they could the gyms, Alexandra's investment company, or Fallon's horses. It seemed they were all free of their grandmother's machinations.

"I'm sorry you got caught up in this mess, Stephanie."

"Don't you dare apologize," she said, sounding outraged at the thought. "I'm just glad we're not stuck sharing breakfast for the next fifty years, especially while you're mooning over someone else."

"Ouch. I never should've talked to you about Anna. Up until a couple of days ago, we were engaged."

"Please." He could almost hear Stephanie's eye roll. "I'm happy for both of you. If you hadn't run into her car when you did, we'd have both ended up miserable. We're lucky it worked out this way."

"Thanks." He appreciated that Stephanie could see the humor in their situation now that everything had worked out. Gabe reached a hand to the back of his neck, nervous but unable to deny the truth. "I can't explain it, but there's not a doubt in my mind that she's the one," he said, confiding in his best friend.

Chapter 26

GABE OPENED THE door and kissed his grandmother's cheek. She wrinkled her nose as she passed the
potted plants. It had taken him three days to plan this surprise. Arranging everyone's schedules had been a pain, but
it would be worth it to see the looks on their faces.

"Quaint."

"Why, thank you. I was hoping you'd enjoy it." Gabe
wasn't about to let her displeasure dampen his excitement
for what he had planned for today. He turned to the woman
behind her and said, "I'm glad you could come, Mother.
Father."

Both of his parents followed his grandmother inside his
house.

"This cabin is so small," his grandmother complained,
looking around herself in disbelief. "Where are we all going
to sleep?" She spun toward him, her purse swinging from
the crook of her elbow. "And why all this secrecy? Why are
we here, Gabriel?"

"Grandmother, this house is almost four thousand
square feet. I'm sure I can comfortably sleep guests in
any of the five bedrooms." He reached for two suitcases
from the mountain piled at the door of the tiled entry.

"And you are here to celebrate my surprise engagement party."

"What?" His grandmother pressed a hand to her chest, turning to look back at his father. "Did you know?"

He shook his head. "I had no clue. We would have thrown a party at home, son." His father's rich voice sounded almost as confused as his grandmother's.

"This is my home." Gabe carried the suitcases down the hall and left them in one of the guest suites, his parents following behind. "Grandmother, is this room big enough for you?"

The room was one of his favorite rooms, with a massive sleigh bed and oak furniture; it gave way to a window seat and the best view of the rolling hills covered in vines.

"I suppose it will do since we are only here for the weekend," she said with a haughty sniff. "Why aren't you holding this party in San Francisco? So many people will be irate to have missed it. Not to mention that the media will not be happy that they weren't afforded the opportunity to cover the Maurier–Radcliffe announcement."

Gabe settled the larger of the bags near the closet and the smaller on the bed before turning to face his family. "About that. That's not the engagement I'm announcing, although Stephanie will be here for the party."

"I'm sure I don't understand." His grandmother's ice-blue eyes searched her grandson for an explanation.

"I'm not marrying Stephanie," Gabe said. "I'm proposing to Anna."

His grandmother's eyes widened and her mouth fell open in uncustomary silent shock. However, it didn't take her long to regain her composure. "No, I won't allow it. Don't make me have to remind you that I can change my will at any time, Gabriel."

A slow, patronizing smile slipped over his lips. "I know."

"You must not. You honestly think that I won't, but I'll change it, and you'll be left—"

"Bankrupt?" he filled in. "Because that's what you are, right? Or almost. You still own the mansion outright, but you invested too heavily in the central California housing market. When the bottom fell out, you couldn't recoup the losses. The only profitable thing you have is the shipping business, but that's not what it used to be, either, is it, Father?"

"Gabriel!" his mother sputtered.

"I mean no disrespect," he assured them. "But this information has made me realize that I will survive on my own merits, building my own fortune from my endeavors. It also means that I refuse to be guilted into a marriage that neither Stephanie nor I want."

"Gabe?" Anna called from the front of the house.

"She thinks we're announcing the opening of her new shop. Please, don't ruin the surprise."

His mother covered her mouth, tears misting her eyes as she reached for his father's hand. But his grandmother arched a brow in defiance, lifting her chin as Anna came to the door carrying two of the smaller bags.

"I thought I heard you back here. I brought these." The words had no more fallen from her lips when she tripped on the edge of the doorframe and tumbled into the room. Gabe caught her just before she hit the ground. She smiled brightly as she looked up into his face. "This time, looks like I ran into you."

Gabe pressed a quick kiss to her forehead. "Still falling for me, I see." He glanced up at his parents as he helped Anna stand and took the bags from her. "Mom, Dad, this is Anna Nolan."

Before she could react, his mother rushed Anna, enveloping her in a warm hug. "Anna," she whispered, her voice choked with emotion. "I'm so happy to meet you."

"It's wonderful to meet you, too," Anna said as she gave Gabe a concerned look at his mother's overdramatic response to a mere introduction.

"Okay, Priscilla, let the girl breathe." His grandmother tugged at his mother's arm, casting a quick glance over Gabe before giving him a sharp nod.

It was all Gabe needed to see to know that she would accept his decision. The situation might not be the way she'd planned it; but, in her own way, his grandmother still loved him. She would come to terms with his nuptials.

"If I'm not mistaken, Gabe, you promised me a fine glass of wine." Gabe's grandmother pressed her fingers to her temples. "I believe I need it."

Chapter 27

"ANNA, WOULD YOU come up here, please?" Gabe asked, waving her toward where he stood with a microphone, in front of the pond in their backyard.

She rose, smoothing the front of her skirt, and walked to the front of the crowd. She'd been shocked to see so many people coming out just to hear the announcement of Anna's plans to open Rosé. Local media had turned up, but she'd been surprised to see several photographers for San Francisco papers in attendance as well. Butterflies took flight in her stomach, making it twist and knot.

"Relax," Gabe whispered, pressing a kiss against her temple. "I'm right beside you."

She searched the grounds, her gaze falling on Stephanie standing close by. Her date for the event, Gabe's business partner, Brandon, had an arm wrapped around her waist and the two seemed pretty cozy, making Anna wonder if something more than a friendship was developing between them.

A buzz began at the back of the patio as Wilhelmina stepped forward, regally acknowledging several members of the media with a nod as she made her way to the front of the crowd where Gabe's sisters and parents watched. Almost imperceptibly, she gave Anna a nod of acquiescence.

Gabe had even invited Anna's parents for the event. She'd told him that there was no need for him to do so, but he'd insisted that he wanted them to stay involved in her life, in their life. Anna's eyes misted at the thought. Reaching for Gabe's hand, her heart fluttered in her throat, making it difficult to breathe, let alone speak. She was grateful that Gabe was introducing her and prayed her nerves would still before anyone could see her hands shaking.

"For those of you who don't know this woman yet, this is Anna Nolan, the creator of Rosé." He paused to look at her and Anna could see his unabashed pride and love for her in his face. His lips spread into a smile and she couldn't help the throb of longing that pounded through her veins. She loved this man with every breath in her body.

"If you haven't already seen her work or its incredible artistry"—he turned to indicate a square vase filled with orange and yellow pincushion proteas, lilies, orchids, and roses on a nearby table—"here is another example of the beautiful work she does." Gabe turned to lift a bridal bouquet from another nearby table. "Anna will make sure that your event becomes life-altering. That's what she did for me. You see, I first ran into her on the 101, quite literally."

He paused as the crowd's laughter filled the moment. Turning toward Anna, he held out his hand. She'd thought her hands were shaking before, but there was no hiding the trembling now. As if understanding her predicament, he held out the bouquet for her to hold. She wrapped her hands around the ribboned stems, letting the familiar weight of the flowers remind her of where she was, why she was here, and let the realization of her dream soothe her nervous fear.

"Since that day, she has completely changed my life. Before I go any further, there's something I can't wait any longer to do." Gabe reached into his pocket and bent to one knee.

Anna's heart stopped in her chest, and she was unable to catch her breath, the bouquet suddenly too heavy to hold.

"Anna Nolan, I love you. Until the day I met you, I lived a shallow existence. You gave it life and vitality. I want to be your partner, not just in business here in Sonoma, but in love. Will you marry me? Be my wife?"

There wasn't a question in Anna's mind as she threw her arms around Gabe's neck, speechless.

"Does this mean yes?" he asked.

"Yes!" She nodded, trying to stem the tears welling in her eyes. "Yes."

"Is he really doing this?" she heard one of Stephanie's sorority sisters mutter from the front row. Wilhelmina shushed her immediately.

"My family is known for their legacy in San Francisco, but this is only the beginning of our own legacy, Anna. You realize that, right?"

He didn't wait for her answer as his mouth crushed hers in a kiss that probably should have been reserved for a more private moment. But she didn't care. Propriety was part of his old life, not their future. That was filled with honest emotions that overpowered social status. With hope and laughter that would outlast reputations and promises that were stronger than "old money" power. The love she and Gabriel shared was the only legacy she wanted for her future.

THE
HORSE TRAINER

Chapter 1

December

IT WAS STILL dark when Travis Mitchell finished up his shift as security detail at the Los Alamitos Race Course. It killed him that he wasn't currently working as a horse trainer, but after refusing to follow his last employer's instructions to "do whatever it takes to win," he'd been fired and effectively blackballed.

He had no idea what his future held, but Travis was glad he hadn't drugged the horse. Besides, Travis would bounce back somehow, as he always did. But the security job provided him with rent-free housing in one of the one-room trailers on the property and that, coupled with exercising a few horses, was enough to make ends meet. Barely.

"Hey, you son of a bitch, stand still."

The curse echoed in the barn, warranting investigation as to who was in the nearby stalls. Few people milled around in the hours before dawn, mostly grooms and cleaning staff. Since most of these horses were valued in the high six figures, it was Travis's duty to keep them safe.

He hurried down the aisle of the barn and several horses nickered as he passed. He ignored them as three loud bangs sounded a few stalls away. A big bay horse was tossing his head in agitation. Narrowing his eyes, Travis peered into the dark space, lit only by a few dim lights overhead.

"Damn, you ass!" A man jumped backward out of the stall as another loud bang sounded. "You mother—"

"Need some help?" Travis asked, jogging over. He stopped cold when a horse lunged at the doorway, snapping his teeth at the man who'd barely escaped.

"No, I've got it," the man growled, turning toward him, recognition dawning. "Oh! Hey, Travis, I heard you were demoted to working the beat. What's next, groom?"

Travis recognized Casper Dolan, one of the most disreputable trainers on the track. Travis wouldn't even let this man clean his horse's stall. He wondered how Casper managed to convince an owner to hire him. The man was mean as snake spit and had a temper to match his wild red hair. Arching an eyebrow, Travis leaned his head to one side of the stall doorway to get a better look at the horse doomed to suffer this man's "training."

"Shit," he muttered.

Destiny's Dreamer. Travis couldn't for the life of him figure out why Fallon Radcliffe, a woman with a small fortune like hers, would hire a trainer like Casper. He'd heard about the colt and his owner. This was her first real race contender, her first time entering the field with the rest of the big guns of horse racing, and she had no idea what she was doing.

Obviously, since she chose to hire Casper.

Rumors about the woman spread faster than speculations about her horse. As part of the San Francisco elite, Fallon Radcliffe was high society money through and through. And she looked the part. Beautiful, elegant, and practically oozing with sophistication. She looked like an angel and almost as out of place as one yesterday when he'd spotted her striding through the barn in her designer heels and fitted suits, her long, blond waves cascading down her back.

Dreamer banged against the door, hanging his head over and wringing his neck threateningly. "Hey, calm down," Travis murmured, soothing the agitated horse as he glanced back at Casper. "How long's he been like this?"

"Always. He's crazy."

Travis didn't miss the way the other trainer cupped his right hand and reached back to adjust his pants. He was hiding something, and it was most likely drugs. He scanned Dreamer's neck and rump, looking for the tell-tale wetness from an injection, but the horse wouldn't stand still. A half-empty feed tub was on the ground and Travis dragged it closer with his foot, unable to distinguish anything but grain in the mash.

Casper waited, crossing his arms and glaring at Travis. "Since this isn't your horse, why don't you take a hike and let me do my job?"

Suddenly, Dreamer blew out a slow breath and groaned, his eyelids drooping as he hung his head. "Did you drug him?" Travis asked, point blank.

Casper took a step closer, looking up at Travis and shoving him backward slightly. The man had to be at least six inches shorter, but apparently he thought he could look intimidating.

"Get lost, Mitchell. Your advice isn't wanted for this horse." He shoved Travis again, but this time Travis didn't budge. "You're not a trainer anymore, just a cheap rent-a-cop."

"Keep shooting off your mouth, Casper, and I'll shut it for you permanently." Travis took a step toward Casper, forcing him backward. "If I find out that you—"

"What's going on?" A woman's quiet and demanding voice interrupted him.

Travis and Casper both turned to see Fallon Radcliffe watching them, hands fisted on her hips. She waited for the answer like a queen with her subjects.

She was even more gorgeous up close. The sun was coming up, shining through the aisle of the barn and lighting her from behind, giving her hair a halo effect, making her look almost ethereal.

But she wasn't like any angel he'd ever seen. An avenging angel, maybe? There was no mistaking the fact that she was pissed.

"Nothing." Travis glanced back at Casper, a smirk spreading over the other man's thin mouth as he crossed his arms over his chest defiantly. "I was making my rounds when your trainer had some…trouble."

She turned to Casper, her brow arching expectantly. "Dreamer was a little fired up this morning, but now he's fine."

Casper was lying. Any fool could see it, but Fallon chose to ignore the fact. Turning back to Travis, she smiled. "I appreciate your concern, Mr.…."

"Mitchell," he offered.

"Mr. Mitchell," she filled in. "But Mr. Dolan is my trainer. As a matter of fact, shouldn't he be heading out for his exercise rider?"

"Yes, ma'am." Casper reached for Dreamer's lead rope and clipped it to the colt's halter before leading him out of the stall.

Travis stepped aside, his arm brushing against Fallon's. The sizzle of attraction broke over him. He cursed his body's reaction to her. He needed an outlet for his pent-up frustration but, as tempting as she was, he could never get mixed in with the likes of Fallon Radcliffe.

"Again, thank—"

Travis cut her off as soon as Casper was out of earshot. "Don't race that horse today."

Her eyes popped open wide and her mouth rounded to a slight *O* before she caught herself. "What?"

"You need to scratch him. I'm not sure what Dolan did, but someone is going to get hurt if you race that horse today."

She watched her horse exit the barn, dragging his feet slowly. His movements were far too sluggish for a horse about to run one of the biggest futurity races of the year.

"Do you realize how much I stand to lose?" She shook her head. "I can't."

"If you don't, you're going to lose more than your entry fee," Travis warned, stealing one final look back at the horse. He sighed heavily, disappointed that this would probably be her colt's last race.

Travis had seen it before. The horse wouldn't perform if he was drugged and if he wasn't drugged, he'd blow up the way he had in the stall. The colt would end up in a kill lot. It was sad but commonplace in horse racing. Travis shook his head sadly, resigning himself.

"Good luck today, Miss Radcliffe. I think you're going to need it."

Chapter 2

GOOD LUCK...I think you're going to need it.

Fallon paced outside the barn, trying to get the security guard's warning out of her mind. Or maybe it had been the look he'd given her that shook her to her core.

Or maybe it was because he was hot.

And he was. He wasn't like the guys she usually dated. No, this one had a ruggedness about him. Despite his professional appearance, he had an air about him that was mysterious and intriguing. She felt like she was barely glimpsing the real man. It wasn't like he was hiding, just choosing not to reveal himself. And his gray eyes reminded her of a lone wolf.

She shook her head at her fantasies. He was a security guard, and she'd bet money he wouldn't be daydreaming about her hours later. She needed to focus on the task at hand—getting Dreamer into the winner's circle.

She glanced at her diamond-encrusted watch and realized she couldn't wait around for Casper any longer. She had to go get showered and changed and take care of a thousand other last-minute things before meeting her family in a couple of hours in the Vessels Club. She'd reserved a table especially for them. It was the first time they'd ever come to watch one of her races and she was determined to prove to them that she wasn't a fool for wanting to breed racehorses.

As the baby of the Radcliffe family, Fallon had grown up in the shadow of her perfect siblings. She adored her brother and sister, but it was difficult trying to match the acumen of her vintner brother, Gabe, or the Midas touch her sister, Alex, had for restoring failing businesses.

Fallon breathed a sigh of relief as Casper came around the corner. "You look worried. Go, I've got things under control here. I'll see you in the winner's circle."

"Are you sure? Was he okay this morning on his run?"

"Yes." Casper waved her off, exasperated, barely humoring her anxiety. "Go."

Fallon inhaled slowly, trying to calm herself, and nodded. Casper had already left to retrieve Dreamer from his stall for the race.

Hoping that her million-dollar appearance would mask her nervousness, she hurried through the throng of race enthusiasts and gamblers lining the railing, making her way to the Vessels Club as quickly as her Jimmy Choos would allow. She opened the door and was blasted by the hot air. It was a welcome sensation as she tried not to shiver in her silk camisole and jacket. Fallon stepped inside, searching the crowd of people for her brother's tall frame. Instead, she heard a nasally complaint from her grandmother, Wilhelmina.

"Really, I don't think that child could have chosen a more inurbane hobby."

Fallon willed the blush to disappear from her cheeks. She swallowed, putting on a brave smile before approaching her family.

"Oh, you made it!" Alex leaned down to press a kiss to her cheek, her eyes rolling toward their grandmother. "We were about to head out to the terrace. We thought we'd be able to see the race better from there."

"And there are fewer people to overhear Grandmother," Fallon whispered back.

Her sister smiled and nodded as their brother, Gabe, gave her shoulder a quick squeeze, his other arm wrapped around his fiancée's shoulders.

"The horses should be heading toward the stands. We'd better find our seat if you want to see them."

"Yes, let's," Wilhelmina agreed, the sarcasm dripping from her tone as she peered down her nose at the railing below. "Because watching ill-bred clodhoppers throw their money away gambling should make for a delightful afternoon."

The blush burned her cheeks again as Fallon saw several people turn and glance at her grandmother curiously. Fallon knew there was no taming her grandmother's tongue.

Wilhelmina Radcliffe had been born into high society and married into an empire, wielding the power both provided her. She was accustomed to the audacity her wealth allowed, which she felt gave her permission to deliver scathing commentary with the authority of royalty. She saw no need to mingle with the commoners, and she'd made it clear that she felt Fallon was doing exactly that by racing horses.

Grateful for her sister's ability to usher her grandmother out to the terrace, Fallon followed. Butterflies took flight in her stomach when she saw the first horse make its way onto the track.

"I'll never understand, dear, why you'd ever sully the

Radcliffe name with horse racing when there are so many other more prestigious pursuits." Her grandmother frowned, her lips pursing. "Those beasts are so...dirty. I mean, if you must have horses, why couldn't you do something more elegant like dressage?"

It was the same argument each time she saw her grandmother. For nearly twenty-five years, Fallon had lived the life her grandmother had dictated. She'd been a San Francisco socialite who managed the finances of the family shipping business, but it never excited her.

Horses made her feel alive. Seeing the colors of her silks on a jockey made her entire body tingle with electricity. Watching her horse cross the finish line, even if it had only been in small races so far, made her feel like she was soaring with him.

"Grandmother, stop," Gabe said, shooting his sister a wink. "Let Fallon have her moment. We'll see what you have to say after Dreamer wins."

Fallon wished she could muster half of the confidence her brother displayed. Her stomach did another flip as she saw the crowd near the railing scatter and yelp in fear. The horses that were already on the track began to prance nervously and she realized there were already six out, with number seven jolting forward.

It was hard to breathe. Fallon gripped the railing, leaning forward to get a glimpse at what was happening below, but she couldn't see anything.

Her grandmother let out a breath in a huff. "Sport of kings, my foot. More like the sport of the downtrodden unfortunates and misguided saps," she muttered, lifting her champagne to her lips. "Please tell me I don't have to attend all of these."

Her words barely registered because Fallon located the

horse causing the commotion. Dreamer reared straight up, unseating the jockey and lifting the groom off the ground. He pawed at the air with his front hooves.

The security guard's last words came back to haunt her. *Good luck…you're going to need it.*

Chapter 3

"I HAVE TO GO."

Fallon didn't wait for her family to register what she'd said. She ran from the terrace and headed back toward the track, unsure what use she would be. And yet she couldn't sit back and watch her dream get crushed. Not when she was so close to getting her horse to the Kentucky Derby.

Dreamer *would* make it. He was the most incredible horse she'd ever seen. He wasn't just fast—he loved to run. When he moved, his feet barely touched the ground, and he had a stride that covered ground the way eagles soared across the clouds—effortlessly.

Fallon gasped as Dreamer kicked a hind foot at one of the pony horses. Casper stood to the other side, his skin blotchy with embarrassment. Her jockey shot him a pleading look but the trainer simply shrugged. Dreamer's handler, back on his feet, drew the colt's reins slightly tighter, trying to control him.

But the horse only became more aggravated. He began shaking his head, setting the bit between his teeth. Without warning, Dreamer reared back again. The handler clipped a stud chain to Dreamer's bridle, hoping it would stop his antics, as Casper helped the jockey get back into the saddle.

He passed them off to the loading crew at the starting gate, but even from where she stood, Fallon could see Dreamer's eyes were wide with fear.

This wasn't good.

As they tried to load Dreamer into his chute, he balked, backing up and stiffening his legs. Two men hooked arms behind him to shove him in, but he began bucking. Somehow, they managed to get him into the chute.

They closed the gate behind Dreamer but it only made matters worse. Rearing inside, he twisted his body, tossing the jockey out of the starting gate to the gasping awe of the crowd around Fallon.

As the emergency crew rushed down the track, Dreamer continued to thrash in the gate. The clang of metal scared several of the other horses as the crew worked feverishly to get the horses safely unloaded.

Fallon gripped the railing, knuckles white with fear as her jockey's golden silks were stripped off so the emergency crew could inspect his shoulder. Fallon heard the announcer notify the crowd that Destiny's Dreamer had been scratched from the race.

No, no, no!

Fallon raced down the fence to the opening, where Dreamer was being handed off to another handler. Blood was flowing down his beautiful chestnut-colored face, dripping from the gash on his head. The horse was still thrashing, trying to rear, while Casper stood to one side, watching in fearful awe.

"What are you doing? Take him," she ordered, running to his side.

"I'm not taking him." Realizing how cowardly he sounded, Casper cleared his throat. "I mean, these guys know what they're doing. We need the vet to sedate him."

"We can't wait for that. He's never acted like this."

Shoving past Casper, Fallon moved closer to her horse. She knew she was putting herself in a dangerous position, but she prayed she could calm Dreamer. Her horse knew her. She'd been there ever since she'd helped his mother foal him and when she'd imprinted him three years ago, and she prayed it would count for something.

Reaching the security detail guarding the gate, Fallon flashed her pass and hurried onto the edge of the track. Dreamer reared again, striking out and catching the lead, ripping it from the handler's grip. Now loose on the track, he turned, ready to bolt into the pack of horses that were being held at the starting gate.

"Whoa, Dreamer," she called, moving closer as he reared again. "Easy, boy." Her fingers nearly closed around the lead when Dreamer struck out at her.

Fallon was knocked sideways, hitting the soft dirt with less pain than she'd expected. When she looked up, she saw the broad, muscular V of a man's back standing in front of her, facing Dreamer with his hands splayed out and his arms angled down.

"Hey, hey, easy now." The voice was loud enough to garner the colt's attention, but it remained calm. "Come on, boy."

Dreamer dropped back to all fours and snorted loudly. The man in front of Fallon took a step toward the horse, keeping his hands open loosely, relaxed.

"There you go."

Dreamer dropped his head, as if hypnotized, and began licking his lips, stilling immediately. The man took the lead easily, turning away from the horse who followed behind him as docile as a puppy. Fallon's gaze lifted, finally able to see the face of the man who'd saved her from being trampled, and found herself staring into those gray eyes again.

"Mr. Mitchell?"

He walked up to her and stretched out a hand to help her up. "Sorry about shoving you, Miss Radcliffe, but a hoof to the shoulder hurts. You were about to find out."

Fallon took his hand. Warm and calloused, it wasn't what she'd expected. Nor had she expected the heat that radiated from his fingertips, up her arm, before sliding through the rest of her body, making her feel light-headed.

"You okay?" His eyebrows lifted in question and she swallowed hard, unable to vocalize the words to tell him she was fine. "You didn't hit your head, did you?"

"No," she finally managed. She stood and dusted off her cream-colored pencil skirt before realizing it was completely ruined, along with her new shoes. Fallon cleared her throat, taking control of her voice. "No, I'm fine. And please, call me Fallon."

"Let's get him to the barn and have the vet look at him there," he suggested, grimacing at the blood on the colt's face.

She nodded and Casper rushed forward. Dreamer's head instantly shot up in the air, his eyes rolling back slightly. "I'll take it from here, Mitchell."

He reached for the lead but Fallon put a hand out.

"Leave him alone. Since you seem inclined to let others handle him when there's trouble, I'm inclined to find someone else to train him for the rest of his races."

"You're firing me?"

Both men stopped to wait for her answer, watching her expectantly.

"You better believe it," she answered. "I only want my horse in the best hands." She looked over at the security guard whose mere presence managed to calm her horse. "And they certainly aren't yours, Casper."

Chapter 4

FALLON'S PHONE RANG while the vet was suturing Dreamer's face. Luckily for her, Casper had collected his check and left. However, it hadn't stopped him from ranting about how she was an entitled bitch, and the media had eaten his words up. Sighing, Fallon glanced at her phone and saw her grandmother's number.

"I have to take this," she informed Mr. Mitchell, who was still standing with Dreamer. He nodded and she made her way to the end of the barn for some privacy. "Hello, Grandmother," she said in a tight voice. She was worried about what would be waiting for her on the other end of the line.

"I saw that."

Of course, you did. "Dreamer is fine. He's getting a couple of stitches but—"

"I don't care about the *horse*." Her grandmother sighed dramatically. "I care about the fact that you were shoved to the ground. By a groom, no less."

"That's not what happened, Grandmother. A security guard pushed me out of the way before Dreamer kicked me."

"Kicked you? Oh, dear heavens." Her grandmother gasped and Fallon could picture her waving a hand in front of her face to keep from fainting. Then she switched her tone, exasperation coloring her words. "Fallon, dear, when are you going to give up this silly horse nonsense?"

Fallon clamped her teeth together and took a deep breath, pinching the bridge of her nose as she prayed for patience. "It's not nonsense, Grandmother."

"This hobby of yours is going to get you or someone else killed. Not to mention, our family name is being dragged through…well, probably something like the muck you're cleaning in those stalls." Her grandmother sniffed loudly, making her opinion of Fallon's career choice very clear—she hated it.

"I'm not cleaning stalls; I'm breeding racehorses."

"They aren't racehorses if they can't get out of the gate," her grandmother said pointedly.

Never one to hold back, her grandmother was painfully blunt. Yet because she came from one of the oldest and richest families in San Francisco, people not only overlooked it, but sought out Wilhelmina Radcliffe's views. And thus she assumed her opinions were wanted in every scenario, though it wasn't the case now.

"Why don't you sell those beasts and move back to San Francisco? You're a Radcliffe. You should be married by now and taking your place in the *family* business."

Fallon loved her family, but she would never return to accept any position in the family shipping business. It was a dying institution and she'd done that already. It stifled her.

Fallon wanted to prove she could make it on her own, following her passion. What she needed was her family's support, not her grandmother's disapproval and old-fashioned, outrageous demands. Marriage? Well, that was the last concern on her mind. She had enough on her plate right now dealing with Dreamer.

"This is the business endeavor I've chosen to pursue." She glanced down the aisle and saw that the vet was finishing up. "I'm sorry, I need to go. You'll be at the race in two months, right? The El Camino Real?"

Her grandmother sighed into her ear again. "I don't know about the others, but I suppose if you insist on continuing this nonsense, I will go to *one* more. But only with the agreement that if this happens again, Fallon, you'll quit this and come back." Her grandmother's voice lowered. "It was an embarrassment."

Tell me about it.

"We'll have brunch," Fallon suggested, avoiding her grandmother's ultimatum and raising a hand to let the vet know she was coming. "I'll call you later. Give my love to the others. And, Grandmother, I love you."

"Yes, dear."

Before Fallon could respond, her grandmother had already disconnected the call.

Before Fallon hurried back to Dreamer, the vet instructed her how to care for his wound, and suggested that he wasn't ridden for a few days. Fallon knew it would take more than a few days to cure what ailed her colt. Something had gone horribly wrong and she was going to be lucky if she could find a way to ever return him to the starting gates, regardless of her confident statements to her grandmother.

As the vet left, Mr. Mitchell turned Dreamer into the stall, silently watching him, as if he were waiting for Fallon to be the first to speak.

"Thank you for your help today."

He simply nodded.

She bit the inside corner of her lip, feeling awkward. Now that she could get a good look at him, she couldn't deny he was extremely attractive in a rugged, cowboy kind of way. His hair needed a cut and hung in long, dark waves on his forehead, making her fingers itch to run through it where it curled slightly at his nape and over his ears. His eyes were the color of a stormy sky, alternating between blue and gray.

But his mouth. Fallon pressed her lips together in an effort not to think about how kissable it was. Full, but not overly so, and just the thought of it was enough to make her stomach do a flip.

"I...um, I should probably apologize for not listening to you this morning."

He turned back toward her, his expression unreadable. "Probably," he agreed, tucking his fingers into the front of his slacks. "What are you going to do?"

She moved to the other side of the door, watching Dreamer, contemplating his question. What *was* she going to do? The race season was underway. All the good trainers were hired. And it wasn't like she could start over next year. Dreamer only had this one chance.

She'd put her heart into the colt—perfect breeding, foundational training, and all the investment she'd built up for her endeavor. She'd put all her money into this dark horse and now, it looked like the opportunity would be ripped away before she even got started. Tears burned, but she refused to break down in front of this stranger.

"I don't know."

"Can I offer a suggestion?"

She shot him a sideways glance.

"Let me train him."

Her eyebrows shot up in surprise. What did a security guard know about training racehorses? Especially a horse of Dreamer's caliber. But then again, he had been the only one capable of calming her colt, which meant he had some sort of instinct.

As if sensing her doubt, he pressed on. "He needs my help or he may never race again."

"*Your* help?"

He scowled for a moment, but he quickly masked his distaste. His expression softened as he looked at Dreamer. "I'm a trainer, not a guard. I'm just doing this…" He shot her a look. "Temporarily," he finished.

Hope flared in her chest, hot and bright. "Wait! Are you *Travis* Mitchell?"

His mouth pinched slightly. "Yes."

Fallon couldn't believe her luck. She'd heard of him, heard of the miracles he worked, but couldn't fathom why he'd be working security. Or why someone hadn't managed to have him working with their barn. "You'll help me?"

"Before I agree, I need to know one thing. Did you ask Casper to drug this horse?"

Fallon blinked dumbly. "Excuse me?"

"He was doping your horse with something. I'm guessing that we saw it wearing off today. I need to know whether it was your idea or his."

"I… I didn't even know."

He narrowed his eyes as he searched her face. She could see he was trying to decide whether to believe her.

She crossed her arms over her chest. "How do I know you're really Travis Mitchell?"

"Ask around."

He was confident, she'd give him that. "Why aren't you working with horses now?"

"Long story. The short version is while you had a dick trainer, I had a dick owner whose ideas about how to get a horse to perform differed from mine."

So that's why he'd wanted to know if it had been her idea to drug Dreamer. Travis tipped his head to one side and looked at her.

"We're in the same boat here."

"Screwed?"

He gave her a half shrug. "Unless we make this work."

"How much do you want? Don't expect me to pay some exorbitant amount just because you know I need someone."

"Not everything is about money, Fallon." He shook his head. His voice was gravelly but his tone was tender, almost apologetic. She was surprised at what hearing him say her first name made her feel. She found she liked the way it rolled from his lips, like a breath or a sigh. But she could tell that something she'd said disappointed him. She'd definitely touched a nerve.

Note to self, no more money talk. "Can you really help him?"

He studied her but she couldn't figure out what he was looking for. Something in her stance or her expression? She wished she knew because, whatever he wanted, she'd give it to him. She was desperate, but she didn't want to admit it aloud. She bit down on her lip, waiting for a response from him. Travis sighed, tucking his hands into the front pockets of his jeans. She could see the indecision clouding his face.

"Mr. Mitchell," she began, reaching for his arm.

Warm tingles shot up her fingers and he looked at her hand on his bicep, his gaze sliding over her in a slow caress. Fallon jerked it back and clasped her hands in front of her nervously.

"It's Travis. And yes, I can, on one condition."

"Anything," she agreed.

"You don't question my training. We're all-in on this. No changing your mind and firing me like you fired Casper. We do this *my* way, completely, until the season is over. Then you can fire me if you feel the need."

When it no longer mattered.

It was a tall order. He was demanding she give him, a stranger, complete control of her horse's future based solely on his reputation. She stared into his gray eyes, trying to read him, but he was indecipherable. But unless she wanted to train Dreamer herself, she had no other options.

"Agreed. Anything else?"

He walked to the stall door and looked inside, exhaling slowly as if he'd been as nervous about this negotiation as she had.

"He can't go back to your training facility. He needs somewhere private, away from everything he's used to, someplace he's never been."

"How am I supposed to manage that?"

He turned back toward her and tipped his chin down, his expression dubious. "You're a Radcliffe. I'm sure you can figure out a way." His voice didn't brook any room for argument. "Someplace quiet."

Fallon bit her lip, trying to figure out where to take Dreamer. Pulling out her phone, she sent her brother a quick text. He owned a biodynamic vineyard in Sonoma. It was the only place she could think of that would be available immediately and might fit Travis's demands. Gabe immediately responded that she was welcome to the house since he and Anna were heading to Italy the next morning, traveling for business for the next few months. He promised to tell his vineyard livestock manager, Marco, she'd be arriving and ask him to open the house for her.

"Done. We can take him up to Sonoma as soon as he's ready to travel."

Travis shot her a sardonic look. "Must be nice to get

anything you want with nothing more than a text. Give me directions. I'll drive him up myself as soon as the sedative wears off. We'll be there by tomorrow night."

"You sure?"

"Nope," he admitted. "But waiting isn't going to make me any more certain."

She wondered why he sounded like he had more doubts about their arrangement than she did. She was the one taking all the risk.

Chapter 5

THIS IS A *big mistake.*

Travis fought the conflicting emotions roiling in his gut as he slowed the truck and trailer in the massive driveway of the vineyard. On one hand, he'd followed Dreamer leading up to this race and recognized his potential to be a champion. He knew that Dreamer could be the one to bring him back from the brink and boost him back into his career. But, on the other hand, he'd be faced with Fallon Radcliffe.

And he didn't like her.

Okay, that wasn't exactly true. He *did* like her, and too much. But he didn't want to. Especially not if he was going to be working for her.

He wanted to feel contempt for her. To see her as the woman he'd expected her to be. The spoiled rich girl, playing at becoming a famous racehorse owner. He'd seen plenty of them rise and fall, but there was something different about Fallon, and he couldn't quite put his finger on it. But that wasn't really what was giving him pause about accepting this job.

It was what had happened whenever they touched. When she'd reached for his arm. It was what had happened when their eyes met. The heated attraction seemed to sizzle between them like an open current of electricity.

It was dangerous. He didn't want to be drawn to her, but he couldn't fight the magnetic pull between them. He'd given in to it when he said yes.

As much as Travis wanted to believe his motive was to help bring the colt to greatness, he couldn't deny the idea of spending more time near Fallon was tempting, though she was out of his league. Hell, he still wasn't sure how he'd even managed to get into the ballpark. Besides, he knew to keep business separate from pleasure and, as enticing as Fallon was, this was nothing but business.

She was, without a doubt, in over her head and needed someone to keep an eye out for her. She had no clue how men like Casper would talk about her, and he doubted her delicate sensibilities were prepared for the ugly reality she'd be forced to face in this boys' club. She seemed so naive and trusting. And he wanted to protect her from it if he could.

Travis parked the truck as Fallon came out of the house, looking concerned. She hurried toward him as he jumped out and went to the back of the trailer to unload the horse.

"You finally made it." She looked more casual today. Her hair was pulled back in a messy ponytail, and she was wearing a flannel shirt and jeans. Casual and, unfortunately for him, sexy as hell.

Travis untied Dreamer and led him out. He could have put the horse on a flight since driving took longer, but Travis wanted to lower the colt's stress level. Surprisingly, Dreamer remained remarkably calm the entire ride, which made Travis wonder what could have sparked the episode at the track.

Two horses whinnied from somewhere near the barn as

Dreamer backed down the ramp, and his head instantly shot up, but without agitation. At the sharp bray of a donkey, Travis gave Fallon a curious look.

"It's my brother's place," she explained. "He's big on bio-dynamic farming so he has all sorts of animals and habitats here."

"Including a donkey?" Travis patted Dreamer on the neck and said, "Well, boy, you're going to have some fun here the next few weeks."

"This is what you wanted, right?" Fallon glanced toward the barn raucous with a variety of animal noises.

Travis nodded. "It's exactly what he needs." They walked him toward the barn.

"I prepared this stall for him," Fallon said, pointing at an enclosed space at the end of the short row barn, away from the other animals.

"No, let's do the one with the run." He gestured toward an empty stall, situated between two goats and what appeared to be some sort of curly-coated, long-haired steer. Dreamer snorted as Travis turned him into the stall.

"Are you sure he's going to be okay? He won't hurt himself?"

Travis shrugged. It wasn't an impossibility, but at least Dreamer was already settling, sniffing at the goats who had come out to greet him. "I think he'll be okay." Right then, the steer bawled loudly and, startled, Dreamer jumped to the side. He circled his run, kicking up his heels playfully before returning to inspect his other neighbor. Travis laughed. "He'll be just fine."

"Okay, if you're sure." Fallon shrugged slightly as she walked back toward the front of the barn.

He followed down the aisle, peering into the stalls along the way. Most were empty but one held several sheep. The first one housed the donkey he'd heard upon his arrival. "Well, aren't you cute?"

"That's Bubba. He's sort of the guard dog of the barn, alerting us whenever someone is around," Fallon explained. "Bo and Sadie are the quarter horses in the pasture. They'll come in at night." She started to leave the barn, but Travis held his ground. "Aren't you coming?"

"Where?"

She frowned at him and said, "To your room, in the house."

"I can't stay in the house."

"Of course you can. Where else would you stay?"

She gave him a breezy laugh, and it reminded him of the way the wind chimes on his grandmother's porch tinkled in the summer evenings. It was the only time in his life he'd been happy or felt loved. Longing constricted his chest as he realized how tempting Fallon really was. She could give him all the things he'd rarely had in his past.

But Travis couldn't go down that slippery road. He steeled his resolve and said, "I'm staying in the barn, where I belong."

Chapter 6

FALLON TIPPED HER head to one side, her blond hair falling over her shoulder as she stared at Travis incredulously. He didn't have to explain to her that this was the way of the world. He was the hired help. Hired hands didn't cross certain boundaries, and living in the house with her would be leaping over them.

Not to mention, it'd make it too easy for him to forget that this was purely a business arrangement.

"Don't be ridiculous, Travis. You can't stay out here."

"Why not? I'll be near Dreamer so I can monitor him more closely."

It wasn't untrue. She didn't have to know the real reason he didn't want to share close quarters with her, day in and day out. He was good at resisting temptation but even he didn't have *that* much willpower. No man did.

"I'll be fine on a cot out here."

"You can't sleep on a cot!"

Her outrage made him laugh. "Why not? I've slept in worse places." Inside his truck, in stalls, on a folding chair. It was better than a doorway. And hell, he'd done that, too.

"Take the office. I don't use it," a short Hispanic man offered, entering the barn with a large, yellow Labrador at his heels. He thrust his hand out to Travis. "Marco Delgado," he said. "I'm the livestock manager. This is Maggie." He patted the dog on the head and she sat at his feet.

Travis shook Marco's hand before reaching out to pet the dog. "Looks like you've got a little of everything here."

"Yep," Marco said with a laugh. "Everything from dogs and cats to alpacas and a few beefalo. Once that horse lives here for a bit, he'll be used to just about anything." He waved a hand at the office door. "Go on and take over in there and move whatever you don't need into the storage shed out back. Flag me down if you need me. I'll be around. *Mi establo es su establo.*"

My barn is your barn.

"Gracias," Travis called after him.

"De nada," Marco answered with a wave, heading back outside.

"You know Spanish?" Fallon asked.

Travis laughed. "You don't work around the track, or horses, in California and not learn Spanish. You'd be at a disadvantage without it."

He crossed the aisle to the office. It looked almost identical to the other horse stalls from the outside, but inside, it was twice as large and had electricity. An overhead fan circled slowly in the breeze. Instead of the bars across the front windows, the rectangular spaces in the dividing walls were filled with Plexiglas.

Most of the barn offices Travis had seen were filled with ratty, second-hand furniture, but not this one. Plush leather couches and chairs were arranged comfortably in front of a large, walnut desk. Matching filing cabinets were nestled against the wall on the left. An oil painting of the Sonoma landscape hung behind the leather desk chair.

Travis ran a hand over the overstuffed, buttery soft cushions, trying not to look too impressed. "Forget the cot, this couch will be like sleeping on a cloud," he muttered.

"My brother loves this vineyard more than life itself so he's gone all out on every aspect of it," Fallon explained. "Including this office that he never uses."

Travis didn't miss the adoration in her voice when she spoke about her brother.

"Be sure to thank him for me." He turned back to face her. "I should grab my gear from the truck. We'll give Dreamer a day or two to settle in and then I'll get started."

"Doing what?" She tucked her hands into her pockets and shrugged slightly. "What exactly is the plan?"

Well, it hadn't taken long for her to start questioning him.

He almost reminded her of the fact but she'd already turned away from the office and headed back to Dreamer's stall, watching the colt intently, looking genuinely concerned. Maybe he'd judged her too quickly.

Travis leaned over the door. "I'm taking Dreamer back to basics to see where he went off the rails and give him something to feel confident about. Then we'll throw a few new things at him and see how he reacts."

"You really think you can fix him?"

"Yes."

"I mean, in time to race again?"

Irritation swelled in his chest. Like every other owner he'd worked with, Fallon only cared about losing her investment. He should have known better.

Dreamer came back inside and walked toward them. Reaching for a handful of grain from a tub beside her, she held out her hand for the colt. "I just want to see him happy again," she said. "Even if it means retiring him or finding him a new job." She ran her hand over the horse's neck affectionately, something he rarely saw in owners. "You know what I mean?"

That wasn't what he'd expected to hear from her. "What's your end game with him, Fallon?"

She brushed her hands over the colt's cheeks and he nickered softly, nuzzling at her face. She giggled quietly, rubbing under his chin as he stretched out his neck, enjoying the attention.

"He used to enjoy running and everything leading up to a race. Now, even I can see he's spooked. He's too sweet a colt for that to happen to him. If he's better suited to be a jumper or a show horse, then so be it. I want him to enjoy his life again."

He eyed her carefully, trying to judge the truth of her words. If he were to take her at her word, she cared about this animal more than the profit he could bring her.

"Right, big boy?" She moved her hand to rub at his neck again, laughing as he bobbed his head playfully, relishing the rubdown. She patted his shoulder and glanced at the watch on her wrist, the diamonds gleaming in the sunlight. "I'm hungry. Why don't we go out and I'll buy you dinner?"

Travis's gaze crashed into hers, trying to ignore the sizzle of heat churning in his gut at the thought of being in a darkened restaurant with her, as if they were a couple on a date.

Was she asking him out? He wasn't about to let her buy him dinner. She was his employer and he couldn't let himself forget that.

Travis took a step backward, putting some distance between them. "I don't think so. I should stay with Dreamer, make sure he settles in okay."

"Come on." She laughed. "You have to eat and there's no food in the house." She shot him a sly grin. "I heard there's a great place in town," she teased. "Pizza? Thick crust. Lots of cheese."

Her eyes practically twinkled with merriment. Away from the track, Fallon seemed younger, sweet, and flirtatious. It made him wonder what she was like before she was forced to become the mature, responsible society princess she'd been raised to be.

She's out of your league, he reminded himself. *Business, keep it business.*

But seeing her with the horse, in the barn with dirt on her hands, wearing worn jeans and a flannel shirt, he found it easy to forget she was San Francisco elite. It was easy to forget she was off-limits.

"I'll tell you what," she offered. "Let's have it delivered and we'll eat it here."

Crap! Now he had no excuse to stay away from her.

Chapter 7

"I JUMPED UP in the middle of that mud puddle and told him I wanted a job," he said, and Fallon's laughter was so contagious that the walls between their worlds crumbled.

"You did not!"

Travis held up one hand. "I swear to you."

Fallon, sitting cross-legged on the couch in the barn's office, tipped her head backward and laid the hand that wasn't holding her glass of wine on his forearm. Heat traveled through his veins and settled in his groin.

She'd come across as in-over-her-head at first, but as they'd talked over the thick-crust pepperoni pizza and she'd become animated, he could see her zest for life. She listened raptly, excited by his tales of growing up on the track. Her dark eyes revealed all her thoughts as she asked him questions about his experiences. But most of all, Fallon had a smart head for horse racing and what it took to succeed.

She was a beautiful, vibrant woman.

She sipped the wine, blinking slowly as her laughter eased into the enigmatic smile of a woman who might have had one drink too many. "And what did he say to that?"

"He told me I had a long way to go but that he would let me tag along after him." Travis smiled at the memory of

Buck Taylor, the man who'd taught him everything he knew about horses and training. "It was the beginning of my descent down the rabbit hole."

She tucked a lock of honey-colored hair behind her ear and studied him closely. "How old were you?"

"Eight."

Her eyes widened slightly in surprised fascination. "You're lucky," she said on a sigh, letting her head fall to the side, against her shoulder, and he caught the sweet floral scent of her shampoo.

"Depends on your perspective, I guess." Travis shrugged, not wanting to confess the real reason he'd been at the track in the first place. His father had an insatiable gambling habit. It was true that Travis grew up around horses, but it wasn't in the way most people assumed. He didn't see the point in clarifying the assumption. The fantasy was better than the truth.

"My family hates that I'm doing this," she revealed, taking another sip of her wine, playing with the stem of the glass. "My grandmother thinks it's a phase that I'll get over eventually before returning to work in the family business."

"Is it?"

She shot him a guarded look. "I can't imagine doing anything else. And my horse is a winner. I know Destiny's Dreamer is going to win the Kentucky Derby in May."

He sat up straight, shocked. "Fallon, he won't make the Derby. He didn't make it out the gate yesterday."

"I know." Travis saw the flicker of doubt cross her face. "But that's why we are here, right? For you to fix that."

"Getting into the Derby is a one-in-a-million shot."

"The odds have never bothered me," she quipped with a nonchalant shrug before she looked at him again. Her jaw set in dainty defiance. "He can win it. I know he can."

Travis stood up from the couch and ran a hand through his dark hair. "What happened to just wanting him happy again? Do you realize what you're asking of me? Of him?"

"But he *loves* to run. You didn't see him before this."

Stubborn silence filled the room. Fallon finished her wine, watching Travis, waiting for him to agree with her.

He couldn't. There was a good chance Dreamer would never race again. Even if he did, he needed to earn enough points in qualifying races in the coming months to even get a shot to compete in the Kentucky Derby. He kept his mouth shut, but it seemed that Fallon was wasting her time and money on an impossible fantasy.

Travis shook his head as he moved toward the doorway. The animals had begun to settle in for the night. The goats bleated softly to one another. The two quarter horses Marco had brought in were pawing in their stalls. Dreamer hung his head over the doorway, watching the horses across from him.

Normally, the barn sounds relaxed Travis, soothing his stress, but tonight, realizing what Fallon expected from him, he felt overwhelmed.

"I can't work miracles," he muttered, turning back to where she sat.

She slid the glass to the table, almost missing the edge, and unfolded herself from the couch. Travis arched an eyebrow, his gaze wandering to the empty wine bottle on the table, wondering when she'd finished it off. She slinked toward him like a cat, softly smiling at him.

"Yes, you can. I saw the way Dreamer responded to you at the track. The way he listened to you, even when he was going berserk." Her voice was quietly seductive, lulling him. "You bring out the best in—oh!"

Fallon's toe caught on the edge of the rug covering the

office floor. Travis immediately rushed forward, catching her as she tumbled.

She weighed next to nothing, but as he held her close, her soft curves melted into him. Clutching his biceps, she looked up at him and burst out laughing. Lifting her back to her feet, Travis slid one arm around her waist, steadying her with his other.

But once she was standing again, she didn't release her grip on him.

Their gazes met, melding together. The heat from her body, still pressed against him, intoxicated him more than the alcohol had. Without meaning to, he took a step closer to her, drawing her in to him as his arm slid up her back. Her hands moved up his arms to grip his shoulders and her smile turned apologetic.

"Sorry, maybe I should have—"

Travis didn't let her finish, didn't give himself a chance to second-guess his action. His mouth slanted over hers.

Without hesitation, her fingers slid along his neck, curling into his hair, dragging him closer, her tongue seeking the heat of his. Travis tasted the sweet tartness of the wine and the spiciness of the pizza on her lips as she matched the yearning in his kiss. Fallon sighed and the sweet sound reverberated through him like a bolt of lightning. His body grew rigid and desire raged through him like a storm.

He couldn't do this. She was his boss, and vulnerable, thanks to that bottle of wine. He wasn't the kind of man to take advantage.

Gripping her shoulders, Travis took a step back, breaking the kiss. She blinked up at him, confused by his sudden retreat.

As a man, he was having a damn hard time keeping his hands off her. He wanted her. The aching throb in his groin was more than enough proof. But, as a gentleman, he knew he had to walk her up to the house. Chivalry won out.

Travis fisted his hands into the front pockets of his jeans. "Let's get you back to the house," he said, leading the way out of the office, standing beside the door, waiting for her to follow. "We can talk about the plans for Dreamer in the morning."

A frown flitted over her brow before Fallon raised her chin. "I'm a big girl, Mr. Mitchell. I can find my way back to the house myself, thank you."

She brushed past him, leaving him standing in the doorway, trying to pretend he wasn't eyeing her curves and wishing he'd kept his damn mouth shut.

Chapter 8

FALLON ROLLED OVER in bed, draping her arm over her eyes and trying to ignore the pounding in her temples. Her brother might make fantastic wine but it always left her with a killer hangover. She regretted her decision to drink an entire bottle—minus the one glass Travis had—in one sitting.

But dinner with him had set her nerves on edge. She'd hoped the wine would relax her. She enjoyed his company, and that was precisely the problem. He made her forget all the rules of etiquette she'd had forced on her growing up. He made her *want* to forget all the proper behaviors her grandmother would deem necessary for a lady of her stature. If she were honest, he made her want to drag him back to her room and throw him on the bed.

The memories of tripping and falling into his arms came back to her, and, of course, that kiss.

And the way he'd immediately rejected her.

"Ugh!" she groaned. "Nothing like making a fool out of yourself."

She flung back the covers. No point in delaying the inevitable.

After rising, she padded into the kitchen and slid a coffee mug from the cupboard before choosing a single-serve coffee pod for her brother's machine. She pressed two fingers to her throbbing temple. She needed something full of flavor, and as strong as possible, please.

She took the steaming mug with her back to the bedroom, and there, threw on a pair of jeans and a thin, ribbed turtleneck. After making quick work of brushing her teeth and tugging her long, blond hair back into a ponytail, she headed back to the kitchen, sans makeup.

"Why bother? It's not like I'm impressing anyone," she muttered to no one as she tipped her head to one side, gazing out into the faint dawn light as she brewed herself another cup.

She could barely make out the shape of Travis, already up and walking Dreamer toward the pipe round pen. She glanced at the clock: it was barely six thirty. If he was working Dreamer already, that meant he'd been up to feed no later than five. She'd been in the barn until after midnight. Didn't the man sleep?

Feeling slightly guilty and more than a little embarrassed, Fallon brewed a second mug. Hoping Travis liked cream and sugar, she carried both cups out to the corral.

Her stomach tightened as she crossed the driveway. She'd kissed him last night and, while he had kissed her back for a moment, she must have made him uncomfortable since he'd broken it off so abruptly. She needed to apologize for her behavior and assure him it wouldn't happen again. Though she really, *really* wanted it to.

At her approach, Dreamer lifted his head and whinnied a greeting. "Good morning," she called. "I come bearing an apology by way of a steaming offering."

"You're a saint." He sighed in relief. Unclipping Dreamer's lead, Travis turned him loose into the corral and took the mug she offered. "There's a pot in the office, but no grounds. Withdrawal symptoms were imminent."

It didn't escape her notice that he'd glossed over her apology and was careful to avoid touching her. She stood on the lowest rail beside him and watched as Dreamer pranced in the pen, head and tail lifted. He trotted over to them, dropping his head for a quick rub on his face before running off again, playfully kicking up his hooves.

Neither spoke for a long moment. Fallon couldn't stand the silence any longer. She opened her mouth to speak as Travis turned toward her.

"What do you say we—"

"I am really sorry about last night," she blurted out at the same time. "Oh, go ahead."

Travis looked down into the mug before clearing his throat. "Look, Miss Radcliffe." He paused.

She arched an eyebrow at him. He was back to *Miss Radcliffe?* That seemed a bit formal for a guy whose tongue was on hers last night. Just the thought sent a tingle down her spine. Her hands itched to run themselves over the rough whiskers covering his jaw. She gripped her mug tighter.

He cleared his throat again, as if he'd come to the same realization. "Fallon," he corrected. "I think we need to make sure to keep this…"

"Professional," she interrupted.

"Exactly." He faced Dreamer again but she had a feeling it was more of an attempt to avoid meeting her gaze. "I think we were both a bit…off-balance last night. I want what's best for Dreamer, and while I still think you're shooting way too high with this horse," he warned, "I'm going do everything I can to get him to the Derby for you."

"Really?" She didn't mean for her voice to sound breathless. Or for it to carry the surprised relief it did.

He simply nodded in agreement, downing the rest of his coffee before passing her the cup and hopping back over the fence to grab a long nylon rope. He cued Dreamer to move toward the railing, asking him to speed up with a cluck of his tongue. After getting him to gallop several circles, Travis moved in front of the colt and cued him to turn, repeating the movements in the other direction. Dreamer followed his cues as if he could read Travis's mind.

"What are you doing?"

"A join up." His words explained nothing, so she carefully watched him turn his back to Dreamer. The horse immediately broke his pace and walked to Travis, dropping his head. He reached out a hand and rubbed it over Dreamer's face without looking at him. "Want to come try it?"

"Yes," she answered enthusiastically, but then she stopped herself. "I should probably let you work with him though."

He shook his head. "No. It'll help him. Come on." He opened the gate for her as she set the cups aside and entered. "It's a bonding exercise. Take the rope and swing it to get him moving."

She followed Travis's instructions and Dreamer immediately obeyed her command, moving out to the railing and breaking into a trot. Travis stepped close behind her as she twirled the rope at her side.

"Like this," he said, sliding his hands over hers, holding them still and low at her sides. "You only need to toss it toward his rump if he slows before you want him to. If he cuts in, toss it toward his shoulder. You don't want to hurt him, just get him to give to the pressure of it."

Fallon tried to listen to his words but the lazy flame of desire licked over her. With Travis's chest pressed against her back, his calloused hands on hers, her blood ignited. His breath brushed over her ear as he leaned forward slightly to tell her what to do next.

"When you're ready for him to reverse, step sideways into his path, and hold your arms out to the side."

One hand fell to her hip and he urged her to move with him while the fingers of his other hand curled around her wrist. Longing danced low in her belly, twisting and twirling as her pulse pounded through her veins. She looked back, her lips mere inches from his, and caught the scent of him. He smelled like the outdoors. Like hay mixed with horses and a spicy male scent that was all his own.

"Like this?" Her voice was barely a whisper.

"Exactly."

His voice was a husky rasp, as choked as her own. His hand slid forward, splaying over her flat abdomen and she was sure she would burn up from the inside if he stayed close any longer. This was not the way to keep things professional between them.

She dropped her arms and spun away from him quickly, shoving the rope back into his hands. "I'm heading to the grocery store. Is there anything you need?"

He inhaled deeply, picking up the rope that had dropped to the ground and pinching his lips into a thin line. She focused on his mouth—his full, kissable mouth—as he licked his lips slowly. The ache started to build in her as his smoky eyes caressed—

Damn it!

Fallon hurried toward the gate without waiting for his response. "Text me with a list of items and I'll pick them up at the store." Grabbing the mugs, she walked back to the house as fast as possible. Any faster and she would have been running. She had to get away.

It wasn't until she was back in the house when she realized he didn't have her phone number.

Chapter 9

TRAVIS LEANED BACK in the desk chair, staring at the photo in the online article he'd finished reading about the Radcliffe family. He'd known Fallon was from "old money" but he hadn't realized how much or how old. Her family fortune dated all the way back to the Gold Rush.

From what he could tell, Fallon was sort of the black sheep of her family. Her grandmother was family matriarch and controlled the shipping business that had garnered the family their original empire. Fallon's father, an only child, helped his mother. Fallon's mother was the face of the corporation, making public appearances and schmoozing investors at parties. Fallon's siblings had their own business ventures, like this vineyard.

That left Fallon to inherit Radcliffe Industries. But she'd told him last night she'd never do it. And after one look at the pictures online, he couldn't blame her. He could see right through the smile she'd plastered on her face for the cameras. She would be miserable working there.

In fact, Fallon barely resembled the other members of her family. Sure, her fair skin and light hair were similar to her mother's but she'd been chubby as a child with her clothes constantly mussed and her glasses askew. Her thick honeyed waves had been a chaos of curls but her smile was as infectious then as it was last night.

Travis clicked on another picture of her, no more than ten years old, with the rest of the family surrounding her, somber expressions on their faces. But not Fallon. She was sporting a broad, toothy, chubby-cheeked smile.

Joy. That was what he saw in Fallon. When she was happy, she lit up the room.

The next photo was of a slightly older girl, maybe fourteen. The glasses were gone, the wild hair tamed into long waves. Now, the girl wore the same austere expression as the rest of her family. She'd matured, learned to control her emotions, to fit into society's expectations of a Radcliffe. The passion she'd once had had dimmed.

He clicked on a picture of Fallon as an adult, dated three years ago, as she knelt beside a newborn colt who had to be Destiny's Dreamer. Though Fallon looked the part of a debutante, the joy was back in her eyes.

Travis watched several video interviews and could only come to one certain conclusion—Fallon Radcliffe wasn't the woman he'd assumed she was. And he was more attracted to her than ever before. *Damn it.*

"Hey." Fallon's soft voice in the doorway jerked him back to the present. He slammed the laptop closed a little too forcefully. He cringed as she arched an eyebrow. "You okay?"

"Yeah, I'm fine." His voice was tight, probably making him look guilty as hell. He rose from behind the desk. "What's up?"

"Do you like Chinese food?" Fallon smiled and lifted a bag in front of her. "I wasn't sure what you'd want."

"I thought you were going to the grocery store."

She shrugged. "I did, but by the time I finished shopping, I didn't feel like cooking." She came inside without waiting for an invitation and set the bag on the desk. She slapped a hand against her forehead. "Shoot, I forgot plates."

"No worries," he assured her, tugging open the bag as the tangy scent of the food hit him, making his stomach rumble loudly. He lifted the containers out, one by one, and handed her a set of chopsticks from the bottom. "We can eat out of the cartons." She lifted her eyebrows and he laughed. "Trust me, it's better this way."

He opened a container and found chow mein. He dug the chopsticks into the food and expertly lifted them to his lips. After he took his first bite, he sighed with delight. Either this food was amazing or he'd been starving. Maybe both.

He looked up to see the glare on Fallon's face.

"What if I wanted that?" As she spoke, her sour look transformed. Her eyes twinkled mischievously as she picked up another container. From his seat, he could see it was lemon chicken—his favorite—and the sweet citrus tang filled the air.

He plucked several noodles between his chopsticks and held them out to her. "I'm okay with sharing if you are."

Her gaze leapt up to meet his. He saw indecision flicker for a moment before she leaned forward and took a bite. As soon as her mouth closed over the food, he realized why she'd seemed indecisive.

It was an incredibly intimate experience, making him remember the way those lips had felt against his last night. Heat bubbled up in his gut, spreading through him like a California wildfire through a dry field. He watched her eyelids drop as she savored the food. Then her gaze lifted, hooded, as she peered at him through her lashes.

"It's good," she whispered, her voice breathier than the meal warranted.

She wasn't talking about the food and they both knew it. Fallon cleared her throat and shoved her chopsticks into the lemon chicken, looking down abruptly. "So, what is the plan for Dreamer?"

He tipped his head to one side, studying her. Pink dotted her cheeks, so he knew he'd embarrassed her. He turned his attention back to the food, unable to still the warning in his gut. He should be running from her, as fast and far as his truck could get him.

But where would that leave him? It wasn't like he could go back to his old life. There was nothing left of it. His job as track security wasn't going to help him get to where he belonged, training horses.

Besides, he'd agreed to help Dreamer. And he knew he could. Fallon was right. Dreamer *could* make it to the Derby. After working with him today, even Travis could feel it in his gut.

"The plan is to build his trust in me," Travis said.

"That's what the exercise earlier was? Did it work?"

"The join up? Yeah. I'm surprised it worked so well. Now I know he's willing to trust, but it'll still take some more time for him to learn to see me as his herd leader. Considering where he was when I first saw him, I think this is good progress."

"You mean, because of Casper." She shot him a challenging look.

He set the container of noodles to the side. "Since you mentioned it, yeah. Why would you hire him? You had to know his reputation."

She broke eye contact, her brow dipping slightly as she stared at the food in her hand. "I'd heard rumors. But I knew he had a lot of winners under his belt, too. That carried a lot of weight. I mean, I should have done more research into his methods."

"You're in over your head, Fallon. You realize that, right?" He glanced at her, trying to judge her reaction to the truth. "I mean, these guys—"

Her hand tightened on the paper container of food. "You think I don't already know what people are saying or see them pointing out my inexperience? I might be in over my head, but I've still been able to tread water in this pool of sharks. And now I'm asking you to teach me how to beat them, because I know Dreamer has what it takes to do it."

She met his gaze and he could read her worry. Her eyes revealed everything she was feeling, including the doubts she tried to hide.

"You're welcome to walk away, Travis. I won't force you to stay because I understand this is just business for you. It's more than that for me. I'd like you to stay and do it with us."

The soft pleading in her voice killed him. She knew other owners wanted to see her fail, if only to remind her that her world was in San Francisco. They wanted to prove that she didn't have a place in this cutthroat industry of fast horses, jockeys, and dirt.

They weren't wrong; she didn't belong in this world of greed. But Travis knew something they didn't. He'd seen the joy her horse brought her. She might not understand why she wanted this so badly, but he did. Racing had done the same for him. He wouldn't kill that for her. Instead, he wanted to fuel that fire in her, to see her succeed.

Travis stepped in front of her and took the container from her hands, setting it on the desk. "I'm not leaving, Fallon."

A flicker of surprise ran across her face. But there was

something else there, something that made his body respond with a flare of heat that traveled from his chest down to his groin.

Stepping between her legs, his fingers trailed up her arm to cup the back of her neck. Her hands found his ribs and he waited to see if she would push him away. He *wanted* her to push him away. It would have made this easier.

But Fallon pulled him closer. He knew he'd been the one to suggest they keep their relationship professional, but right now, having her this close, with her hands on him, he realized it had been impossible from the start. At least, it had been for him.

Fallon intrigued him, bewitched him, and he couldn't seem to stop himself from getting closer when he was near her.

"And this isn't just business," he whispered. "Not for me."

His head dipped, his mouth brushing over hers lightly. She sighed, her fingers gripping his torso tighter, as if worried he'd try to escape. His other hand came up and cupped her face, his thumb brushing over the satin skin. A soft whimper came from her throat as Fallon arched into him, her tongue sweeping past his lips to meet him. It was more than he could take when her hands moved up, lightly trailing the hard wall of his chest to his shoulders. She was sweet, vulnerable, and so very tempting.

Holy hell. He couldn't let this happen, even if it was physically painful for him to pull away. Travis forced himself to break their kiss, dropping his forehead against hers and trying to catch his breath. "Damn it," he muttered.

Fallon smiled slightly, biting her bottom lip and looking up at him through her thick lashes. "Does this mean you *don't* want to keep this professional?"

What had he been thinking? She was practically San

Francisco royalty, or as close as he'd ever come, and he was nothing more than a poor kid from the wrong side of the tracks with a gambler for a father. Not exactly her type. Or the right guy for her, whatsoever.

"Travis?" she whispered, lifting her face to kiss his mouth lightly. He took a deep breath and rolled his lips inward, pinching them together. "Okay, I see," she said, clearly hurt. He couldn't blame her.

"Fallon," he began, wanting to explain himself, to apologize for his lack of control, but he wasn't sure what he could say to excuse his behavior. It wasn't like he could tell her who he really was.

She patted her hand against his chest lightly and slid past him. "Don't worry about it, Travis. I get it."

Chapter 10

FALLON AWOKE IN the morning, stretching her hands over her head, arching her back, unsure why she felt so content. She decided not to fight the feeling and snuggled under her covers, tugging the down comforter tighter around her. She wished she didn't need to venture out to the barn. Just the thought of what—or better, who—was waiting for her caused a shiver of anticipation to work down her spine. And it had nothing to do with the chilly winter air that swept over her.

"Shit," she muttered, throwing back the covers. If she was this cold in the house, Travis had to be freezing in the barn.

Fallon hurried through her morning ritual—brushing her teeth, running a light coat of mascara over her eyelashes, and tugging her brush through her hair—before she found a clean pair of jeans and flannel shirt. After brewing two cups of coffee, she grabbed a quilt from her brother's hall closet and hurried outside to find Travis.

The barn was empty but for Bubba, who greeted her with his happy braying.

She heard Travis's muffled voice outside. "Hey, hey… right there. That's a good boy."

Dropping the blankets on the couch in the office, Fallon

headed to the back of the barn and into a small, enclosed turn-out pasture. She skidded to a stop as she saw Travis working with Dreamer, her mouth falling open as she watched the colt practically dancing with the man. If Travis turned to the left, Dreamer turned with him, pivoting on his back foot. If Travis backed up, the horse followed. When Travis jogged across the pasture, the muscles in his thighs bunching under the denim of his jeans, Dreamer elongated his stride, following his new trainer like a playful puppy.

Fallon leaned over the fence, watching the pair intently. It was magical, as if they were two parts of a whole. Travis jumped sideways and Dreamer froze, his attention focused, ears twitching. Using a short crop, Travis touched the colt's shoulder and Dreamer took a step away from it. Travis jumped to the side again, repeating the movement with the horse until he did it without the crop cuing him.

A sharp bark from Maggie broke Dreamer's focus and his head shot up. The dog had seen Fallon, and once the horse had, too, he whinnied.

Travis followed Dreamer's gaze and Fallon saw his gray eyes crinkle slightly in the corners as he smiled. "Good morning. About time you got up," he teased, moving toward the fence and accepting the mug she held out to him.

"I'm the boss. I'm allowed to sleep in." She gave him a smirk as she took a drink of her quickly cooling coffee. His brow dipped quickly, almost imperceptibly.

"You don't have anything planned today, do you?"

She was surprised by his question. "Not really." Dreamer pranced away from them, circling the pen before dropping his head to nibble at the short grass.

Travis gave her a lopsided grin. "Good. Because I wanted to take him out for a ride today and it's probably best to ride with someone in case he acts up. Want to saddle up?"

"Are you sure that's a good idea?" She glanced at the horse, nibbling on the grass, but thought of Travis's reaction to their kiss last night.

"Yes," he drew the word out slowly, as if unsure why she would ask.

Fallon shrugged, not one to beat around the bush. "It's a valid question. Whenever you're around me you can't seem to make up your mind whether you want my company. If we go on a trail ride, how do I know you won't kiss me and leave me stranded in the hills?"

She waited while his expression went from suspicious to mildly annoyed before, finally, a grin tugged at the corner of his mouth. "Okay," he said with a sigh. "I apologize for last night."

"And the night before?" She arched an eyebrow and lifted the mug to her lips. Then she sighed, too. "Look, I don't want your apology, Travis. I just want you to make up your mind."

"What?"

"I think you're a lot like Dreamer. You know what you *want* to do, but you're afraid to let yourself do it. Maybe he's not the only one around here who needs to relax and go with the flow."

Travis turned around and leaned his elbows on the fence railing, looking at Dreamer thoughtfully. "You might be right."

Chapter 11

FALLON SAT ASTRIDE Sadie, waiting as Travis led Dreamer out of the barn. There'd been a moment when he'd been worried Dreamer wouldn't tolerate the western saddle but the horse had remained remarkably still as Travis placed it on his back. It looked like Casper hadn't screwed up this one aspect of Dreamer's training after all.

"Ready?" Fallon asked.

"Yeah." Travis gathered the reins in his left hand and slid his foot into the stirrup. He couldn't help but feel slightly bewildered as he settled into the saddle, waiting for Dreamer to act up. Instead, the colt remained still, twisting his neck to look back at Travis when he didn't cue him to move. "Huh?"

"What?" Fallon carefully moved her mare toward Dreamer. The colt simply dropped his head, completely relaxed.

"I expected…" He gave her a slight shrug as he squeezed his thighs, cuing Dreamer to move out, as calm as a rocking horse. As the colt began walking beside the mare, his head and ears relaxed. Travis let his fingers loosen on the reins, rewarding the colt for his positive behavior.

"What?" She raised her brow in curiosity.

"I expected something. Some sort of blow up. I didn't think he'd be this calm."

Fallon flashed him a bright smile. "He's always been like this under saddle."

"I have to admit, I didn't think Casper would have started with the basics. He doesn't seem that patient."

"Oh, Casper didn't. I hired him only a few months ago. I started Dreamer."

"You broke him to saddle?"

She nodded. "It was a piece of cake. I've never had any trouble with him. He's always taken new things in stride."

And just like that, Fallon surprised him again. He watched her closely as she held the reins easily between her fingers. She was a natural in the saddle, relaxed but with perfectly balanced body position. Hell, he felt himself grow hard as he watched her hips rock in rhythm with the mare's movement.

He tore his eyes away and asked, "How long have you been riding?"

The corner of her mouth quirked up mockingly. "Not all of us rich girls take riding lessons at the country club, you know."

"I wasn't suggest—"

She tipped her head toward him slightly. "You didn't have to, I could see it in your face. You think I'm just another spoiled, rich girl who only knows how to ride because she's been on million-dollar grand prix horses with half-million-dollar trainers." She rolled her eyes. "As much as I wish I'd taken riding lessons growing up, my parents were too busy running the business to take me, and, more importantly, my grandmother never approved of the sport. No one contradicts my grandmother."

He nodded, pretending to focus on Dreamer as Fallon fell quiet. He wanted to allow her the privacy of her thoughts.

"I was twelve when Grandmother decided it was time I learn how to be a proper lady. The next six years were the worst years of my life. But then, when I finally went to college, I noticed the school had an equestrian team. I started hanging around the barns—watching only—until one of the guys on the team took pity on me and offered to teach me how to ride."

Fallon cleared her throat, reaching down and sliding a hand over her mare's neck. "He taught me the basics and said I was a natural," she said with a sly smile.

"How long did the two of you date?"

Her gaze leapt up to his. "How'd you know?"

Travis chuckled, his shoulder bouncing in a guilty shrug as he looked away sheepishly. "I've used that line a time or two."

She bit back her smile. "Ah, so, you were a player, too, huh?"

"Hardly," he answered quickly.

This wasn't a conversation he wanted to pursue, even in jest. He certainly didn't want to open a discussion about his past with Fallon. He'd have to confess that he'd never actually owned a horse of his own. That he'd ridden animals worth millions but none of them belonged to him. Or how, most of the time, he didn't have two nickels to rub together.

Her eyes widened slightly but she didn't push for more. "We dated for about a year. That was long enough for me to join the team and realize I wanted a future with horses, and *not* with him."

"How'd you end up involved in racing?"

"I went to a charity event and saw my first claiming

race. I didn't have a place to keep the horse but it didn't stop me from putting my money down. I left the race with Dreamer's mother, Destiny."

Travis shook his head and scoffed in disbelief. It was shocking how Lady Luck had simply smiled on Fallon. Born into the right family who loved her. Money rained down on her. As did brains and beauty. She'd been gifted every advantage. Then she'd happened to be at a race where she won a filly that would later give birth to a horse as talented as Dreamer.

"How'd you choose a stud for her? Or learn to break him?"

She pursed her pretty, pink lips at him. "I questioned professionals and reviewed race stats. As for breaking him, I learned what makes him happy. You spend some time with him. And then you just know."

She'd mentioned before how she wanted to see Dreamer happy. Travis had assumed she was anthropomorphizing the colt, or at the very least, viewing a horse's psyche as an unqualified layperson. But he was quickly finding out that Fallon understood this animal. She might not use the same terms he or his mentor, Buck, would have, but Fallon had a gut instinct that he couldn't deny. True, she'd researched stallions while deciding which one to breed with Dreamer's dam, but he'd bet she'd ultimately made that decision on her intuition as well.

He shook his head. "You're full of surprises, aren't you, Fallon Radcliffe?"

She lifted her face toward the sun, the rays dappling her face through the trees, and smiled broadly. The sight made his chest ache with longing. If only things had been different. If only he was somebody. If only he was a man with a future, instead of one of her hired lackeys.

Her laughter fell over him—light, carefree, and making him feel like he'd walked into heaven. It drew him away from his morose thoughts.

"You have no idea."

Chapter 12

FALLON SLID THE heavy western saddle and blankets from Sadie's back. Travis hurried over to take it from her, looking shocked to see her carry her own gear.

"Get out of here," she said with a laugh, brushing past him. "What kind of prissy girl do you think I am? I can saddle and *un*saddle my own horse."

She hated when people assumed they knew who she was because her family was wealthy. Just because they'd read articles or had seen the public images of her didn't mean they should assume she only fit that portrayal. Just because her family donated money at charity events didn't mean Fallon wasn't willing to get her hands dirty working behind the scenes. Whether it was building homes with Habitat for Humanity or working at one of San Francisco's many homeless shelters, Fallon cared more about the people she helped than the image she portrayed. It was also probably the main issue of contention between her and her grandmother.

Lifting the grooming caddy from the tack room floor, Fallon carried it into the aisle where both horses were cross-tied, facing one another. She reached for a brush at the same time Travis did. When their hands met, he jerked back as if he'd been burned. She pressed her lips together, trying not to take it personally.

She was surprised by how hesitant he was. When it came to horses, Travis was confident, taking immediate control. But when it came to her, he seemed on edge and nervous.

Fallon brushed the mare down and said, "You said you worked with Buck Taylor. What was that like?"

"Incredible. The man could get a horse to do pretty much anything." She could hear the note of hero worship in his voice.

"You know, you're not too shabby yourself, Mr. Mitchell," she teased. "I saw you this morning, dancing with Dreamer." She carried the brush back to the caddy and retrieved a hoof pick, tucking a small face brush into the back pocket of her jeans.

"That was liberty work," he corrected as he wandered closer, watching as Fallon carefully picked the mare's hooves clean.

He was quiet for a few minutes and she looked back over her shoulder. His gaze was focused on her rear. She wiggled the hoof pick at him. "You waiting for this or enjoying the view?"

His eyes darkened slightly but he didn't move or apologize. Instead, he continued staring at her. "You want to help me train Dreamer next time?"

"I've never done it before."

"Maybe we should both try new things."

She stood upright, cocking her head to one side, watching him carefully, trying to be sure she'd read the correct meaning behind his words. It was clear he wasn't talking about horse training any longer, but he looked confused, torn. And he'd left her hot and bothered too many times before.

Besides, there was something else in his expression. Something she wasn't sure he'd want to put a name to—hunger.

"Do you…" She paused, biting the corner of her lower lip, wondering if she wasn't about to make a mistake. It seemed she'd made so many of them with him.

But this didn't have to be a regret. She could be reaching out as a friend, as someone who shared her adoration of Dreamer and horse racing. It was safe. She cleared her throat. "Do you want to have dinner with me tonight?"

Emotion flickered in his face. Confusion. Doubt. Perhaps a little anxiety. Apprehension began to take root in her belly. She could practically hear her grandmother's voice, reminding her that a lady should never throw herself at a man.

"I…I mean—"

She wasn't sure how to cover for her stupid idea. She'd made them both uncomfortable and now he was about to reject her again. Why did she keep putting herself in this position with him?

"Sure."

She hadn't expected that. "Really?"

Travis nodded slowly, his gaze caressing her. He didn't move, but his eyes were stormy again, cloudy and fathomless, and Fallon felt her knees weaken.

"It'll give us time to talk about Dreamer and the training planned before his next race."

"Oh." Even she could hear the disappointment in her voice. She had to get a grip. Fallon cleared her throat and nodded. "That makes sense."

Turning away from him, hoping he didn't see the embarrassment in her face, Fallon took a deep breath to calm the unwelcome desire washing through her veins. She wasn't some teenage girl with a crush. She was an intelligent and successful woman who could tell when a man wasn't interested.

She unclipped Sadie and backed her out of the barn quickly. She'd made a fool of herself and, thankfully, Travis was enough of a gentleman to let her save face. She needed to figure out how to get rid of this crush for the sexy horse trainer she'd hired because it obviously wasn't mutual.

"Fallon, don't rush off."

Travis had seen the hurt on her face when she turned away from him. He needed to get a grip on this attraction to her. She was his boss, off-limits, and far more woman than he'd ever deserve.

"No, I forgot that I have to…" her words trailed off as she exited the barn.

To get the hell away from you, he finished in his head.

Travis turned his attention back to Dreamer. He hadn't meant to embarrass Fallon, and knew he should have never agreed to dinner. And he shouldn't have asked her to go on a ride with him today. It was one thing to torture himself wanting someone he could never have, but it wasn't fair to lead her on.

He was a nobody. Hell, he *wished* he was a nobody. That would be a step up. Growing up, he was the kid people felt sorry for. The one with the ratty clothes and no food in his cabinets. The one who slept in the track barn with the horses because it was warmer than his dad's one-room apartment since the power had gotten shut off after he gambled away the money for the electric bill.

Dreamer nickered softly, as if he could read Travis's dark thoughts. Travis ran a hand over the colt's face. Dreamer's success was the key to changing the way people saw him, but that required him to keep his distance with Fallon Radcliffe. A fling with her wouldn't be media fodder—it would be career suicide. People would assume he'd only gotten the position by seducing her. And he needed to prove himself to everyone.

He clipped the lead rope on Dreamer and turned him back into his stall before heading back to the office. He was going to cancel his dinner plans with Fallon. Then he would go find himself a hotel room in town.

Travis scrubbed his face with a hand, exhaling the breath he hadn't realized he'd been holding. It wasn't a perfect idea, since he'd have to be up at the ass-crack of dawn to feed, but it was better than fighting his attraction twenty-four/seven. He swiped the keys from atop the desk and stepped out of the barn in time to see her car head through the gate.

Damn it!

Travis juggled the keys in his hand, needing something to distract him from the fact that it was too late to bail now. He might be an asshole, but he would never stand up Fallon Radcliffe.

Chapter 13

FALLON TRIED TO ignore the sound of the shower down the hall as she laid the ingredients for spaghetti on the granite counter. What had possessed her to think she could figure this recipe out? The video online made it look so easy, but staring at the various items strewn over the kitchen, she wished she'd bought the jarred sauce and pre-made meatballs. The sight of the packaged ground beef turned her stomach.

This was going to be a disaster.

Especially when, thanks to said shower, she couldn't quite get the image of a wet, naked Travis from her mind. Or the way the water must be trickling down those hard muscles of his chest and abs to trail—*nope!*

She bit her lip, tugging her hair back before twisting it and securing it with a band in a messy bun on top of her head. Travis had made it clear he wasn't going to cross the line he drew between them again. She'd asked him to make up his mind and, obviously, he had. She was going to have to respect that.

After searching several cabinets, she found a cutting board and a couple pots. After filling one with water, she set it to boil, and then she grabbed the tomatoes and began chopping.

She reached for the bunch of parsley and chopped that as well, dumping the whole mess into the other pot. That's when she realized she'd forgotten to wash the produce. Cringing, Fallon prayed they wouldn't get *E. coli*.

She examined the contents of the pot again, certain it didn't look anything like the sauce in the video. She must have forgotten a step. As she reached for her phone to watch the instructional video again, Fallon bumped the handle of the pot, tipping it over.

The pot flipped toward her, and she was instantly covered in tomato guts before she could jump out of the path of destruction. "Shit!"

She ran to the sink for a towel as the other pot boiled over, hissing and sputtering, splattering water on the stove. She ran to move it but her foot hit the tomato mess on the floor and she screeched as she slid on the tile, crashing to the ground.

"Need some help?"

Fallon looked up in time to see Travis step around the mess on the floor and turn off the burner. Her heart stopped for a moment at the sight of him, his hair still damp from the shower and carrying the delicious scent of soap into the room.

"No." She pushed herself back to standing, but her right foot nearly slid again. "Ugh! I'm completely covered in tomato."

"But you're okay, right?"

"Yes," she said as she heaved a sigh.

Travis bit back a smile.

"It's not funny," she said.

He eyed the mess on the floor, the ingredients on the counter, and the water all over the stove. "What on earth were you trying to do?"

"I was trying to make you spaghetti."

Travis was trying not to laugh. Fallon didn't find the situation humorous. She felt like a failure. She couldn't even do something as simple as fixing a meal. Fighting back the tears, she threw her hands in the air. "I've never cooked anything, okay? I wanted to do something nice, but—"

"Wait, you've *never* cooked? Not anything?"

She rolled her eyes, hating to admit something that made her sound spoiled. "I've never had to. I mean, I've heated things up and have had food delivered, but most of the time, we have a chef at home. I've never actually cooked anything from scratch."

"At home? As in the Radcliffe mansion?"

She nodded.

"Wow, it must be nice to be a Radcliffe," he muttered, blinking a few times before clearing his throat. "Okay, you go get cleaned up and change your clothes. I'll take care of this mess and we'll figure out something else for dinner."

Fallon ducked her head as she hurried out of the kitchen. She may have been born into wealth, but she couldn't do the most basic tasks. It seemed like no matter how hard she tried to be "normal," she ended up flat on her ass.

Travis eyed the slump in Fallon's shoulders as she walked out of the room. He hadn't expected it from her and wondered how an inability to cook—which he still couldn't quite fathom—warranted that sort of surrender. He wasn't sure what had caused the brimming tears he'd seen, but he was willing to do just about anything to make sure they didn't fall.

He heard the water turn on in one of the bathrooms down the hall and tried to distract himself from the visions of Fallon stepping into the shower, warm water sliding down her satiny skin, using enough soap to make her body slick as his hands—*that's enough!*

It would be easy for him to drive into town and grab them dinner, but because she was upset about not being able to cook, he decided to teach her a few basics instead. Travis quickly cleaned up the counters and floors before washing the pots. Then he rummaged through the refrigerator, which was still practically empty even after her shopping trip, and he found cream and a block of mozzarella cheese. A quick search of the pantry yielded a loaf of sourdough bread and tomato juice.

Fallon returned as he set the ingredients on the counter, her long hair still damp, making her eyes look large and luminescent. His breath caught in his chest and heat spread through his veins slowly, inching toward his groin. Travis tried to fight the longing, but it was a losing battle.

"Why'd you stop wearing glasses?"

Fallon looked surprised at first, but then she smiled. "How did you know I wore glasses?"

Think of something, Mitchell.

He watched a wide smile curve the lips he desperately wanted to taste again. "You googled me, didn't you?"

He must have looked as guilty as he felt. He was busted and he knew it.

She arched an eyebrow and crossed her arms. "And what did you find out?"

"You've always been a bit of a tomboy, for one thing."

"Is that all?" She eyed him suspiciously.

He wasn't about to tell her how much he suspected he knew, even without reading the media puff pieces. Her lack of confidence was obvious when she stood with her family. She doubted her abilities around them, and she simply wasn't happy. But he also knew what made her smile.

"I can see how much Dreamer means to you," he said, thinking about the picture of her with the newborn colt. Travis took a step closer and lifted a wet tendril of hair, letting the curl twirl around his finger. "And that you've managed to get this mop under control."

Fallon's cheeks blazed pink and he laughed as she covered her face. "You saw pictures of me as a kid, too?" She shook her head. "I guess that's one of the joys of being part of a famous family. My awkward years of frizzy curls and thick glasses were documented for public consumption."

A smile tugged at the corner of his mouth. "You were adorable."

"Sure, I was." She rolled her eyes and frowned at the items on the newly cleaned counter. "What's all this?"

Travis followed her gaze. "I'm giving you a cooking lesson."

She looked at him warily. "My last attempt didn't turn out so well. I'm not sure I'm up for round two. Maybe we should go out and get something instead."

"Trust me." Travis reached for her hand, dragging her toward the stove, and trying desperately to ignore the electric shock that shot up his arm when his fingers touched hers.

He stepped behind her, and placed his chest flush against her back. Then Travis reached for the tomato juice. The heat of her body scalded him, but he tried to ignore his body's response to it as he leaned closer to her ear to give her the instructions. Her wet hair was cold against his lips, yet did nothing to cool his raging lust.

"Everyone should know how to make a grilled cheese sandwich. And, since you've got the fixings for tomato soup, we're going to have a feast."

Chapter 14

FALLON SHIVERED AS Travis's breath fanned over her neck, igniting her desire for him. She inhaled sharply as he let his hands fall on her hips.

"This is going to be easy," he promised, his voice hungry, and she quickly prayed for focus. "First, open the cans of tomato juice and pour them into the pot."

"Okay." Her voice was barely a whisper of sound.

Fallon reached for the electric can opener, wondering if it always took this long to get a can open or if it only felt that way because Travis's hands were on hers. She fought to keep herself from leaning back into him.

"Now what?"

He turned on the burner. "Pour those into the pot and add some cream."

"I have cream?"

He chuckled and she felt the rumble against her back, goose bumps breaking out over her arms. "You don't remember buying it?"

Fallon didn't trust herself to speak and simply shook her head.

"Now, grab the whisk and stir it while you pour it in so it doesn't separate."

"Which one?" She turned her face toward him and gasped when it put her lips a fraction from his. She could kiss him if she chose to move just an inch.

Travis's eyes went stormy, going dark as he slid his hand down her arm and reached for the utensil in the holder on the counter. "This one."

His lips nearly brushed against hers as he spoke and she tried not to acknowledge the longing swirling in her like a tornado, out of control. Placing the whisk in her hand, he dropped his to splay against her stomach and her body arched in response.

"Fallon."

His lips brushed against the hollow behind her ear, the tip of his nose trailing over the curve of it. The sensation sent delicious spirals of heat swirling through her, coming to rest low in her belly, beneath his hand. Something about this man made her feel like she didn't have to impress him, that being herself was better than being *the* Fallon Radcliffe she'd been shaped to pretend to be.

She sighed softly, melting against him as his thumb rubbed over the soft cotton of her shirt, slipping between the buttons and brushing against her bare skin. That simple touch was enough to ignite the inferno in her. White-hot lust shot through her, making her quiver in response, and she dropped the whisk into the pot.

"Careful," Travis said, shifting her away from the stove and turning it off, keeping one hand still at her hip. "You don't want to get burned, do you?"

Too late.

Somehow, Fallon managed to keep the thought to herself as she turned in his arms, facing him, thrilling in the forbidden pleasure of her body arching into his. She wanted to regain some sense of self-control and laid her hands against his chest to move away, but when his gaze met hers, she saw a desire that matched her own.

"Aren't you hungry?" she asked, her voice more breathless than she'd intended.

A shadow flitted over his eyes, darkening them. "Not for food."

Without warning, his mouth slanted over hers, his kiss deep and insistent. He wasn't demanding, but easily coaxed the response she was so willing to give. Nipping at her lower lip, Travis plundered her mouth, leaving her gasping for air and clinging to him, her fingers digging into the flesh of his arms. His skin was hot, branding her, but she wanted more. As his mouth moved over her jaw and her neck, she couldn't stop the soft moan when his tongue traced the column of her throat where her pulse raced.

Fallon slid her hands to his back, feeling the muscles clench and bunch beneath her fingertips. She had to touch him, to feel his skin under her fingers. She tugged at his shirt as his fingers deftly found the buttons on the front of hers. He released them, and then his hands played over her ribcage. As he pressed open-mouthed kisses along her collarbone, his palm cupped the mound of her breast, and she felt the explosion of need from within. Travis curved his arm around her waist, drawing her closer. His mouth closed over the material of her bra, ripping another moan from her throat. Her response was shameless.

"Fallon?" His voice held a note of doubt and she didn't think she could stand his rejection again.

"Travis, if you stop, I might have to kill you."

She felt his smile against her skin, and then her nipples hardened as his tongue swirled over them, one by one. "I don't think I could, even if I wanted to," he admitted.

There was a flurry of hands, mouths, and tongues, her

clothing was cast wherever it landed, and Fallon found herself pressed against the closed door of her bedroom in nothing but her sensible bikini briefs. She wished Travis would hurry up and remove those as well, so she finally hooked her thumbs in the sides, determined to do it herself, but he wrapped his fingers around her wrists and stopped her.

In the same way he effortlessly convinced Dreamer to follow his lead, she let him guide her to do the same. Lifting her hands to either side of her shoulders, he held her wrists against the door, letting her feel each glorious inch of him pressing into her. Then he rocked his hips into her.

If she'd wondered about his attraction to her, his rock-hard erection dispelled her doubts.

"I want to see you, Fallon." His voice was hoarse, tortured, as he slid down her body. His mouth explored every inch of her. "Let me."

Travis released her hands to cup her breasts, teasing the nipple to a taut peak with his thumb before tasting her. Fallon whimpered as waves of pleasure washed over her. Her knees gave out when his hand moved down her belly to cup her gently, his finger slipping beneath the material of her underwear.

"This isn't going to be slow and sweet," he growled against her skin. "I…I can't."

Fallon dug her fingers into his hair and tugged his face back to her, the scruff of his day-old beard scratching against her skin and making her shiver with need.

"Good," she whispered. "Because that's not what I want."

She ran her hands over the breadth of his chest, easing him backward toward the bed, before reaching for the button on his jeans and pulling them open. She shoved them down his muscular thighs and let her nails brush over the rough dusting of hair as she reached for the band of his boxer briefs. His impressive erection strained against the material.

Travis's gaze crashed into hers, searching for answers to questions she wasn't aware he'd asked. She gave him a light shove to sit and straddled his lap.

"What is it that you *do* want, Fallon?"

"I want the natural feeling I have with you, how instinctive it seems." She wanted his strength, and the confidence he brought out in her. Fallon gave him a smile, feeling surer than she had in a long time. "I want you, Travis."

Travis slid his hands around the curve of her butt and inhaled slowly, his face tipped up. He watched her with passionate yearning in his eyes, though they were shadowed with doubt. "You might regret it."

Not waiting for his argument, she dipped her mouth to his. Then she slid her hand to cup the back of his head, meeting his desire with her own, and said, "No, I won't."

Chapter 15

FALLON DROVE HIM wild. Like a siren, she mesmerized him and put him under a spell.

There was no other explanation for the way he seemed to lose all self-control when he was with her. But it was too late for him to turn back now. Travis was lost. In her eyes, in her confident assurances, and in her touch. He needed to bury himself in her more than he needed to breathe.

Grasping her perfect ass, he rose from the mattress, settling her on her back and leaning over her. She sighed as his hands slid into the back of her underwear, as his fingers instinctively clenched into her flesh, and when he pulled the garment down her thighs, dropping it on the floor. Then he quickly shed his own and stepped between her thighs. Running his thumb over her seam, he rejoiced in her gasp of delight. He'd never had a woman respond to his touch with such desperate yearning, and he loved it.

"Condoms?"

He needed her now.

"Bathroom, under the sink."

When he returned, she rose on her elbows, watching him with appreciation as he walked back to the bed.

"You're like a work of art." The words slipped out, unbidden, and she bit her lip.

Travis ran a thumb over her mouth, growling as he tried to hold himself back. "Fallon, you have no idea how sexy you are, do you? Or what you do to a man when you talk that way."

He tore open the wrapper and slid the latex over his length before hovering over her, positioning himself between her thighs.

"Who, me?" She sounded surprised.

She was Fallon Radcliffe, beautiful debutante, wealthy socialite, and intelligent businesswoman, yet she didn't seem to realize her own attributes.

Travis trailed a finger between her breasts and over her flat stomach, taking in every gorgeous inch of her. "Yes, you. You're enough to make a man forget himself." His gaze met hers. "You're sure?"

Wordlessly, she reached for his hips, pressing the head of him against her core—he groaned in agonized pleasure. It broke him. He buried himself in her, nearly coming unglued in the first stroke. She was heaven. Her body cradled his, taking her own pleasure as her hips rocked to meet his thrusts, her nails digging into his back. The doubts he'd harbored about the two of them faded. They fit together perfectly.

Every touch sent him spiraling higher. He wanted to draw out the exquisite torment but when Fallon gripped his hips, her body arching into his, and he felt her tremble as she found her own release, her body milked every ounce of pleasure from him. Relief gripped him as he plunged into her one last time, following her to ecstasy as she clung to him.

Travis dropped his forehead against her neck, holding

his weight off her with his elbows. He was unsure if he would ever be the same. She'd done something no woman had ever done. She'd managed to make him forget who he was and where he'd come from. She'd made him want more and had convinced him, for a moment, that he could achieve it. And that made Fallon dangerous.

Because come tomorrow morning, he and Fallon would be back in their rightful places. She'd be completely out of his reach.

Chapter 16

FALLON WOKE THE next morning, pleasantly sore, to the scent of freshly brewed coffee. She stretched as the sultry memories of last night swirled through her mind, making parts of her tingle with anticipation as she wondered what today might bring.

In spite of the fact that she and Travis made love, and that he'd curled his body behind her, allowing her to fall asleep tucked in his embrace, he hadn't completely opened up to her. She'd sensed he was retreating from the moment he came out of the bathroom after cleaning himself up. He'd been gentle, tender, and attentive, but there was a sadness in his eyes as he pressed a lingering kiss to her lips before she'd curled against his chest.

Sliding from the bed, she tugged on a pair of jeans and a sweatshirt. Fallon smiled, knowing the sight of her grungy, comfortable clothing would have given her grandmother a heart attack if she saw it, because for the first time in a very long time, Fallon didn't care what anyone else thought.

She piled her hair into a messy bun atop her head and brushed her teeth quickly before padding into the kitchen, looking forward to spending the day working with Travis.

This was a man who not only understood what she needed in the bedroom, but believed in her dreams and her ability to accomplish them. He believed in Dreamer.

Unfortunately, Travis was nowhere to be seen.

His coffee mug, the only sign he'd been in the house at all, was in the sink. Even the dishes from the meal they'd left behind last night had been cleaned up. It was almost as if last night had never happened.

Fallon stared out the window as she poured herself a cup of coffee and added milk and sugar, expecting to see Travis with Dreamer in the round pen. The early morning fog made it difficult to see, but the pen appeared empty.

She grabbed her cup and headed for the barn, catching a glimpse of Travis in the pasture behind it. Deciding to play it cool, she leaned over the railing. "Morning. How's he doing?"

"Good." Travis barely glanced her way, keeping his focus on the colt as he cued him over a jump right before Dreamer trotted over several poles on the ground.

"Cavaletti training?" It was a training used most often for jumpers and eventing horses. She'd never heard of it being used for a racehorse.

"Something new for him to think about." His tone was clipped.

He obviously wasn't going to make this easy on her. She sipped the brew as Dreamer leapt over the small jump again. "You okay?"

"Fine." He kept his head down.

"Because you seem like you're not."

"I'm fine," he assured her, his gaze flicking toward her briefly before returning to watch Dreamer take another set of poles. "Just concentrating."

She could see the tension in his shoulders. Something

was wrong but he was stonewalling her and she didn't know why. "Dreamer's okay?"

"Yeah, he's actually doing great. I've changed up his feed from what Casper was giving him and he's mellowed a lot."

"Enough to—" A car coming up the driveway tore her attention from the pair in the arena. "Oh, no."

Fallon cursed her luck as the limo drove past her and slowed in the circular drive. Her heart began its slow descent into the pit of her stomach and she closed her eyes, praying it was her brother returning home unexpectedly. Any hope she had crumbled as the driver held the car door open for her grandmother.

Even from this distance, she could see the sour look on her grandmother's face. The green hills, fed by the recent rains, shimmered in the crisp Sonoma morning dew like a fairyland, but it didn't impress Wilhelmina Radcliffe in the slightest. She wrinkled her nose as she moved aside, allowing Fallon's parents to exit the car behind her.

This was the last thing she wanted to deal with today, especially when she was already trying to navigate an unpredictable horse and an emotionally detached man.

Chapter 17

"OH, GOOD HEAVENS, child!" her grandmother exclaimed. "What in the world are you wearing? And what happened to your hair?" She reached forward, plucking at the pile of wayward curls atop Fallon's head with her gloved fingers.

Ignoring her grandmother's criticism, Fallon leaned forward and pressed a quick kiss to her grandmother's cheek before repeating the same with her parents. "What are you guys doing here? Why didn't you call?"

"Your father and I are on our way to Rachel Prescott's wedding in Napa. You remember her, don't you?" Her mother rolled her eyes. "The chubby girl with that messy long hair."

Fallon remembered Rachel. A sweet, kind girl whose father was some sort of politician. Rachel had carried a little baby fat into high school and had been tormented about it, until she'd ended up in the hospital for anorexia.

"Will you be staying for lunch?" she prompted.

"I should hope more than that! They're heading to Napa and I thought I'd come visit with you for a few days until they return," her grandmother filled in. "Won't that be lovely?"

Lovely wasn't the word Fallon would have used. *Misery* and *torture* were the first words that flitted through her mind. She loved her grandmother, respected her, but the woman was the definition of trying. Not that Fallon would admit that aloud. A much safer response was simply to smile and nod.

"I'll set you up in a room, then."

Her grandmother took a step past Fallon. "Just a moment. That's that security guard from the race who shoved you. What's he doing here?"

"He's a trainer. Why don't we go inside and I'll explain."

Her grandmother turned back to her and shook her head. Fallon didn't miss the disapproval in her ice-blue eyes, nor in her pursed lips. As her grandmother allowed Fallon to guide them toward the front door, Fallon couldn't resist one last look at the man working with Dreamer.

She needed to talk to him so they could at least lay their cards on the table, but that conversation was going to have to wait until her family left. And right now, she had no idea how long they would stay.

Her grandmother scrunched up her face as she sipped the coffee Fallon had prepared. It might not be as tasty as their chef's at the mansion in San Francisco, but it wasn't *that* bad.

"So, are you going to race that beast in the El Camino Real Derby or not? I can't keep my schedule open indefinitely, you know."

Fallon gave her a slight shrug.

Her grandmother frowned. "That's not an answer," she scolded.

Her grandmother's harsh words haunted her from her childhood. *A lady always uses her words. Don't look ignorant by shrugging, Fallon.*

She'd lived most of her life trying to alter her grandmother's opinion of her. Fallon had never been smart enough, never quite pretty enough. She couldn't dance as well as her sister and didn't have her brother's charm. In her grandmother's eyes, she'd always been lacking in one way or another. She swallowed the bitter retort that fought to be released.

"Travis doesn't think he's quite ready yet."

"Travis?" Her grandmother arched an eyebrow expectantly and Fallon's stomach clenched as she realized her mistake.

"Mr. Mitchell," she corrected. "My trainer."

"Since when is *Travis* the one making the decisions?" She poked a fork at the store-bought Danish in front of her before pushing the plate away. "He is *your* employee, not the other way around, dear. You are the one calling the shots when it comes to your business. Never forget that."

"I understand that, Grandmother, but he's the professional. He knows how to prepare Dreamer for a race better than I do."

"Hmph." Her grandmother's face didn't hide her disagreement. "I was under the assumption that you were the one in charge of your future. Isn't that what you told me?" She let out a disappointed sigh. "And I was so looking forward to watching your horse win a race in front of all of my friends. I had planned to brag about what a success you've become."

Her grandmother wanted to show Fallon off to her friends? She was proud of her? That was a first. The envy Fallon had always felt for her siblings suddenly bubbled up, gnawing at her good sense. Sure, she'd originally agreed to let Travis have full rein with Dreamer, to train him how he saw fit, but that was before she knew that her grandmother wanted to take an interest in the career she'd chosen. That was before her grandmother had exhibited anything other than disdain for Fallon's pursuits.

Travis had even said this morning that Dreamer was doing well. In fact, she'd never seen him this relaxed and limber.

"I'll ask him if he thinks it might be possible," Fallon offered.

Her grandmother scoffed with a slight laugh. "My dear, someday you'll realize that we are Radcliffes. We don't ask for permission."

Chapter 18

TRAVIS TURNED DREAMER out into the pasture, watching him kick up his hooves before running over the hill to meet up with the other two horses.

"There you are."

"Rough morning?" Fallon sounded exhausted. Sympathy for her rose up as she ran a hand over her eyes and sighed. He'd been keeping his distance all day. He had to.

He'd spent last night making love to his boss. And she wasn't just his boss—she was Fallon Radcliffe.

He'd crossed a line and wasn't sure how to go back.

"You could say that. My grandmother is staying with me for the next two days."

Her grandmother, *the* Wilhelmina Radcliffe? His brow lifted in surprise but he remained silent.

She turned toward him and threw her hands into the air. "Are you not much of a talker, Travis? Or is it me? Because it's exhausting trying to figure you out."

"I—" He shrugged slightly.

It would be better for her to think he didn't like her than it would be to admit the ridiculous truth—that he was falling for his boss, a woman so rich and powerful, a woman so beautiful, that he didn't stand a snowball's chance in hell of being anything but a quick roll in the hay to her.

She nodded, biting at the corner of her lip. His gut twisted at the insecurity he could see in her eyes, knowing he was the cause of it.

"Okay, then, I get it. Last night was fun, but we need to focus on the task at hand—getting Dreamer ready for the El Camino Real."

"What?" He spun to face her, his hand gripping the halter he held. "He's not ready to race yet. I told you this had to be slow. He needs time."

"And I'm telling you that he's racing in the El Camino Real. Make sure he's ready." Her voice was hard, making her a woman unlike the one he'd seen so far. She spun on her heel, squaring her shoulders and hurrying back toward the house. "I pay you for results, Travis. Make sure he places so we aren't too far behind in points to qualify for the Derby."

"The agreement was that I train *my* way, and that you wouldn't interfere," he reminded her.

"Well, guess what? Since you seem inclined to change your mind with whatever direction the wind blows, so can I."

Chapter 19

February

TRAVIS AVOIDED FALLON for the next few weeks, and he knew it'd be even easier to avoid her in the hustle and bustle of the El Camino Real at Golden Gate Fields. He figured he could bunk in his truck until the race. Or maybe he'd stay in the barn, if there was room, but Travis doubted it. Either way, he wasn't about to waste his limited funds for one of the expensive hotels nearby.

He loaded the horse into the trailer and slid behind the wheel when Fallon appeared at his truck window with a thick envelope. She held it out to him. "Here."

"What's this?"

"Cash for expenses. Food, a room, and whatever else you might need while you're there."

Her words were short, to the point, and tense. The same as they'd been in every other conversation they'd had since making love. If that wasn't an indicator of how she felt about him, he didn't know what was.

He opened the envelope and stared at the stack of hundred-dollar bills. He didn't think he'd ever held so many at one time. There had to be at least five grand here.

"That's a lot of expenses. Where do you think I'm staying? The Claremont?"

She shrugged as if she hadn't handed him a crap-ton of cash. Hell, he wasn't even comfortable carrying this much at once. "I'm sure hotels will be expensive this weekend. Consider it a bonus for making sure he does well. I know you aren't keen on racing him yet." As she spoke, she avoided his gaze.

Travis clenched his jaw and shoved the envelope back at her. "You think? Keep it. I might be the only person you know who can say this, but I don't care about your money, Fallon. If I don't think he's ready on the morning of the race, I'll scratch him. No amount of your blood money is going to change that."

He twisted the key, disgusted by the thought of risking Dreamer's health for money, and drove away without looking back.

Okay, that wasn't exactly true. He looked back once to see her standing in the driveway watching him, her hands helplessly at her sides.

Chapter 20

FALLON SLID THROUGH the doors of the Turf Club at Golden Gate Fields, brushing past several waitstaff to find her grandmother at the wall of windows overlooking the track. "Sorry I'm late. I was making sure there weren't any problems getting Dreamer to the track."

"And?"

"He's good."

Her grandmother's gaze slid over Fallon's designer pantsuit before nodding slightly and turning back to the group gathered around her. Biting back the bitter words on her lips, Fallon ignored her grandmother's friends and held her breath, watching the parade of horses below.

Dreamer's jockey was once again in her gold silks, shimmering brightly under the cold Bay breeze. Her bay colt pranced onto the track, his head bobbing as if he couldn't wait to get out and show off for the crowd.

Fallon's eyes fell on Travis, who was leading Dreamer himself. Unlike most trainers, he must have refused to turn the job over to a groom. His level of care warmed her, but it also made her worry about her decision to ignore his warning and race Dreamer today —even if the El Camino Real was one of the only races where Dreamer could pick up precious qualifying points for the Derby.

"Your grandmother says that Destiny's Dreamer is quite the colt. She makes him sound like the next Secretariat." Fallon turned to a portly gentleman beside her. "After listening to her, I had to bet on him."

Several of her grandmother's friends murmured in agreement and Fallon felt her stomach twist into a tighter knot of fear. People were betting their money on her success. This was no longer just about her gaining her grandmother's approval.

*If Dreamer loses…*she reined in the thought quickly, sending up a quick prayer as she watched Travis hand Dreamer off to the gate crew. Fallon leaned forward, her face practically pressed against the window as she watched them try to load him into the starting gate. He immediately balked and she heard the titter of laughter from one of the women in their group.

"They say all the winners hate going into the gate."

Fallon didn't respond; she couldn't. She was barely breathing.

"I'm sure he's antsy to run," another male voice chimed in, right next to her ear. Her grandmother's associates had crowded closer.

Fallon could feel the crushing weight of her grandmother's expectations. Dreamer had to win. He *had* to.

Behind the gates, Dreamer reared, but the crew managed to get him down. Seconds later, the gates burst open and the horses charged out, bunching against the rail. The animals practically merged into one body. Only the bobbing of their heads and flurry of hooves were distinguishable as the jockeys fought for the lead. A chestnut horse with blue silks pulled ahead and two horses fell behind the pack. One of them was Dreamer.

Stretching out, his stride lengthened as he ate up the synthetic material that covered the ground as he made the first turn. Fallon's heart raced almost in time with his gallop.

A gray horse tried to break from the pack along the rail, but then got caught in another group farther up. Excitement erupted around her as the horses came around the last turn.

Fallon could see Dreamer on the outside, giving him the disadvantage of having to run harder, farther, and faster than the rest. He fought for every inch he gained, tearing past the other horses and closing in on the leaders, who were now grouped three wide in the front. As the animals strained toward the finish line, Dreamer crept closer.

Hands reached for Fallon's shoulders, shaking her as cheers roared in her ears. Several of the men began yelling instructions to the jockey, as if he could hear them from here. In a pounding thunder of hooves that Fallon could feel in her chest, the horses crossed the finish line, neck and neck. It was too close to determine the winner.

They had to wait for the final call.

Her grandmother's friends were laughing, cheerful at the prospect of the horse they bet on winning even third place. But when Fallon met her grandmother's gaze, excitement wasn't what she saw. It was the same expression she'd seen in her grandmother's face most of her life.

Disappointment.

Chapter 21

"TWO FREAKING POINTS." Fallon paced the aisle of the barn, wishing she could lose her temper. She wanted to throw something—anything. "Damn it. He was so close. Winning only two points won't get us to the Derby."

"And now he's hurt again," Travis pointed out.

She glared at him. The last thing she needed right now was another "I told you so." She'd heard it from her grandmother, right before she'd pulled Fallon aside and informed her that she'd had enough of this "horse nonsense" after Dreamer had placed third. She'd insisted Fallon write off her losses and be back in her position as the Marketing Director for Radcliffe Shipping before June.

In Fallon's mind, that gave her four months from now to prove herself. With Dreamer's injury, though, she didn't know when, or if, he'd race again.

Thanks to the dressing-down she'd taken from her grandmother, Fallon hadn't arrived at the barn until after the vet had already left. She eyed the bandage on Dreamer's leg. "What did the vet say?"

"Physically, he'll be fine. He must have cut his pastern when he reared in the gate. Just a few stitches." Travis turned his back on her and looked in Dreamer's stall, where the colt was eating. "Emotionally, I don't know." He shook his head and looked back at her accusingly. "I told you he wasn't ready."

His words only fueled the doubts racing through her mind. Why *was* she doing this? She didn't know the first thing about training racehorses. She knew marketing, and should have stuck with that. Everyone expected her to fail. She was out of her element. Now, she was beginning to believe they were right.

"Santa Anita's almost two months away, and we only have two points toward the Derby—and the winner of Santa Anita is guaranteed entry to the Derby."

"Forget the Derby, Fallon. I'm not sure I can even get him into the starting gate again. Don't you understand that?"

Fallon pinched her lips together, reminding herself that Travis was the professional. She'd begged for his help. Ignoring him had caused them to end up here—with Dreamer injured.

If she was being honest with herself, she hadn't entered Dreamer because of her grandmother. She'd been angry with Travis for being so dismissive after they'd made love. For making her feel used. In a way, she had been testing Travis, reminding him who called the final shots, as least in this part of their relationship.

She nodded, defeat slumping her shoulders.

"Good." He turned to walk away, stopping as he reached the doorway. "One more thing. I don't want you there while I work with him. If you aren't there, you can't interfere."

Chapter 22

April

TRAVIS GALLOPED DREAMER across the field. After weeks of being confined to a stall, then several more of slow rehabilitation, Dreamer couldn't wait to stretch his legs. Loosening the reins, Travis felt the colt pick up more speed, his stride eating up the turf. He was fast, and he wasn't running full-out yet.

Slowing the colt, Travis cued him to walk as they returned to the pasture near the house. The other horses whinnied in greeting and he could hear Bubba braying. Nothing more than the noises he'd grown accustomed to over the past very quiet eight weeks.

Sure, he'd visited with Marco and a few of the field workers who remained on the vineyard, but they were busy. Unlike him. Travis rose early and fed all the animals, even though they weren't his responsibility. Even with his double workouts, Travis could only do so much with Dreamer. The rest of the time he wandered the property, trying to find anything to keep him busy. Anything to keep his mind off Fallon.

Nothing worked.

He couldn't count the number of times he'd typed a message, asking her about her day or whether she might come visit the vineyard, only to delete it without sending. Sure, he'd texted her pictures and kept her informed with updates on Dreamer's progress, but they were the same sort of things he would send to any owner whose horse he was training.

But Fallon was different and Travis couldn't deny it. And yet, he'd been the one who put up this wall between them in the weeks leading up to the El Camino Real. Once they'd made love, he couldn't pretend she was just his boss. And he didn't want to be a one-night stand to her.

He wanted to be more.

More than he'd ever deserve, especially from someone like Fallon. It didn't stop him from missing the way she'd meet him at the round pen in the morning. The way she smiled, looking up at him shyly through her lashes. The way she whispered his name like a prayer when he touched her.

He was an idiot.

Dismounting to open the gate, Travis spotted the car parked in front of the main house. Marco had mentioned that Fallon's brother, Gabe, had been called away again and wouldn't be returning for another few months. Apparently, he'd been wrong.

As the woman exited the driver's seat of the sparkling new Audi, her long legs made his mouth go dry. Blond waves swung loose at the waist of her skirt, fitted to show off luscious curves that his body instantly recognized.

Dreamer whinnied loudly, as if he also recognized the person slowly turning toward them. Fallon's smile widened, but then quickly fell. That reaction had to be because of him. Taking a deep breath and rebuilding the wall around his heart so she didn't see straight through it, Travis walked up to her.

"I'm surprised to see you." The words came out far more antagonistic than he meant them to.

"I..." She bit her lip, then squared her shoulders, standing straighter. She probably remembered who employed whom, something he wished he could forget. "The Santa Anita Derby is next week. I'm surprised to see him out."

She ran her hands over the colt, her palm sliding over his coat. Squatting down to inspect his injured leg, she glanced up at Travis. "It looks good. You can barely see where he cut it."

"He's fine. With a couple more days of prep work, you'll see a different horse at the track."

She rose to face him, looking concerned yet oddly smug. "And you? How have you managed the past few months?"

I've felt alone. I've missed you. Been wanting you, even though I know it's what I could never have.

"It's been perfect."

"Good."

But the sentiment didn't quite reach her eyes. In fact, the flicker of disappointment made him feel like Dreamer had kicked him in the gut.

Chapter 23

PERFECT?

That had been the last thing Fallon wanted to hear. She'd hoped that he might have missed her, at least a little bit. Especially after the many texts he'd sent her over the past two months, all cautiously friendly. Apparently, she'd mistaken professionalism for friendliness. Like a fool, she'd thought he might want her to return, might want more than this working relationship they had.

Well, you were wrong, again.

They stood in silence as Travis studied her so intently she began to feel like a specimen under a microscope.

"Well…good," she repeated. She turned and opened the trunk to retrieve her bag. He watched her tug at it, struggling to lift it from the back of the car.

"Here." Travis reached forward, lifting the suitcase effortlessly, although she knew for a fact it had to weigh at least fifty pounds. "What's in here? Boulders?"

"Shoes, clothes." She shrugged. "Necessities."

"Ah." His head bobbed but she could see the lopsided smile tugging at the corner of his lips.

"I'm having dinner delivered. Why don't you join me and update me on Dreamer?"

He looked suddenly uneasy. "I've got a routine and I'd rather not jinx it this close to a race."

"Jinx it," she repeated. He was obviously avoiding her. "Okay, then I guess I'll get my things inside and you can update me tomorrow."

She turned her back on him, refusing to let him see how much his rejection hurt. Again. She wouldn't continue putting herself out there only to have him turn her away.

She was Fallon Radcliffe, damn it. Maybe it was time she started acting like it.

He was a coward, plain and simple.

Travis's stomach growled viciously as the caterer pulled out of the driveway. He could go over to Marco's place and mooch dinner off him or head into town and grab a burger. But all he wanted to do was accept Fallon's invitation.

He was still kicking himself for the hurt he'd seen in her face, knowing he'd been the cause of it. Travis ran a hand through his hair and clenched his jaw. If nothing else, he owed her an explanation for the cold shoulder he'd been giving her.

Travis took a deep breath and rolled his shoulders back, forcing himself to choke back his sense of self-preservation. Then made his way to the house, finally willing to share the demons he'd been facing for so long. He raised his hand, but before he knocked on the door, it opened.

"Oh!" Fallon jumped backward, nearly dropping the plate she held in her hands.

"Sorry, I…" He wasn't sure what to say. "I came up to talk to you."

"Come in. I was about to bring this dish out to you." Fallon stepped backward, letting him inside.

The perfect hostess, always knowing exactly what to say

and do. Even when he'd been a dick and hurt her. "Fallon, I need to explain."

"No." She shook her head, tossing her long waves over her shoulders and turning away. "You really don't. I saw that you didn't leave for dinner and didn't want you to go hungry."

He noticed that she didn't meet his gaze. "Fallon?"

She glanced at him over her shoulder. "So, Dreamer's really improved, huh? You think he's ready for the race?"

Travis followed her into the dining room where she slid his plate onto the table. "Fallon, stop."

He'd come here prepared to tell her his story. He was ready to explain why he'd pushed her away, why she deserved so much better than him, and why the night they'd spent together had been a mistake and couldn't happen again.

She froze in place, her hands on the table, as if trying to brace herself for whatever he might say next. His hands slid to her arms as he moved closer, the heat from her body burning him through his shirt. The scent of her invaded his senses, making him dizzy with desire for her. Dropping her head forward, he heard her sharp intake of breath. But then her back stiffened against him and she moved away.

"No, I'm not doing this again." She turned around, wrapping her arms around her waist. "You can't have it both ways, Travis. There's no revolving door here."

"I know." His hands gripped the back of one of the chairs, needing something to distract him. "You deserve more than this."

"What is *this*? I can't figure you out. Do you even care about me?"

"It's not about you. You—you're perfect. But me…look, I told you I grew up at the track, but I didn't tell you why." He lifted his eyes to meet hers. A small part of him prayed she'd accept him despite his past, but he knew to expect the worst. "My father was an addict, and his drug of choice was the horses. I could read a racing form before I read chapter books in school." He shook his head, disgusted by how he'd been raised. "I learned math by making and collecting side bets for my father." Travis scrubbed a hand over his face. Just admitting this story from his past made him sick. "The man was either placing bets or drinking whatever money came in from the few he won."

"Travis." Fallon reached out a hand, but he jerked away. Her touch burned, and right now he had to get it all out. Then she'd understand why they couldn't be together—maybe agree with him—and he could bury the past again.

"Buck was the only person who knew. He saw me sleeping in the barn one night after my father lost a crap-ton of money. He'd gotten blitzed and forgot me at the track. Or got arrested, who knows. It was the last time I saw him." He shrugged, and a bitter laugh escaped him. "No one even looked for me. But Buck took me in, raised me from the time I was eight years old."

"You lied," she said quietly. "That story about the puddle."

"No, that happened on the same night—that was why I was in his barn in the first place." He glanced down at his hands, gripping the chair so tightly that his knuckles had turned white. Letting go, Travis willed himself to not let Fallon realize how important her reaction was to him.

He shrugged a single shoulder. "Now you realize why *this* can't happen. I'm a nobody. Literally. I didn't even have a real identity until I got my driver's license and that was only because Buck helped me. Pitied me."

Fallon rolled her lips inward and studied him. He let out a slow exhale, preparing to leave.

"I never meant to hurt you, Fallon, and that's why you need to know. I'm not good enough for you." He turned away, back toward the doorway. "I'll pack my things."

"What? No." She moved forward, reaching for his arm and spinning him to face her, colliding against his chest. "You can't leave."

Unable to help himself, his hands slid up the length of her arms, cupping the smooth curve of her cheek. "I can't stay."

"Travis," she began. A slow, sweet smile spread over her lips. "You promised to help Dreamer, to prove to the world he's more than the long-shot everyone thinks he is." Her hands moved up his chest to circle his neck and he felt his entire body tense. "Both of you have so much to offer. You can't give up so easily."

"Facing the reality of limitations isn't giving up."

Fallon stood on her toes, her lips brushing against his. "Your version of reality is flawed. Let me help you see mine."

After she tugged him down toward her, Travis gave in, wanting—no, needing—what Fallon offered him. Her mouth captured his, her fingers delving into the thick waves of his hair, pulling him closer as her tongue swept against his. Their kisses grew more frantic, hungry, and desperate. His pulse raced; blood pounded in his ears. He ached to fill her again.

Hell, who was he kidding? This wasn't just a physical need. He was falling for Fallon, hard.

He let his lips find the curve of her jaw, the racing pulse throbbing at the side of her throat. He relished the sweet sigh of his name on her lips. "You deserve so much more than I can give you, Fallon."

She drew back from him, looking deeply into his eyes.

Hers were soft with yearning, completely vulnerable and open, revealing her heart to him. "I don't want anything more than you, Travis. No matter what that is."

"You don't care about—"

"I care," she whispered. "But only because it's made you who you are today. We're shaped by our pasts, but they don't have to define us. We choose who we become." She cupped his face, forcing him to look into her eyes. "We both can."

He couldn't believe this incredible woman wanted him, even though she'd seen the baggage he dragged along. "You're sure?"

Her sultry smile returned. "Don't ask me again." She took a step away from him, her fingers reaching for the buttons on her blouse. Walking backward, she edged her way toward the hall, dropping her shirt from her arms. "You should probably come see how certain I am."

He wasn't dumb enough to ask again.

Chapter 24

THE TRIP DOWN to the Santa Anita track before the race was a blur. Travis had insisted on driving Dreamer down to keep an eye on the colt and she insisted on riding with him. It had been worth taking nearly twelve hours to complete the seven-hour trip to see Dreamer prancing playfully when they walked him to the barn. He was completely fresh thanks to the stops they'd made along the route for him to stretch his legs. Unlike her, he'd arrived with energy to spare.

But it had been nice to fall asleep against Travis's shoulder and to spend the night in his arms, even if it had been in a run-of-the-mill motel. In fact, since his confession to her, they'd come to an unspoken understanding. There were no discussions about their pasts or futures beyond the Derby.

She hadn't told him about her grandmother's demands—that she sell Dreamer and walk away from horse racing—or that she'd given in to her grandmother's pressure to return to the family business. For now, she wanted to bask in the warmth of spending her days working alongside Travis, and her nights making love to him. It was a fantasy that she knew would come crumbling down eventually, but for the time being, they were both content to pretend it would never end.

She watched Travis help the jockey onto Dreamer's back for a couple of warm-up laps before the parade of horses. After leading Dreamer to the pony rider, he paused at the end of the barn and watched the other horses heading to the arena. Fallon wrapped her arms around his waist from behind and laid her cheek against the hard wall of his back.

"I feel good about today."

Travis turned, his arms dropping around her and pulling her against him before he placed a lingering kiss on her mouth. "I do, too. He's ready to go."

"The break has been good for him."

"It's been good for me, too." He nibbled against the hollow of her neck.

Fallon tipped her head back, laughing, unable to remember the last time she'd felt this happy and carefree. Somehow, she and Travis would make things work. They'd already found a way to make their differences work for them.

"Well, isn't this cozy?"

It had been months since Fallon had last seen Casper Dolan. In fact, she hadn't seen him since the day she'd fired him. Though she didn't care what he, or anyone else, thought about the way she and Travis held one another, she didn't like the way Travis's mouth had pinched into a thin line. The muscle of his jaw twitched.

"Mr. Dolan," she said with a smile. She turned toward him while keeping Travis behind her, hoping he'd follow her lead. "Do you have a horse running here today?"

"Funny."

He glared at her and she instantly realized her error. Not only did he not have a horse, but it was likely he wasn't training due to her dismissal. His gaze flicked to Travis behind her. "If I'd known it would have ensured my job, I'd have offered my stud services, sweetheart."

Travis tensed behind her. Fallon felt the furious rage building in him. Over the intercom, the announcer called the horses to post.

"Come on." Fallon ignored Casper and tugged at Travis's hand.

"When you're done slumming, honey, feel free to call me again. I could show you the difference between a gelding and a stallion."

Travis spun faster than she'd thought possible and lunged for Casper. He grasped the smaller man by the jaw and pressed his face so close their noses almost touched. "Apologize to her."

"Screw you. I'll call the cops."

"Apologize now."

Travis shoved Casper against the wall, a gasp escaping as Travis knocked the wind out of him. Fallon heard a slight squeak that she chose to assume was an apology.

"We have to go, Travis. The race—"

"Don't you ever come near either of us again, understand?" Travis shoved Casper one last time before letting the other trainer fall. Grabbing her hand as he walked past, he headed for the rail where they could see the race.

"Take a breath," Fallon said soothingly, when they were out of earshot. "Today is about us. Don't let him ruin it."

She watched Travis's breathing return to normal.

They stayed by the rail, because there wasn't time to head up to the box, not if Fallon wanted to be able to see anything. From down on the ground, it was going to be tough to make out much, but Travis pointed out Dreamer in the third stall.

"He's ready."

The sound of the bell cut her off as the gates burst open and thirteen horses flew out.

Fallon forgot anything she might have said as she clutched at Travis's arm, leaning as far forward as she could in order to see Dreamer. Four horses had immediately hunched in the front of the pack as they ran past, and her colt was even with the leader, on the outside. They made the first turn and she could barely see them. As they crept past, she watched her jockey holding Dreamer steady.

"Come on, Dreamer," she muttered. "Why is he holding him back?"

"To keep him from losing steam before the final turn."

Fallon could feel the tension emanating from Travis. He was as nervous as she was. As the horses cleared the last turn and came to the home stretch, she saw Dreamer open up, his stride lengthening, ears pinned to his head. His feet didn't seem to touch the ground as he pulled farther from the pack, leaving them behind in the dirt he kicked up. The anxiety that had been tightening in her chest exploded as Dreamer crossed the finish line a full five lengths ahead of any other mount.

Leaping into the air, Fallon spun, throwing herself at Travis and letting him catch her as they spun together in a circle.

"He did it!"

Travis sounded as awestruck as she felt. The little colt she'd helped deliver, the foal she'd raised against everyone's predictions, had just won. They were going to the Derby.

"You did it, Travis!"

He smiled at her broadly. "The Winner's Circle staff is going to be looking for you. Go. I'll get Dreamer and meet you there."

He started to walk away but she held his hand, tugging him back to her and pressing her lips against his. "Thank you."

His eyes gleamed with mischief. "Thank me later, sweetheart."

"Miss Radcliffe?"

"Yes." Several microphones were pressed toward her as reporters circled her, making her nervous. She tried to ease her way into the Winner's Circle, where Travis was waiting for her. When she was with her family, Fallon avoided the media whenever possible and let her mother act as the family spokesperson. She might be a marketing expert, but Fallon had absolutely no skills when it came to communicating with the media. Most of the time, she simply embarrassed herself.

"Miss Radcliffe—"

"Over here!"

"What do you think—"

Too many voices surrounded her, creating a buzz of sound and making it difficult to tell who was calling her, let alone what their question might be.

"You've just moved up from being an unknown to being a contender for the Kentucky Derby. How did you do it?"

She scooted through the throng, hurrying into the Circle where Dreamer began prancing, acting uncomfortable with the crowd closing in on him. Travis pulled her to his side, holding Dreamer's lead a bit tighter, and leaned down to her ear.

"We need to make this fast. He's not happy."

"Miss Radcliffe, how?"

The voices and questions kept coming as she tried to figure out which camera to smile at, which reporter to answer, all while trying to keep her eye on Dreamer. She struggled to listen as she was congratulated by others in the Winner's Circle. Coupled with his win, the noise made Fallon dizzy.

"Wasn't he injured in his last race? He's been questionable in his past starts. To what do you credit the change?"

"Dreamer is a fantastic horse—"

"So, you credit the horse's natural talent?"

"Well, yes, of course."

A photographer called out to her and snapped a quick picture. Dreamer shook his head, trying to jerk the lead from Travis, attempting to rear slightly.

"You should take him to the barn. I'll meet you there."

Travis's brow lifted slightly but he didn't argue. Several photographers followed him as he led Dreamer away but the reporters remained behind, circling her like a pack of wolves moving in for the kill.

"Were there any other changes you made that you would attribute your win to?"

Prying eyes focused in on her expectantly. She had to be careful what she said or it would create a maelstrom of speculation and rumor. Fallon wanted to get away from these vultures and get back to the barn, where Travis waited.

"I made several changes to his schedule," she admitted, thinking of how Dreamer had seemed to relax during his time at the vineyard. "But more than anything else, I allowed him to be a horse. His training reflected that and his win today was the result of a horse that loves to run. If you'll excuse me."

Fallon nudged past the crowd and jogged to the barn where she could finally celebrate their success, with her arms around Travis.

Chapter 25

TRAVIS INHALED SLOWLY, trying to ease the knot of betrayal threatening to strangle him. He'd heard every word Fallon had said, including the way she took credit for the changes in Dreamer. This win should have thrust him into the limelight and earned him a reputation as a premier trainer, but she had stolen it from him—the one person he'd trusted.

You did a job. You were paid for it. She doesn't owe you.

Admitting the facts didn't lessen the feelings of hurt from rising, threatening to drown him again. Telling Fallon about his past should have drawn them together, but maybe it had given her ammunition against him.

Fallon's voice was excited as she hurried into the barn with her phone to her ear. "I'll tell him."

He waited at the stall for the groom to return from walking the colt until he'd cooled down, watching as she tucked her phone into her purse. "We have a celebration party tonight at the mansion. I tried to talk her out of it but my grandmother insisted."

Travis barely grunted and Fallon cocked her head to one side, studying him. "What's wrong?"

"Nothing." He wasn't about to get into this with her here, where anyone could overhear them. "You want me there?"

Fallon took a step back, looking confused. "Of course, you're responsible for today."

A bitter laugh escaped him. "You sure about that?"

"Travis?"

He couldn't stay or he'd say too much. He stormed toward the doors. "I'm going to get Dreamer ready for the trip back in the morning."

"Wait, Travis—"

He barely slowed long enough to glance back at her. "Don't expect me there tonight. If I'm not good enough to share the win in the Circle, then I'm not good enough for your fancy shindig, either."

Fallon smoothed her hand down the side of her scarlet cocktail dress, taking another glass of champagne from the tray a waiter held out to her. She searched the crowd for Travis. After he left her in the barn, he'd disappeared completely. If anyone around the barn knew where he was, they weren't talking. Fallon smiled politely, thanking another one of their shipping clients when he congratulated her on Dreamer's win. Tonight should have been a celebration of a near impossible task, but it felt like a trial.

Fallon didn't care about any of this. She only wanted to find Travis, to understand why he'd been so angry. He couldn't possibly think she hadn't wanted him in the Winner's Circle.

Anna, her brother's fiancée, moved beside her. "Don't look now, but your grandmother is headed this way. She's not happy about the article in the paper this morning."

"What article?"

Anna's eyes widened. "You didn't see? There's a big front page article about you, Dreamer, and your new trainer."

"Okay? Why would Grandmother care…"

"It's a picture of you and the trainer *together*," Anna filled in. "Gabe and I, on the other hand, are thrilled for you."

"Travis and I aren't—"

Anna smiled mischievously. "Sure, you're not," she said with a laugh. "And neither were Gabe and I." She lifted her glass to her lips. "Oh, shit. There she is. Go, I'll cover for you."

Travis hadn't planned to come at all. And now that he was here, he knew why he wanted to stay away. This was definitely not his crowd.

The women were decked out in sequins and jewels; the men in designer tuxedos. Travis stood out like a sore thumb with his Levi's and button-down shirt, though he was wearing a sport coat.

He was about to turn around and leave, despite the doorman's instructions to head toward the ballroom, when Mrs. Wilhelmina Radcliffe appeared. *Shit.*

"Ah, Mr. Mitchell. Just the man I wanted to see." She waved a hand at the doorman. "I'll take you to Fallon. She's this way."

Left with little choice, Travis followed as Wilhelmina escorted him to a sitting room and closed the door.

"There," she said as she made her way to a bottle on a table against the wall. "Perhaps you'd like a drink?"

"Fallon isn't in here," he pointed out. His gut churned.

Wilhelmina shot him a calculated smile, carrying two glasses of amber liquid and holding one out to him. "Nothing gets by you, does it?"

She lifted the glass to her lips and he did the same, tossing back the drink and setting the glass aside, leery of her game, whatever it might be. "What do you want?"

Arching an eyebrow, she looked him over. "That was forty-year Glenfiddich scotch."

Travis shrugged. "Okay..."

"It's almost four thousand dollars a bottle."

"Well, you were ripped off," he said with a scoff. "Why am I here?"

"I was hoping you could tell me. What is it you're hoping to gain from Fallon?"

Travis shrugged. "She's my boss. I'm training her horse." It was the truth, even if it was oversimplified. And with him and Fallon, nothing was simple.

"I see." Wilhelmina walked back toward the bottle, setting her own glass back on the table before turning back and holding a folded newspaper out to him. "This doesn't look like a typical employer-employee relationship."

Travis took it and scanned the headline. While the article should have detailed Dreamer's win and Fallon's success, instead it speculated about their relationship and why she'd kept his involvement with Dreamer a secret. Irritation bubbled in his chest when he noticed a quote from Casper Dolan.

"This is nothing but bullshit."

Her chin lifted at his language. "I'm willing to offer you a million dollars to walk away from my granddaughter."

He carefully inspected her expression. Nothing in her face indicated she was anything but serious about her offer. "What?"

"Come now, Mr. Mitchell, we both know that Fallon has no business being at the race track. She's naive and doesn't realize how far in over her head she is. But you belong there."

She wasn't saying anything he hadn't already thought to himself, but he'd also seen the joy Dreamer brought Fallon. Ultimately, that was the only thing that was important to him, regardless of how he felt about the infuriating woman right now.

"Fallon belongs here, with her family," Wilhelmina insisted.

"Under your thumb, you mean."

Wilhelmina didn't deny his accusation. "One million dollars to walk away."

"I don't want your money."

"Of course you do. Who wouldn't?"

"I'm not doing this for the money. Not everyone can be bought."

"Yes, they can, you simply need to find the right currency and negotiate the price." Her ice-blue eyes slid over him before narrowing. "You aren't in love with her, are you?"

He wasn't going to admit anything to this woman, but deep down, he knew it was true—he was in love with her. If he wasn't, Fallon's betrayal wouldn't have cut so deeply. Travis clamped his jaw shut, unwilling to form a response, but it seemed Wilhelmina didn't need one.

She pursed her lips, mocking him. "You poor man. Fallon would never fall for someone like you. You have nothing to offer her. Why, she's simultaneously dating far better prospects than you, men more suitable to her station. Be reasonable. I'm sure I have enough connections to get you a job at a training facility. Where would you like to work? Kentucky?"

There was no point fighting her. Wilhelmina Radcliffe had said enough to remind Travis exactly who he was, and who he wasn't. Especially where it concerned Fallon.

Of course Fallon had plenty of men to choose from, waiting to give in to her every whim and desire—money, cars, houses, vacations, even horses. He, on the other hand, had nothing to offer.

"Keep your money." He walked to the door. "I'm training

Dreamer until the Derby. And after that, I'll find my own position." He shook his head, unsure whether he was more disgusted with her or himself, and stepped into the hallway. "I don't want to be part of anything you have your hands in."

"I'm protecting my granddaughter." She followed him with an authoritative click of her heels.

"I guess that must be what you tell yourself so you can sleep at night." He turned back toward the woman, crossing the hall to look down at her. "You're suffocating her, trying to fit her into that mold you created. One day, she'll either run away or shrivel up and die. Either way, you're going to lose her if you don't let her live her own life."

"Travis?"

Fallon's tentative voice stopped him cold. He spun to see her in the hall, staring at them, her eyes wide with shock. She looked exquisite with her flowing gown hugging every luscious curve of her body. Her long, golden waves were pulled to one side. He wanted her, not just physically. He wanted every part of her. And for forever.

He held his hands up. "I'm leaving. Dreamer and I will fly to Kentucky tomorrow to ready him for the Derby. I'll see you there in a month, Fallon. Act like an owner and let me be the trainer. It's what we do best."

Ignoring the crowd that had begun to gather, Travis walked out the front door and started heading home. He didn't even wait for the valet to bring his car around. He needed to put as much distance between him and Fallon as quickly as possible. If he didn't, he'd turn around and make a mistake neither of them could afford.

Chapter 26

FALLON BLINKED BACK the tears as she faced her grandmother. "What did you do?"

Shrugging, she took a deep breath, moving closer and pointedly glancing at the observers. "Now isn't the time," she said, leaning close and reaching for Fallon's arm.

Jerking herself free, Fallon stepped back. "Now is the *only* time. What happened?"

"I asked him about his intentions. He informed me that he was quitting after the Kentucky Derby. There was mention of a position in Kentucky."

Fallon's heart stopped in her chest before splintering into fragments. She should have suspected something like this would happen. Travis wasn't going to stay. He'd taken on this opportunity with Dreamer with hopes of using it to spur his career. His win today had shocked and impressed plenty of people. Job offers were sure to roll in, but she hadn't expected him to walk away so easily.

It's not his fault you were living in a fantasy. He never promised you forever.

Travis had warned her all along that they should keep things professional. And yet she had chosen to pursue him. Now she was reaping the painful result.

"I'm sorry, I have to…I have to go." She eased through the circle of people watching them raptly.

"Fallon," her grandmother called.

But Fallon ignored her, kicking off her shoes once she reached the second level of the house. Away from prying eyes, she finally let the scalding tears fall freely and allowed the fragments of her heart to break apart.

Chapter 27

May

FOUR WEEKS SHOULD have been enough time to put her heart back together. By now, the thought of seeing Travis today shouldn't send her pulse racing. But apparently, she was wrong.

Fallon stood in the doorway of the barn as Travis groomed Dreamer, his muscular frame silhouetted. She heard him speaking in soothing tones to the colt. Warm desire slid through her veins, heating her blood, pooling it low in her belly and making her wish she could flip it off with a switch, the way he had.

"Last day, Dreamer. Today you need to run like your ass is on fire," she heard him say as he ran the brush down the horse's back. He paused with his hands on the colt's shoulder. "I'm going to miss you, boy."

"You don't have to," she informed him as she neared. His head jerked toward her and she saw him stiffen when he realized who she was. Dreamer nickered a greeting. "You don't have to miss him. You could stay."

She waited a beat before moving close to him, letting her hands glide over her colt's neck. "If he wins—"

"You need to find someone else." Travis tossed the brush

into the grooming caddy and retrieved the saddle for the warm-up session. "This won't work. It was a mistake from the start."

"I see," she murmured, trying to pretend his words didn't feel like a knife to her heart.

"Do you?" He buckled the cinch.

Anger swelled in her like a sudden typhoon, washing over her. "You know what? No, I don't. I thought we had something. We might have had a few bumps at the beginning but we turned a corner, Travis. I thought we had. Then, all of a sudden—"

"You realized you were better than me?"

"What? I never said—"

"You didn't have to," he interrupted her. "Your dismissal at Santa Anita was sufficient. If it wasn't, watching you take credit for Dreamer in the Winner's Circle was."

"That wasn't what I did."

"No? Then why did you have me leave as soon as all the reporters arrived and began asking questions? You sent me off as if I was just like the rest of the hired help."

"I was scared to death, Travis. I didn't want to talk to them. I make a fool out of myself in front of the press." She reached for his arm. "I wasn't dismissing you. I was worried Dreamer would freak out and hurt someone again. When he gets like that, you're the only person who can calm him."

His jaw clenched and she could see his indecision. She needed him to touch her. As if he could hear her thoughts, Travis slid his hands to her arms, the heat of his fingers causing goose bumps to break out on her flesh. Butterflies danced in her stomach.

"Travis, I never meant to take credit for your work. I'm sorry. For the record, I have never, ever thought you weren't good enough for me." She reached up to cup his face. "If anything, you're more than I ever dreamed of."

She knew the moment his control snapped. Travis's eyes blazed with hunger and she was certain it was reflected in her own. Without warning, his mouth captured hers, his fingers delving into her hair as he walked her backward until she was pressed against the stall. Fallon's arms wound around his neck, arching into him, letting the heat of their passion fuse the pieces of her heart together again.

His lips found her throat and she heard his growl. "But wait, what your grandmother said—there's no one else?"

"There never has been. No one could ever measure up to you." The words spilled from her unchecked. "I love you, Travis." He drew back and she realized what she'd revealed. "I..."

Fallon bit her lip as Travis tipped her chin up with a finger, searching her face. A slow smile spread over his lips as he said, "You mean that."

She nodded.

"I don't know what I did to deserve you, Fallon, but I can't let you go. I don't know why I ever thought I could."

"I'm not going anywhere." Her palm ran over the rasp of whiskers he hadn't yet shaved this morning. "I was hoping to convince you to see things my way."

"I love you, Fallon. I have since I arrived at the vineyard."

He didn't give her the opportunity to respond before his mouth covered hers again, their tongues dancing.

"Ahem." They parted to see an exercise rider approaching. "Should I come back later?"

Fallon smiled up at Travis, reveling in the desire that

shone brightly in his eyes. "We have a race to win. I need your mind on the task at hand."

"Fine by me." Then he lowered his voice to a whisper and said, "But afterward, we're going to celebrate properly."

"I'll hold you to that," she warned.

Chapter 28

TRAVIS FELT FALLON'S hand tremble in his as they watched Dreamer approach the starting gate of the most important race of his young career—the Kentucky Derby. Unlike his other races, he loaded inside without any trouble, standing quietly as the rest of the animals made their way inside. Pride welled up in Travis when he saw the change in the colt.

"How was he this morning?"

"Ready to run, enjoying the cold." He brushed his thumb over her wrist and felt the steady thrum of her pulse, sending a sizzle of heat shooting through him.

"He's never run out of California."

"He's been down here long enough that it won't matter. You'll see." He moved behind her, wrapping his arms around her. "Trust me."

"I do."

Fallon looked up at him, a joyful smile on her lips. The vulnerable honesty in her voice made him forget the race and the horse they'd worked so hard to get there. He could only focus on the woman in front of him and the gift she'd given him. He'd seen this look on her face before, in the picture of her with Dreamer. It seemed the colt was no longer the only thing that brought her purpose and joy.

The bell sounded and the horses broke out of the gate, tearing down the track in a blur of flexing muscle and graceful beauty. Dreamer didn't move to the outside as he had in his past races. This time, he took the lead right away, worrying Travis that he might fade before the final turn.

They came around the bend and Dreamer found another gear. His lean body stretched out farther, eating up the track, leaving the pack of horses in the distance, crossing the finish line seven lengths ahead of his competition.

Fallon leapt into Travis's arms, winding herself around him, pressing kisses to his face. "He did it! You did it!"

"*We* did it!" He captured her mouth, their kiss quickly moving from celebratory to hungry. "You realize what this means, right? It means he's eligible for the Triple Crown now."

A slow grin slipped over her lips. "Does that mean that you're not quitting?"

"We have work to do. Fallon, you're stuck with me for the long haul."

She cupped his face in her palms and kissed him. "Promises, promises."

But Travis knew that this promise was the honest truth.

THE
GOURMET
CHEF

Chapter 1

ALEXANDRA RADCLIFFE GLANCED at the glittering Rolex on her wrist, took out her phone, and thumbed the button for her office. Her assistant, Caitlyn, immediately answered.

"Alex, you can't be finished with the meeting already."

"I'm not. Traffic was terrible and I just got here."

Caitlyn sighed into the receiver and Alex knew she was pressing her fingertips to her temples, the way she always did when she was frustrated. "I made your driver download Waze to avoid this. I guess he didn't bother to use it."

Alex might be late, but she still knew how to control a meeting. She was here to discuss a deal with Doug Kincaid, the CEO of Eco-Tech, which was an upcoming technology firm that needed more cash flow to pursue their eco-friendly products. They were on the cutting edge of technology and, therefore, exactly what she wanted to get her hands on, but Alex wasn't about to let Doug Kincaid know that. Within the hour, Eco-Tech would be part of her company's client profile and she would be on her way to meet with two more potential overseas investors.

"I'm just fashionably late," Alex quipped as she opened the front door of the massive eco-friendly high-rise. Just one more of many altering her precious San Francisco skyline. "Anyway, any quick tips for me? What does he look like?"

"He's very serious about the environment, so don't brag about your gas-hog limos, but that's probably stating the obvious. Good looking, early thirties, dark hair and eyes. I don't know exactly what you expect me to say. He's a techie, so I'm sure he'll be dressed casually."

"Aren't they always?" Alex brushed off her stylish Dolce & Gabbana suit, wishing she'd toned it down a bit for this meeting. Since her meeting immediately afterward was with high-profile clients at the Four Seasons, she'd opted for style over comfort. She stepped into the lobby and wrinkled her nose. "The floors are made of cork."

Caitlyn laughed. "Don't forget to call Mrs. Radcliffe back."

"My mother called?"

"Your grandmother," Caitlyn corrected. "She's called three times this morning."

"It's only ten a.m."

An exasperated sigh slid through the receiver. "Tell me about it. She's tenacious. You have to give her that."

"It's no longer a viable investment. I'm not throwing any more money into Radcliffe Shipping."

"A sinking ship?" Caitlyn offered as Alex groaned at the bad joke. "Oh, come on," her assistant teased. "That was a good one."

"If you say so." Alex glanced at her watch impatiently as the elevator slowed its ascent. "Next time she calls, tell her I'm in meetings all day and will call her tomorrow. Maybe by then she'll move on to nagging my brother for funding."

"Will do. Let me know when you're finished at Eco-Tech

and I'll get started drawing up the documents. Mr. Tanaka and Mr. Ryland will be waiting for you in the View at MKT Restaurant and you *cannot* be late."

"Now who's nagging?" Alex teased. She'd hired Caitlyn nearly four years ago, when she'd opened the AR Group, and the woman had proven herself indispensable. She was more than her employee. Alex counted Caitlyn as one of her few close friends.

"Shoot, I forgot to call my sister and find out where she and Anna want to meet tonight. Can you—"

"Already on it. You're meeting them for drinks at the High Five on Market."

"The sports bar?"

"I guess."

"Gotta go. I'm here." The elevator chimed and the doors opened as Alex disconnected the call.

Stepping out, she looked past the empty reception area to where glass windows lined the wall on one side of the wide-open interior space. A man stood inside next to a table against the back wall, arranging the breakfast items. His tall, tan, lean frame hinted at someone who took care of himself, while dark curls caressed the nape of his shirt, not quite long enough to look shaggy or unkempt, but just enough to need a trim. Alex's fingers clenched slightly around the handles of her Ferragamo briefcase, itching to see if those waves really were as soft as they looked.

She frowned at the wayward sentimentality of her thoughts and forced herself to remember where she was and why she was here—to make a deal. She assumed the man was Mr. Kincaid, but why was he alone in the conference room?

Where was the rest of his staff? The CFO or lawyers?

Then he turned around, his gaze falling directly on her.

The air shot from her lungs as warmth circled places that had been void of any heat for too long. Alex felt her breath catch in her throat.

He didn't look like any techie she'd ever met. This man didn't have any geeky qualities. In fact, he looked like he'd just stepped off the cover of some sports magazine. His dark eyes lit up with pleasure as he welcomed her with a brilliant smile. His square jaw sported a five-o'clock shadow—*at ten a.m.?*—and there were those full lips. He had the kind of mouth women fantasized about, imagining long hours spent kissing slowly.

He waved a hand at her, indicating she should enter the conference room and, not wanting him to think she was ogling him, Alex cast aside her hesitation. Lifting her chin slightly, she pasted a confident smile on her lips as she entered the room.

She was a professional and prepared to do what she did best—negotiate the hell out of this contract and walk away a winner. Well, she would once she could convince her brain to start functioning again.

Chapter 2

NICOLAS DONACELLI HADN'T expected to turn around and find the most beautiful woman he'd ever seen staring at him. Her stormy gray gaze slid over him slowly, as if weighing his value, before lifting to meet his again. Her blond hair, pulled back in a loose bun, was mussed enough for a few stray wisps to fall loose around her face, softening her perfect angular features. Doug had already mentioned that he was running late and she was obviously here for the meeting, but she looked uncertain. Since everyone else was still downstairs, he lifted a hand, waving her into the conference room.

This woman was high class; she practically oozed wealth and prestige. Nico wondered what business Doug had with her. They didn't exactly run in the same circles. Doug and his college-friends-turned-coworkers who ran Eco-Tech were grassroots guys. The kind who preferred jeans and flannels to power suits. Doug was going to need every person in his boardroom arsenal to not get completely blindsided in this meeting. Now he understood why Doug had ordered the full breakfast menu from Martinelli's, instead of the usual pastries and coffee.

Nico met the woman's gaze again and she smiled at him. His heart stopped as it plummeted into his gut. Not that it was his heart throbbing below his belt. This woman wasn't just pretty; she was stunning. Enough to dry his mouth and send the blood rushing from his brain to settle farther south. It had been a long time since he'd been around such a gorgeous woman, but it hadn't been *that* long. Yet his body continued its impersonation of a teenage boy on his first date.

Think about prepping lunch at the restaurant. Think about washing dishes. Think about football and drinks tonight with Aaron. Anything but the woman in front of you.

Nico fought to drag his attention back to the job at hand. Turning away from her, he focused on arranging the last breakfast tray before Doug arrived with his team. He needed to get his ass back to the restaurant. He had a busy day in front of him. There was a lunch menu for him to prep and he still needed to convince his boss to let him try his new pasta dish, which meant getting back in plenty of time to make the fettuccini from scratch.

From there, he'd have to hurry to his second gig as a personal chef at a family estate. Though stifling at times, it was a decent gig with good pay.

Just a few more months and he could stop answering to others and start making his dream a reality.

Nothing was going to feel more liberating than the day he'd be able to turn in his notice and walk away from cooking what other people told him to prepare. In a few months, he'd have enough experience as a head chef and the down payment necessary to open his own restaurant—the Don—where he'd blend traditional Italian cuisine with molecular gastronomy techniques. It would be a tribute to his grandfather, the man who'd taught him to cook. He just needed a little more experience and a little more money. Well, that and a solid business plan.

Her bold voice jerked him out of his reverie. "Excuse me, I'm Alexandra. I believe you're expecting me."

She walked up to him confidently, and he was surprised to see that the woman was *even more* beautiful up close. His brain shut down, refusing to comprehend the slightest response, even as she slid her designer briefcase onto the conference table and held out her hand to shake his.

Instinctively, Nico held out a hand and she gave it a quick pump.

"It's a pleasure to meet you in person, Mr. Kincaid. I apologize for the delay. I'm afraid I need to get right down to business. Unfortunately, I have another appointment in…" She glanced at her watch, the diamonds blinding him as they caught the sunlight from the floor-to-ceiling windows. "Less than an hour, actually."

Mr. Kincaid? Wait a second. "I—"

"Not to worry. I can assure you that the AR Group is fully prepared to offer you a significant investment, but I do have to ask for a bit more than your original offer."

"No, you don't understand—"

She narrowed her eyes for a quick beat before the corners of her lips tugged up in a slow smile. She gave him a slight nod. "What I understand is that you are seeking investors because you need the assistance my firm can offer, Mr. Kincaid. I also know that while your company is on the cutting edge of several technological breakthroughs, unfortunately, they have been stalled due to lack of funding. Funding that my firm is now offering."

She crossed her arms and arched a brow victoriously. "You see, I've done my homework and I know exactly what this company is worth with those projects sitting uncompleted." She waved a hand at the projector and computer at the end of the table. "Why don't we dispose of the unnecessary theatrics? Neither of us really wants to rehash what I'm sure the lawyers will quibble over later. My firm is prepared to offer you seventy-five million dollars in corporate funding with forty of that earmarked for your research projects. However, the AR Group is going to require a seventy percent share of Eco-Tech in contrast to the forty-five percent you originally offered."

"Seventy-five…million?" Nico nearly choked on the words.

Just the thought of anyone having that much money, let alone tossing around the number so casually, boggled his mind. It had taken him years to save up the fifty thousand dollars to get his restaurant off the ground.

"Mr. Kincaid, I really don't have a lot of time thanks to the horrible traffic, but if we could just sit down for a moment, I'm happy to explain our position. You'll find that this offer is very generous and that seventy percent would be…"

She narrowed her eyes at him as he stared at her mouth, unable to stop watching the way her lips curved as she spoke, the way the pillowy pink flesh moved around each syllable and the way her voice washed over him, breathy with just a slight huskiness.

"Mr. Kincaid?" She reached for his arm. "Are you okay? You look like—"

"Alexandra!"

They both spun toward the doorway. Nico saw Doug leaning against the frame with a smug look on his face. Several of his staff watched behind him, waiting to enter the room. He nodded at Nico as he pushed thickly framed glasses higher on the bridge of his nose. "Thanks, Nico. I'll take it from here."

The last thing Nico needed was to get into trouble while delivering for Martinelli's. He wasn't ready to strike out on his own and he really didn't want to get fired. "I didn't—"

Doug shook his head and, wordlessly, gave him a slight wave of his hand.

"Wait a second." The woman turned back to Nico before her gaze returned to Doug as he pulled out a chair, directing the rest of his staff to sit. "*You're* Mr. Kincaid?"

"I am." Doug chuckled, obviously enjoying her discomfort and the elevated position it now put him in. "And this is Nico Donacelli, our caterer, and here is the rest of my staff. Now that Nico understands the inner workings of this business proposal, we should probably sit down and nail down that *forty-five* percent I originally offered you."

Her cheeks colored a bright pink and she slid into one of the chairs, glancing at several of Doug's staff who were barely trying to contain their mirth. Alexandra pressed her lips together, glancing at Nico as he made his hasty retreat. The tempestuous look she gave him with her gray eyes made two things clear: first, he'd just ruined her deal, and second, she never wanted to set eyes on him again.

Chapter 3

"HAVE YOU EVEN called Grandmother back yet?"

Alex pressed her lips together, willing herself to have patience as she tried to ignore the laughter in her younger sister's voice. "Would you? I mean, seriously, Fallon, do you realize how much money I've already sunk into the shipping company? My investors aren't going to be coerced into giving any more."

"Well, if Radcliffe Shipping goes under, Grandmother will be forced to face the fact that she might not be the businesswoman she thinks she is. Time and technology have changed operational procedures but she hasn't. Do you know how long it took Gabe to even convince her to give her employees cell phones on the docks?"

"If she doesn't have a company to run, she's going to have free time on her hands and you know what that will mean, right? 'Gabe's vineyard and your ranch are far too *primitive*,'" Alex said, mimicking her grandmother's arrogant tone. "We'd become the recipients of all her time and attention."

"And you'd become her new favorite hobby," Fallon commiserated.

Alex groaned. "I'd suffocate."

Her sister giggled. "I don't think suffocation is likely in that huge house."

"She'd smother me," Alex insisted.

"So, what are you going to do?"

"I don't know." She slid into her limousine and directed the driver back to her office. "I guess I have some investments I could liquidate if I have to. It might buy her a little time. I'll go back to the office and look into it."

"Oh, no, you don't," Fallon warned. "You have to go home and change. Anna and I have been waiting for tonight for weeks. Don't you dare bail on us."

Alex pinched the bridge of her nose. After the fiasco at Eco-Tech that morning, she'd forgotten about their girls' night out. "Can't we reschedule? It's been a hell of a day and I've got a splitting headache."

"Come on, Anna and I came all this way. We're stuck staying with Grandmother to plan Gabe's wedding," she reminded Alex, as if that should be enough reason for her to give in. "We need to escape for a while."

Alex sighed. "Fine. I guess after my morning fiasco I could use a drink."

"Why? What happened?"

"I'll tell you about it tonight. Suffice to say, I made a fool out of myself and it's going to cost me."

"Don't keep me waiting."

"Later. I don't even want to think about it right now."

"Oh, no! That bad? Well, there's your excuse not to drop any more money into Radcliffe Shipping then."

"That won't work. Wilhelmina Radcliffe doesn't take no for an answer. She won't give up until I give her something. You know that."

"True." Fallon laughed quietly, but Alex heard the respect in her voice. They might not agree with their grandmother's morals or her methods, but they did respect what she'd accomplished over the years, in spite of her late husband's gambling addiction. "But *you* can't exactly fault her for it."

"The hell I can't. Our grandmother is so focused on *her* business pursuit that she forgets we each have our own enterprises to run. It's all she talks about."

"Really? You don't say. I can't imagine anyone else in this family who might act that way," Fallon teased. "Hey, pot, meet kettle."

"What's that supposed to mean?"

"It means the apple didn't fall too far from the tree. You're exactly like her."

"I am not." Alex didn't like the implication. Her grandmother was stuffy, stubborn, demanding, and, well, overbearing. She wasn't like that.

"Alex, I love you, so I'm going to be honest with you. You're so busy being a businesswoman that you've forgotten all about the woman part. You don't even remember how to be a friend or have anything but business relationships."

"I have friends," Alex interrupted.

"Like who?"

"Caitlyn, for one."

"She's your assistant," Fallon pointed out.

"That doesn't mean she's not a friend," Alex argued.

"It's not the same when you're signing her checks."

"Says the woman marrying the man she once employed," Alex retorted, quickly regretting it. She knew what Fallon was getting at. It had been a long time since Alex had gone out to a dinner that didn't include a negotiation of some sort. She was always either wooing investors or making a deal. She couldn't even remember the last time she'd done something because it sounded fun or relaxing.

"Lexie," Fallon scolded gently. "When was the last time you went on a date?"

Fallon using her nickname for Alex was her undoing. "Okay, I promise to leave work behind tonight."

"Prove it. Show me that you can let your hair down. That means no talking about work, money, investments, or dividends. For one night, forget that you're a Radcliffe. Tonight you're not going to be a socialite, you're going to just be social."

"Who sounds like our bossy grandmother now?" Alex rolled her eyes, wondering what she'd just agreed to.

Chapter 4

NICO GRABBED HIS uniform from the backseat of the car and headed for the back door of the kitchen, opposite from the main entrance to the mansion. The staff manager glared at him as he burst through.

"You're late."

"I have five minutes before my shift begins," Nico pointed out. "I'm good."

"You'd better be dressed and ready to start promptly at four. Dinner service cannot be delayed." The old man pressed his thin lips together so tightly they practically disappeared. His eyes slid over Nico as his nose wrinkled slightly. "This is the only warning you're going to get."

"Yes, sir."

"Go," the manager ordered with a sniff, "and make it fast."

Nico hurried into the staff bathroom to change clothes. Leaving his jeans and T-shirt in his locker, he shoved his arms into his chef coat, slipping the buttons into place. Then he headed back to the kitchen and, ignoring the curious looks from Dylan, his sous chef, he tugged a bunch of basil from the rack and began chopping it roughly, dropping it into the food processor before reaching for the pine nuts.

Dylan paused in his vegetable garnish prep. "I thought we were doing lobster tonight? Want me to go double check?" Setting his knife aside, Dylan started to move away from the counter.

"No, we're doing a fresh fettuccini with pesto and scallops instead." The meal had been such a success at Martinelli's today that he decided to repeat it for the family for whom he worked as a private chef.

"But—"

"Trust me. Prep the scallops."

"Me?"

Nico rolled his eyes and inhaled slowly before pausing his hands. "Yes, you. I'm going to make the pasta, the sauce, and the gelato, but I'm trusting you to prep and sear the scallops. Please don't screw this up. My ass is in your hands."

Dylan gave him a sly grin as he turned away with a quick wink. "No thanks. You're not my type."

Nico chuckled as Dylan headed for the freezer and then came up beside him. "You sure about this, Chef? You know how the lady doesn't like changes made to her menu."

"Then we'll have to make it so amazing she forgets what she originally wanted. You're going to help with the gelato. Grab the ingredients for me while I work on the pesto."

"We don't have time for gelato."

"We do if we use liquid nitro."

Dylan's brows shot up and he smiled. "Yes, Chef."

This was where Nico was happiest, his most confident. Standing in the kitchen, making decisions and running his crew. He loved cooking and the artistry of putting it all together to make something beautiful and delicious. He had since he was a boy, standing beside his grandfather in his family's little Italian restaurant in Oakland. He'd thrived as they created *zuppe* and swelled with pride when Papa Don proclaimed his mushroom risotto the best he'd ever tasted.

For years, he worked in the restaurant with his grandfather, taking notes as he passed down the detailed recipes he'd brought with him from northern Italy. If Papa Don told him he had a gift, he believed him. It was where Nico learned the basics, but, a stickler for tradition, his grandfather had never let Nico put his own twist on the recipes.

Culinary school had struck a fire in Nico. It was there that he learned to play with flavors, to become creative. He'd had access to state-of-the-art equipment and the freedom to cook what he wanted, and to make mistakes. And now, he'd had a taste of both worlds and wanted to combine them.

It was a decent gig, working as a private chef in the kitchen of a wealthy family. He only had to make dinner for them five nights a week when their regular chef left for the day, and though he had to follow their rules most of the time, soon he'd be able to pick up where his grandfather had left off, opening his own restaurant. Someday soon, the Don would open to rave reviews. Until then, he would satisfy himself by taking pride in the meals he made for the family he served.

They were as rich as King Solomon himself and Nico still wasn't certain how he'd landed the job. There'd been at least twenty applicants in the kitchen the day he interviewed. But somehow, his grandfather's chicken cacciatore and tiramisu had won over the staff manager, who'd hired him on the spot. And, at least for now, the family seemed pleased with his dinner menus.

Nico tasted the finished pesto sauce and set it aside as he went to work on the lemon gelato, mixing the cream, sugar, eggs, and lemon juice. Sliding on his protective gloves, he called Dylan over to help him with the final steps. As he whipped the mixture, Nico poured the liquid nitrogen in slowly, using a technique he had mastered in school. It wasn't something he was able to do often and he was still surprised he'd convinced the staff manager to stock it, but he was going to make sure he proved its value in the kitchen with an unforgettable dining experience for the family.

Dylan finished up the scallops while Nico prepared the pasta. As the pieces were brought to him, Nico plated them with the pesto fettuccini and decorated the dish with a basil leaf, pine nut, and freshly grated Parmesan garnish. Wiping the edge of the dish as the server waited, Nico eyed the food. The color was perfect, the presentation was aesthetically pleasing, and the aroma was divine.

Dylan, standing beside him, eyed the pesto fettuccini and seared scallops. He slapped a hand against his stomach as it let out a loud rumble. "We get to eat the leftovers, right?"

"This is good to go. Take them," Nico instructed the server.

Turning back to Dylan, he smiled broadly. "Absolutely not. Now I'm going to dish up the gelato. And you," he said, pointing at Dylan, "are going to freeze lemon chips."

Satisfaction rushed through him. He couldn't imagine being anywhere else right now; this was exactly where he belonged. Today, private chef. Tomorrow, restaurateur.

Chapter 5

"SO? WHAT'S IT really like working for people who are that rich? I mean, are they snobs or what?" Aaron tipped back his beer and signaled the bartender for another as he reached for another hot wing and shoved it into his mouth. "You sure you don't want some?"

Nico shook his head and slid a tortilla chip from his plate of nachos. "No thanks, these are more than enough."

He barely registered the spice of the food as he began mentally checking off the last-minute to-dos before he could set up another meeting with the bank. The most pressing was to write up a business plan and he had no clue how to start. The bartender slid two more pints in front of them and Nico thanked him, turning his attention back to Aaron, who was staring up at the football game on the television over the bar.

Nico's best friend of twenty years shook his head. "I'm not sure I'm ready for this beating."

"Aw, come on." Nico slapped a hand on the bar. "Don't jinx them. The Raiders are doing well this season."

"So far." Aaron dropped the wing bones into a paper-lined basket. "But that just means the other shoe is going to drop, or the refs are going to kill them with penalties. Something."

"Sadly, you're probably right," Nico said with a chuckle.

Aaron spun around to glare at him and his eyes suddenly widened. Nico turned to see what had garnered that sort of reaction when Aaron shoved Nico's shoulder and started to rise from his stool. "Oh, no, you don't. I saw them first."

"Fine. You can have whoever it is," Nico agreed, turning around anyway. "I'm here to watch the——"

Standing in the doorway of the bar was the woman he'd met at Eco-Tech this morning. She looked different now. Her power suit was replaced with a flowing skirt and blouse combo and the top of her hair was pulled back while long waves cascaded over her shoulders. But there was no mistaking her.

He watched as she entered the High Five, looking around at the various television screens, all blasting the same football game, before her stormy gray gaze fell on him. Immediately her smile slipped from her lips and her brows lifted skyward in surprise. Just as quickly, a frown appeared. She nodded slightly as she passed him on her way to their table. For a moment, he thought she might stop and say something, but she continued past him wordlessly.

"Dude, stop already," Aaron hissed.

"What?" Nico tracked her every move, unable to tear his gaze from her. *What in the world was a woman like her doing in a sports bar?*

"Do you know her? Because if not, you look like a stalker."

They'd barely taken their seats when one of the women with her leaned forward. He heard her ask, "Do you know him?"

"Remember my morning meeting?" she asked, averting her gaze from his.

Her friend's brows shot skyward and Nico was curious what about had been said about him. Before he could get up to ask, she slid from her chair and approached him.

Aaron leaned sideways, trying to look inconspicuous. "Please tell me you don't know her and she's coming to talk to me."

"You wish." Nico smiled as Alexandra approached him, looking more confident than he felt. His pulse was pounding so hard he couldn't hear anything but the roar of it through his veins. Not that it mattered, because his mouth had dried up and he doubted he could speak anyway.

"I'm sorry for interrupting, but I wanted to apologize for the way I acted this morning."

"No apology necessary. I should have—"

"Spoken up sooner?" she finished for him.

He wasn't sure if she was deliberately being abrasive or was simply direct, accustomed to being the one to take charge of every conversation. Nico was beginning to wonder if she wasn't just like the diamonds she wore: beautiful to look at, but cold and hard as stone.

He'd known plenty of people just like her. Old Money, like the high society crowd of San Francisco, who looked down on everyone else, especially the type of people who worked in a kitchen. The distinction between dishwasher and chef never seemed to matter to them, but he was going to try to give her the benefit of the doubt.

The bartender approached and she leaned toward him. "Two cosmos and a Sierra Nevada IPA."

"You know, I might have spoken up this morning if you'd paused long enough to let me say anything."

Her chin lifted slightly but she didn't argue.

"Let's start over," he said. "How about if I buy you and your friends your drinks?"

"I don't think so," Alexandra answered, glancing back at her table, where both of her friends watched them expectantly. The blonde, who looked very similar to Alexandra, stood up and waved at them.

"I think they want you to come back."

Alexandra sighed. "I think they want you to come with me." She glanced up at him apologetically. "It's my sister and my sister-in-law. Well, she will be in a few weeks."

"And why would they want me to come over?"

If the roles had been reversed and it were his friends, they'd want to give him shit in order to embarrass him in front of her. But the women at the table weren't cut from the same cloth. He could hardly imagine them acting like his friends.

Alexandra turned those gray eyes on him apologetically. "Maybe because I told them about what happened this morning and they think it will be funny to watch me squirm."

"Squirm?" he repeated.

She sighed and her cheeks turned pink as she averted her eyes. "I might have told them you were…attractive."

Heat spread through him and Nico tried to ignore the way it pooled in his groin. He felt himself smile as he looked back at Alexandra. "You think so, huh?"

She cocked her head to one side. "False humility doesn't become you."

He laughed aloud at her blunt statement. She certainly didn't pull any punches. The bartender slid her drinks on the counter and Nico motioned to him that he'd pick up the tab before grabbing his beer and the Sierra Nevada. "Then let's go."

"Wait, I don't think—"

He didn't give her the chance to shoot him down. Nico heard her sigh from behind him as he headed for the table.

"Fine," she said. "Just don't cry to me when you wish you hadn't come over."

"I consider myself duly warned," he tossed back over his shoulder, waiting for her to follow him.

"Hi," the blonde said as she leaned across the table, offering her hand. "I'm Fallon. My sister didn't mention that you were so…tall."

The other woman burst into laughter and quickly covered her mouth. "I'm sorry," she said when Alexandra shot her an incredulous look. "But after everything you told us, that's pretty funny. I'm Anna." She reached for the Sierra Nevada and then they shook hands.

"It's nice to meet you both. Now, I'm curious," Nico said, giving Alexandra his most charming smile. "What exactly did you tell them about me?"

A slight smile tugged at the corner of her lips as she slid one of the cosmos in front of her sister. "I might have mentioned that you're obnoxious."

He tipped his head conspiratorially at the two women. "That would be a lie. Besides, she couldn't possibly know that from the two words I said to her today."

"She *did* mention your curls and your bedroom eyes." Anna pinched her lips together to keep from laughing when Alexandra's eyes widened.

"I swear I didn't…" Alexandra's cheeks blazed. "Anna, Fallon, this is Nico, uh…"

"Donacelli." All three women looked at one another expectantly, as if unsure who should speak next. "So, what brings the three of you out tonight? Celebrating your big boardroom win this morning?"

"Hardly," Alexandra scoffed before taking a long drink from her cosmo.

Nico glanced up in time to see Anna drop the beer bottle

from her lips and swipe her fingers sideways at her throat, the universal signal to quit while he was ahead.

"Sore subject." Fallon smiled across the table at him. "Lexie doesn't consider anything a win unless she gets exactly what she wants. That didn't happen this time."

"Because of our interaction?" he asked.

Alexandra shrugged a shoulder.

"Aw, damn, I'm really sorry."

He knew exactly what it was like to work hard for a goal and then have something stupid screw up your plans. Like being short a business plan and the ten thousand more dollars he needed to get a start-up loan.

"Anything I can do to help?"

"No, I'm just going to relax tonight and show my sister that I can have fun."

"We'll see." Fallon sounded less than convinced but shot Nico a shrewd look. "You're already talking about work, which was a no-no, remember?"

Alexandra rolled her eyes. "That wasn't my fault. He brought it up," she said, pointing at Nico accusingly.

He raised his hands in front of him. "I'm just here to watch the game and eat nachos. We can talk about anything you want."

Her gaze lingered on his mouth for a moment before the tip of her tongue snuck out to wet her lips. Every inch of his body leapt to attention as his body nearly burst into flames. Her gaze rose slowly, connecting with his, and he saw her eyes darken. She had no clue what she was doing to him.

Or maybe she did.

Chapter 6

"SO, FALLON AND Anna are quite the pair, huh?"

"That's putting it mildly." Alex glared at the backs of the two women. She'd felt more than a little betrayed when they excused themselves to go to the ladies' room, leaving her alone with a man who sent hot pricks of desire racing up her spine.

He was a nice guy and she didn't blame him for her mistake this morning at the meeting. It wasn't his fault she'd been in such a hurry or that she'd jumped to conclusions. She'd been the one to rush head-first into selling him on her position before he'd even introduced himself.

Truthfully, what CEO would have been setting up the breakfast buffet? She'd been off her game and allowed her grandmother's never-ending requests to distract her, and paid the price for her inattention. She'd had to give up 10 percent of the stake in Eco-Tech to make the deal happen. But there was a bright side. She'd closed the deal with the AR Group afterward as the majority shareholders...*and* she'd somehow run into Nico again.

Alex leaned back in her chair, sipping from her second cosmo. "How did you know I'd be here? Did you follow me?"

He laughed. "I was here first, remember? Maybe it's just my lucky day."

His dark gaze slid over her, heating every inch like a caress. Her heart pounded against her ribs as the blood rushed through her veins. Alex took a deep breath to combat the sudden light-headedness that left her dizzy and reaching for the table to steady her.

"You're saying it was sheer coincidence?" Her voice was lower than she'd intended, sounding seductive, even to her own ears.

He leaned forward, closing the distance between them, his gaze locking with hers, his voice gravelly and oh-so-sexy. "I prefer to call it luck."

He was close enough that she could feel the warmth of his breath fall over her lips. Alex instinctively tipped her body closer to his, drawn to him despite her earlier humiliation. Conversation flowed easily with him and he seemed almost familiar, as if she'd known him most of her life.

Alex watch his lips move and wondered for a moment what it might be like to be kissed by them, to let the fullness of them brush over her skin. Goose bumps broke out on her arms and a shiver of delight whispered over her as her fingers played over the stem of her martini glass.

What was she doing? This was supposed to be a girls' night out. She wasn't supposed to pick up the sexy caterer tonight.

Alex cleared her throat and sat back in her chair, taking a quick drink of her cosmo and looking at him over the rim. "Mr. Donacelli, I should really—"

"Nico," he corrected her with a laugh. But this time the sound was tempting, deep and rich, making her wonder if that wasn't how his voice would sound in the morning. "I think we should be on a first-name basis by now, don't you?"

"I suppose, it's just..."

Alex bit the corner of her lip, unsure why she was bothering to fight this attraction she felt for him. Fallon and Anna would encourage her to go for it. He was an incredibly good-looking man, intelligent, witty, and sexy enough to melt her panties. And in truth, she wanted him. But the logical side of her brain kept reminding her that she needed to be responsible, to consider the consequences. She'd almost blown a deal this morning because she'd been blinded by him.

"Just what?"

He brushed a finger over the side of her hand and she jumped at the electric spark that ignited deep in her belly. Alex took another long sip from her drink, praying it would help her relax. Then she looked around the room, trying to latch on to any topic since her attraction to this man seemed to overwhelm her senses.

"Breakfast was delicious this morning. Please send my compliments to the chef."

"Thank you."

"I meant that you should tell—"

"I'm the chef," he interrupted.

"Oh!" That surprised her. Her gaze slid over his T-shirt and jeans. The attire of a "regular" guy that didn't exactly speak of wealth. "Does that mean you own the restaurant that catered—"

He took a sip of his beer. "Not yet."

"Oh, so you're just the chef?"

Alex, stop being rude! She inwardly cringed. She never spoke without knowing exactly what she wanted to say and always said what she meant. But what was it about this guy that made her keep blathering incoherently?

"Yep, that's me. *Just* a chef."

She didn't miss the annoyance in his voice. He smiled

at her but it didn't quite reach his eyes the way it had before. It seemed like no matter what she said to him, it was wrong. Alex finished her drink, stalling for time as she wondered how best to apologize—*again*—without making matters worse, but he didn't give her the opportunity.

"What about you? Are you just another suit?"

She narrowed her eyes at him over the rim of her glass. Was he playing some sort of game? Her family was the richest in San Francisco, not to mention one of the most widely recognizable. Every one of the Radcliffes had been featured as part of the new generation of San Francisco elite at one time or another. How could he *not* know her on sight?

She opened her mouth to tell him exactly who she was and that she didn't appreciate his artifice, until she realized there was nothing but open authenticity in his dark gaze. Suddenly, the idea of anonymity thrilled her. The ability to just be herself, to be vulnerable and not worry about someone dating her for the power, status, or prosperity that her family name suggested, was refreshingly enticing.

She coyly tipped her head to one side and smiled at him. "I guess I am. I work at AR Group."

"The investment firm?"

She nodded.

"That explains why you were trying so hard to convince me to up the shares…I get it. So, you're a high-power suit." His eyes shone with humor.

She held up a hand. "Let's *not* talk about work anymore. I'd like to forget what happened this morning."

He winked at her. "Let's start over, Alexandra."

"Alex," she corrected, biting back the smile that was tugging at the corners of her mouth. He had a boyish charm that was difficult to resist.

"Well, *Alex*, it looks like you could use another drink." He slipped her empty glass from her fingers and went up to the bar to get her another cosmo.

Alex clenched her hand, digging her nails into her palm, trying to ignore the heat swirling through her at his touch. She worried it was the result of too much alcohol drunk too quickly, but she knew better. This man was intoxicating.

He slid another cocktail on the table and glanced past her, toward the bar, and she felt disappointment shoot through her. She didn't want him to feel obligated to wait for Anna and Fallon to return. Following his gaze, she saw his friend watching them expectantly.

"Do you need to get back? I'm fine if you do." She hoped he wouldn't. As unorthodox as their meeting had been, she found she was enjoying his company.

Nico sighed and shook his head. "Do you mind if I invite my friend over? I promised him we'd watch the game together."

"Of course."

As his friend dragged a chair over from a nearby table, Anna and Fallon came back from the bathroom.

"I'm Anna, this is Fallon and Alex. What's your name?" Anna asked as she took her seat.

"Aaron. Nice to meet you."

"So, who's playing?" Alex asked, looking at the televisions lining the walls. Football? She didn't know much but she thought she'd be able to fake her way through a conversation about the sport. "Is it the Forty-Niners?"

Nico shot her a puzzled glance. "No. The Raiders and Chiefs."

"Oh. I just saw the red outfits."

She saw Aaron frown and Nico bit back a smile. "You're a big Niners fan?"

Before she could answer, Aaron threw his hands into the air and groaned, along with several other men who were surrounding the bar. "Aw, man, seriously? Another penalty?"

"Well, sure," she said, turning her attention back to Nico. "Isn't everyone in San Francisco? Who else would you root for but the home team?"

Anna's eyes were wide as she stared at Alex.

"I don't know, the Oakland Raiders?" Aaron suggested as he shook a handful of nuts just before dropping them into his mouth and throwing back the rest of his beer.

Anna shook her head but Alex wasn't sure what she was trying to say. She wrinkled her nose and Nico snickered.

"Something wrong with the Raiders? Is it the silver and black *outfits?*"

Aaron let out a loud guffaw but Alex wasn't sure what was so funny, although she suspected they were laughing at something she'd said. "No. I mean, it's Oakland."

"What does that mean?" She had Nico's full attention now.

She rolled her eyes and glanced over at the screens again. Maybe football wasn't a subject she could fake her way through. This seemed to be getting a bit out of her control, and from what she could see, it was nothing but large men running into one another on a field anyway. She couldn't even tell who had the ball or where it was supposed to go.

She looked back at Nico. "I mean, they're from Oakland. Does anything good ever come from there?"

Aaron snorted, nearly spitting out his beer. Nico's head dropped back as he laughed, the sound reverberating through her, making her senses hum. She couldn't figure out what she might have said to cause the reaction in him.

"Oakland, born and raised." Nico clinked glasses with Aaron and Alex closed her eyes, hanging her head.

Would this humiliation ever end? She slid a hand over her eyes and shook her head. "I'm sorry. I didn't…"

She heard his laughter, rich and vibrant as it fell around her, making her feel dizzy. Unexpected desire swelled in her, hard and fast, curling in her belly and warming her from the inside out.

Nico reached for her hand. "Don't worry, Alex. I don't take offense. It just means that we're the *only* good things to come from Oakland other than the team, right, Aaron?"

Chapter 7

NICO HAD NO idea how much time had passed. The game ended hours ago and Aaron had found his way back to the bar for the postgame wrap-ups, but he was still at the table with Alex. Anna and Fallon had disappeared again. And he suspected they'd done it deliberately to give him and Alex time to get to know each other.

So far, he liked what he'd discovered about her. She was an intelligent woman who could talk about a great number of topics, even if football wasn't one of them. She was as confident and sophisticated as she was beautiful, but she was quick to laugh at herself when the opportunity presented itself. As they continued to drink, it happened more and more.

The simple fact was that he liked her a lot, but it didn't take a rocket scientist to see that they were from different worlds. She was white collar while he was lucky his blue one wasn't stained a dingy gray. She was Ivy League educated; he had barely worked his way through culinary school, scrimping for every dime. But despite their differences, he could see the same yearning in her eyes.

He brushed his thumb over the top of her hand and she paused mid-sentence, looking up at him curiously. He could tell she'd had too much to drink, as had he, but neither of them were driving. It didn't matter.

"What is it you want out of life, Alex?"

Nico wasn't sure where the question had come from, or how it had managed to slip out. She suddenly looked sad, looking down at their hands. She flipped hers so that their palms were pressed together and wound her fingers between his, sending electric shock waves up his arm.

"I just want to be able to be the real me."

His gaze lifted to meet hers and he leaned closer. "Have you been yourself tonight?"

She nodded slowly, a soft smile tipping the corner of those perfect pink lips.

"Good. I like the real you." His lips barely touched the corner of hers and she inhaled sharply. "Do you want me to stop?" he whispered against her mouth.

"No." Her hand squeezed his tighter and she leaned into him, pressing her lips fully against his.

Nico felt his entire body thrum with an electric longing as he tasted the tart cranberry juice that still lingered on her lips. Her fingers curled tighter, silently begging him to move closer, to give her more. He slid his tongue over the seam of her lips and she parted them, welcoming him into the heat of her mouth. It was heaven on earth.

"Oh! Sorry, it's just—" Anna looked mortified when she realized what she'd interrupted.

Nico withdrew, not sorry at all for kissing Alex, but not willing to embarrass her again after what had happened that morning—well, *yesterday* morning now. Alex gave him a slight smile but then he saw the color in her cheeks as she quickly turned to face Anna.

"Gabe's calling to see when we are heading home, and they're going to be closing down soon."

Nico couldn't stop the feeling of disappointment that covered him like a wet blanket. "That means I should probably make sure Aaron gets home okay."

His friend was leaning heavily against the bar with two other men and a woman in a red bustier and skin-tight leather pants. They were tossing back shots as they celebrated the Raiders' win. He had no interest in leaving Alex's side to spend the evening dragging a drunk Aaron to his apartment and getting him settled inside. But that's what friends did, even at the expense of their own love lives.

"Can I call you?"

Alex's eyes brightened at the thought and her brilliant smile brightened his mood. "Really?"

"Absolutely." He slid his phone from his pocket and handed it to her, his fingers lingering over her hand. "Would ten minutes from now be too soon to call?"

She laughed and typed in her number before she quickly added, "But please don't give it to anyone else. That's my personal number."

"You better believe it, Alex. I don't want anyone else ever getting this number again."

She gasped slightly as she caught her breath and seemed to process what he'd just inadvertently revealed. Nico rose, knowing he needed to go before he made a complete fool of himself over her. He leaned down and pressed a quick kiss to her cheek.

"I'll call you tomorrow. I promise."

Chapter 8

ALEX WATCHED NICO walk away as she tried to will her heartbeat to slow. She didn't dare stand to follow him or she was sure she'd pass out from lack of oxygen.

"Why didn't you get his number?" Fallon shoved the middle of Alex's back, urging her toward the bar. "Go after him."

She shook her head. "I can't do that."

Her denial made her realize just how much she wanted him. Maybe it was the alcohol loosening her up, or maybe she was finally taking her sister's advice, but she'd enjoyed talking with Nico. And the man was hot enough to turn her limbs and her brain, apparently, to mush.

"Why can't you? You like him, right?"

"Yeah."

"Well, he's obviously into you," Anna pointed out. "That kiss was *hot!*"

Alex covered her cheeks with her hand. PDA had never been her thing. She was all about looking prim and proper in public, the way a Radcliffe should. But tonight had been different. Nico hadn't been like anyone she'd ever met, and he made her feel free to follow her heart.

Fallon turned to Anna. "I told you she wouldn't do it."

"Do what?"

"Loosen up," Anna offered.

"You're so tight-laced that you don't know how to relax." Fallon shook her head sadly. "I worry about you, Lexie."

"I'm fine." Alex bristled at the judgment in her sister's tone but even she could hear the feeble denial for what it was—a complete lie.

"You're a workaholic who's so focused on dollars and cents that you're losing touch with your humanity. So have fun." Her sister leaned close. "Go get laid. That man is gorgeous."

"Fallon!"

"She's right, Alex," Anna encouraged.

Alex looked from one to the other, unable to believe that they were both encouraging her to have a one-night stand. "Thank you both, but I'm not going to sleep with him."

"Why not?" Fallon asked and shrugged as she took her seat again. "You must be getting soft. You never used to be afraid to go get what you want." Her sister slid a sideways glance in her direction.

"I know exactly what you're doing."

"Is it working?" The corner of Fallon's mouth quirked upward.

"I don't do one-night stands," Alex reminded them.

"Who says it has to only be one night? It could be a wonderful week or a glorious month. Who knows?" Anna pulled her phone from her purse. "You'll never find out until you give it a chance."

As appalled as Alex tried to sound at the idea, her entire body seemed to hum at the mere suggestion of it. She stared at Nico's broad back, those curls that begged her to run her fingers through them, and those hands with long, tapered fingers. She remembered how those lips had felt on hers. He was the opposite of the men she usually dated—successful businessmen who drove luxury cars, traveled the world, and were too focused on what dating Alexandra Radcliffe might do for their career to even inquire about her wants or desires. Maybe that was exactly the reason she needed to walk over to the bar. Maybe she needed to remind herself that a man could be genuine without wanting something from her.

Alex tossed back the rest of her drink with a grimace. "Fine, but you realize that if I wind up on the front page of the paper tomorrow, it's your fault."

"No one would believe it about you anyway," Fallon promised. "Now, go, before that girl in the red bustier gets her talons into him." She pointed toward the woman in skin-tight pants, knee-high boots, and an overflowing bustier.

Oh, hell no.

Chapter 9

RHIANNA WINKED AT him and Nico quickly looked away. He didn't want anything to do with her. It wasn't just that she had a reputation, it was that she liked her reputation. She was quick to tell stories of her conquests.

Nico saw her lean close and whisper something to Aaron before he frowned and looked over at Nico. Aaron turned back to Rhianna and shook his head but she gave him her best pout. Dread welled in the pit of Nico's stomach as his friend walked toward him.

"Yo, what do you have planned for the rest of your night?" Aaron looked like he'd rather eat rusty nails than talk to Nico right now. "Rhianna wants us—"

Nico had no interest in anything Rhianna might have planned. "Let me stop you right there."

Before he could say any more, he was pressed against the bar as a hand curled in the front of his shirt and sweet curves pressed into him. Nico reached out to balance himself as another hand slid into the long hair at his nape, dragging his face downward.

The moment she touched him he knew it was Alex. Now he inhaled her as their lips met, their breath mingling, the taste of her striking the match of his desire. His fingers curled into the dip of her waist, dragging her against his chest, and she sighed into his mouth as his tongue dueled with hers.

Breathless, she dropped down from her tip-toes and looked at his throat, too embarrassed to meet his gaze. "Come home with me," she whispered.

Nico knew it was probably the alcohol talking but his body didn't care. Every muscle seemed to contract with need and his brain stopped thinking logically. He wanted to go with her—he wanted *her*—but he also knew he couldn't take advantage of her inebriated state.

"Neither of us can drive." The words were a gruff rasp and neither of them could mistake the desire in it.

"I have a car waiting outside."

Ignoring the glare he could feel burning across the bar from Rhianna, he tipped Alex's chin up, forcing her to look into his eyes. "You're sure?"

She nodded, her eyes glazed with yearning.

"Then what are we waiting for?" Nico reached for her hand and tugged her away from the bar.

"Hey!" Rhianna called from where she and Aaron stood watching the exchange. "I thought you'd—"

Aaron waved at him. "I've got it. Get the hell outta here so I can work my magic."

Chapter 10

NICO WAS READY to ravish her in the back of the limo, but somehow managed to (mostly) keep his hands off her during the ride to her house. Besides, Alex was more than a little tipsy. He'd had a buzz when he left the bar, but it faded as they drove, and the minutes stretched into what felt like hours. Her head rested on his shoulder and the scent of her shampoo teased his senses, making his body ache with need. He'd contented himself with stroking her arm from her shoulder to elbow, her warm breath fanning over his chest as he waited to see where she led them once she sobered up a bit. If she changed her mind, he'd simply make sure she got home all right. Then he'd take a cab back to his place where a cold shower would be waiting.

"*This* is your house?"

Nico picked up the keys when they slipped from Alex's fingers onto the tile steps of the porch of her Seacliff home. She giggled as he opened the door for her, resting her weight against him as he held her up with an arm around her waist. Nico tried not to think about the way her breasts pressed against his side, or the way her fingers hooked around the waistband of his pants. His discomfort was a testimony to how badly he was failing. Nico stared around him in awe at the Spanish Colonial that had probably been standing on this spot at the turn of the century. The sweeping entry opened to a staircase on one side, a dining room on the other and, in front of him, a wall of windows showcasing the view of the Pacific Ocean bathed in moonlight. He took a few steps forward, wondering what it must be like to wake up in this home each morning.

Her hand slid around his waist. "I didn't ask you here to see the view."

"Alex, you've been drinking and I like you. I *really* like you, but—"

"You don't want this?" She took a step back, suddenly hesitant.

His hand cupped her cheek. "I do. You have no idea how much I do." He closed his eyes, willing his body to come back under control. "But I'm just not that guy."

She smiled, her eyes smoldering with passion as she stared up at him. "I'm not that drunk. I know what I'm doing."

"Do you?" His fingers traced the line of her jaw. "I'll tell you what. We sober up for the next hour and if you still want this, I'll stay."

"Then I guess I only have one question for you."

"What's that?"

Alex stood on her toes, pressing her lips close to his jaw, her breath fanning over his neck and making his entire body feel like it had been engulfed in flames.

"How do you take your coffee?"

Chapter 11

ALEX BROUGHT OUT two steaming mugs of coffee and slid his across the table. Her buzz from the alcohol was gone but her body still hummed at the thought of Nico's kiss. From the first moment, he'd stirred something primal in her, reaching into her core and making her lose control. The poker face she'd cultivated for business had served her well through all aspects of her life, but it wasn't working now. Nico had a way of seeing right through it, or making it disappear altogether.

"So, what should we talk about?" She lifted the mug to her lips, blowing on it gently as she glanced at him.

What she saw caused her heart to jolt in her chest. The raw hunger in his gaze as he watched her made her freeze with the cup against her lips. And then it was gone, like shutters snapping closed over windows.

"Let's talk about you." He rose, lifting the mug from the table as he made his way to the bay window, taking in the view of the ocean. He glanced over his shoulder at her. "You're not just another suit, like you said. A *suit* couldn't pay for this place, and wouldn't get driven everywhere in a limo."

Her heartbeat stuttered in her chest. She didn't want to

tell him who she really was. She liked the fact that he was here for her, not for the status of her family name or the connections it could offer. "I worked for everything I have," she said carefully as she wandered closer to him at the window. "But I did start off with a good-sized boost most people don't get. What about you?"

"I'm afraid I'm the lowly chef I claimed to be. I grew up working in my family's restaurant and hope to open one of my own someday."

"Well, if everything you cook is as good as that breakfast I had at Eco-Tech, you'll make it happen."

"Hmm," he murmured, looking back out over the water and sipping the coffee. "You're not really drunk, are you?"

"I told you I wasn't. I don't lie, Nico."

"And you still want me here?"

She slipped the mug from his hand and set it on the side table nearby before slipping her arms around his waist and looking up at him. "I wouldn't have asked you to come over if I wasn't certain."

His hands found her shoulders and held her firmly. He didn't push her away but didn't pull her close, either. Alex wondered what was going through his head.

He slid her hair back from her shoulder, the back of his fingers brushing against her jaw, and she wanted to moan at the pure pleasure of his touch. Instinctively, her body arched into him, seeking the heat of his. His fingers moved against her hair and she realized he was pulling the pins out. As her hair hung loose, he tucked the pins into his pocket and ran his fingers through the length of her waves. Tipping her head into his hand, she sighed with sheer ecstasy, the touch sending tingles down her neck and raising goose bumps on her arms.

Without another word, his mouth found the curve of her

jaw, pressing hot kisses along the length of it. Her fingers clenched in the hard muscles of his back, trying to hold herself upright as his mouth ravished her neck. A storm of need swelled in her. She tugged at his shirt and, as if reading her mind, he reached for the bottom of it and jerked it over his head, letting it fall to the floor. She released him only long enough to unbutton her blouse as his hands found her waist again. He pulled her close before his hand trailed up her ribcage to the lacy edge of her bra.

She shivered against him, her nipples tightening in anticipation as his thumb brushed over the lace covering her breast. Her hands splayed over his chest, her back arching as his lips pressed against her collarbone before moving lower. His tongue swirled over the lace and Alex gasped as icy heat shot to her core. Her hands plunged into his curls, drawing him closer to her. His hands slid down her hips, pulling at the skirt as he lifted her up. Alex wrapped her thighs around his waist.

"Down the hall, second door on the right," she whispered, her body trembling as her bare flesh pressed against the muscles of his chest.

As he made his way down the hall, his tongue slipped into her mouth. Alex couldn't get enough of him. She needed him inside her, but also prayed this would last for an eternity. Her hands cupped his face as he entered her room and she slid to the floor. Her skirt was bunched between them, giving him access to her bare thighs. His fingers caressed the length of them, as he pressed his face between her breasts, traveling down the length of her body, tasting every inch of her.

The roughness of his palms against the sensitive skin of her thighs made her throb with hunger. When his hands cupped her rear, he pressed her against his mouth, and she squeaked in surprise. He was gentle, yet demanding. Insistent but yielding. She reached back to unzip the skirt, letting it fall, and Nico moved back up, pressing kisses to her stomach as he reached behind her to unclasp her bra. After sliding it down her arms and allowing it to pool on the floor with the rest of her clothing, he looked down at her.

"You're exquisite," he whispered, his voice raspy with desire.

She stepped away from her clothing on the floor and smiled up at him, her fingertips sliding down his chest to reach for the waistband of his pants. "Thank you. But you're still dressed."

With a flick of his wrist, the pants were unbuttoned and he slid them down his legs, standing before her wearing nothing but boxer briefs and a smile. She stared at him, his erection boldly straining against the material, and licked her lips.

"Alex, I have to warn you that if you do that again, I'm a goner."

They moved together simultaneously, neither waiting for the other. Arms and legs tangled as he carried her to her bed, falling with her onto the mattress.

"Condoms?"

"Nightstand drawer." He moved away and she shivered without the warmth of his body pressed against hers. "Need any he—"

"Got it," he said, his voice strained as he stripped off the briefs and tore open the packet, sheathing himself.

Nico moved toward her and Alex sat up on the bed, her fingers tracing the ripples of his abs, urging him closer. She reached behind him and gripped his butt, pulling him down on top of her as she opened to him.

"Now."

"Alex," he argued, his eyes closing as she arched into him, wrapping her legs around his hips, and he fought for self-control.

"Please, Nico, now."

He didn't argue. With agonizing slowness, Nico slid into her, and Alex felt her body tighten from the inside out. Pleasure coiled in her, threatening to break her as he moved, his body carrying her closer to the precipice with each stroke.

"I can't," he groaned, dropping his forehead against her neck. "You feel too good."

Good didn't begin to describe what she was feeling. Alex was euphoric, her entire being wanting more as she reached for her climax, clinging to him. Nico filled her and his every thrust drove her closer until she gave in to the pleasure and lost herself to the explosion of ecstasy. Her body quaked against him as he plunged into her and came.

They were both still gasping for breath, their bodies slick with sweat, as he raised himself onto his elbows, lifting his weight off her. Looking down into her eyes, Nico brushed a tendril of hair from where it had fallen over her forehead. "Are you okay?"

"Maybe?" She met his gaze and the tenderness there made her want to weep. "I don't know," she answered, honestly. "That was…"

"Incredible," he finished for her.

"Yeah," she agreed, awestruck.

There was a part of her that wanted to insist he leave now. A part of her needed to close the door on this once-in-a-lifetime experience. But when Nico leaned down and nipped her mouth, pressing kisses over her face before deepening them in an erotic dance of lips and tongues, she knew she couldn't ask him to go.

When she felt his erection twitch, still buried within her, desire raged again as if they hadn't just found their release.

Alex moaned softly into his mouth. "So soon?"

He chuckled, the sound vibrating deliciously against her flesh. "Apparently." His mouth sucked at the curve of her breast and her back bowed in response. "This time I want to make love to you in the moonlight."

Nico didn't ask for permission as he lifted her, carrying her in front of the windows where the light of the moon cast its glow over the ocean, and proceeded to ravish her once again.

Chapter 12

ALEX WOKE TO the sound of metal clanging in her kitchen and the delicious aroma of bacon and coffee wafting into her room. Light poured in from her windows where the drapes had been opened wide, and her gaze fell on the view of the ocean. Usually it brought a sense of satisfaction to Alex, but this morning it made her entire body warm as memories of last night flooded her: Nico rising over her, burying himself within her for the first time. Later, pressing her against the wall between the windows as moonlight bathed the beautiful features of his face in soft light as they came together. Then, tucking her against his chest and tracing patterns over her spine while she fell asleep curled in his embrace.

She'd never felt this way with a man before. In the past, she'd focused on the progress of the relationship, and she'd always been in charge, calling the shots and deciding how fast or slow the relationship would move.

But Nico didn't demand anything of her and didn't even know who she really was. Instead, he offered her a choice and gave her as much as she wanted to take. Last night, her mind had succumbed to her body and heart. It wasn't like her. It was as if she had been tossed into the ocean waves outside her window.

"I hear you up in there. Breakfast will be ready in about five minutes," he called, his voice husky, making her entire body throb with want again.

She reached for her phone on the nightstand and realized she'd been too preoccupied last night to remember to take it out of her purse and charge it. Glancing at her clock, the numbers glared back at her, striking a chord of panic.

She was already almost two hours late for work. Caitlyn must be frantic. She'd probably called the Missing Persons Unit by now. Alex jumped out of the bed and tugged a pair of lounge pants and a T-shirt from her dresser, throwing them on quickly. Hurrying into the living room, she jerked her phone from her purse and plugged it in. As soon as she turned it on, it vibrated wildly with text messages and missed calls.

"Shit," she muttered.

"Trouble?" Nico left the kitchen and made his way to her, wrapping an arm around her waist and dragging her to him before covering her mouth with his.

Alex melted against him, unable to resist the brush of his lips against hers, or the feel of his heartbeat, strong and steady, or relishing the warm skin beneath her palm. He smelled like sunshine and cinnamon. Her breath caught at the sudden elation she felt in his arms.

Nico withdrew with a pleased growl, smiling against her lips. "Good morning."

Alex sighed happily. She could get used to this sort of start to her day.

Again, her phone vibrated in her hand. She had to take it, even though she dreaded it. Normally, she ate, slept, and breathed her job, so the feeling was as foreign as the contentment wrapping itself around her heart when she thought about last night with Nico.

"It's work," she murmured.

"Take your call, but keep it short. Your French toast will be ready in just a minute."

Her mouth watered, both from the sweet smells coming from her kitchen and the sight of his bare back and tight rear as he walked away.

Holy cow, I have to get my hormones under control!

"Hi, Caitlyn," she said.

"Where have you been? I've had to cancel two meetings for you already this morning and you weren't answering your phone. Were you in an accident? Please tell me you're okay."

"I'm fine. I just forgot to plug in my phone when I got back home last night."

"Did you forget to come into work, too? Or to call your assistant so she could reschedule your appointments?" Alex pinched the bridge of her nose at Caitlyn's admonishment.

"I'm fine," she repeated, sidestepping Caitlyn's questions. She tried to ignore the dull thud pulsing behind her eyes. "What's on the schedule for the rest of today?"

"You were supposed to meet with your grandmother for lunch—I'm sure you know what she'll want to talk about—and then you have a meeting with Mr. Barker later today to discuss the Eco-Tech deal and your progress with the clients from yesterday's meeting."

She glanced at Nico in the kitchen as he held up a plate, indicating her breakfast was ready. Alex nodded her acknowledgment, wanting nothing more than to spend the rest of her day getting lost in this man again.

Where in the world had that thought come from?

She had work to do, meetings to take. Her business wouldn't run itself. Spending the day in bed with a stranger—albeit a very sexy, talented stranger—just wasn't on her schedule for today.

"Tell my grandmother I'll meet with her for lunch next week and push my meeting with Barker back until two. I'll be in as soon as I shower."

"Wait, you haven't even—"

"Caitlyn, please." Alex raised a hand to massage her temple. "I'll be in soon, okay?"

There was a slight cough on the other end of the line as Caitlyn cleared her throat. Alex knew she'd probably hurt the other woman's feelings but she didn't want to get into this now, not with Nico only a few feet away and watching her.

"Okay. Call me when you're on your way in. I'll have them set up the conference room for you and Mr. Barker."

"Thank you. I'll call when I'm leaving."

She disconnected the phone and listened to her messages before checking the texts. Then she dropped the phone onto the table. They could all wait. At least until she'd taken a couple aspirin for the raging headache she was quickly developing.

"Emergency at work?" He slid into the seat next to her at the table.

Alex shrugged. "No, I'm just late and should have called." She sipped the coffee and moaned as it slid down her throat. "Did you use my coffee to make this? Because it doesn't taste this good when I make it."

Nico chuckled. "No, I borrowed your car to run to the market a few streets over and grabbed a few things. You don't cook much, do you?"

Her stomach rumbled quietly as she cut into the French toast. "I'm never really here except to sleep, shower, and change before heading out again."

His brows arched but he refrained from commenting.

She bit into the sweet bread. "Oh...oh, my! This is..."

She closed her eyes, savoring the sugar and cinnamon as the vanilla flavor nearly burst in her mouth. "Amazing."

She heard the slight clatter of silverware and opened her eyes to see he'd dropped his fork and was staring at her, his eyes gleaming with hunger. It was the same look she'd seen last night, before he'd made love to her.

"What?"

"You're killing me."

"What did I do?"

Nico simply shook his head as he picked up his fork and went back to eating, leaving her to speculate.

"You know," she said, "you should just open your own restaurant and serve just breakfast all day."

"Just breakfast?"

"Well, this is the second time I've eaten your breakfast and both meals have been incredible."

"You should taste my tiramisu."

"I love tiramisu." She smiled over at him. "If it's even half as good as this French toast, you'd be a millionaire in no time."

"Not sure being a millionaire is likely, but having my own place is the plan."

She looked up at him, wanting to know more about the subject he'd barely touched on last night. "Soon?"

"I hope so. My grandfather owned an Italian place and I grew up cooking with him. I'd like to continue the family tradition but with my own style."

"The world will thank you." She stabbed another bite with her fork, swirling the bread through the maple syrup.

Nico nodded and grinned as he reached over to wipe a bead of syrup from her lip with his thumb. Alex instantly froze, his touch sending spirals of heat through her and making her clench her legs together to try and deny the desire he so easily woke. As if reading her thoughts, he brought the digit to his own mouth, sucking the sweetness from it, and she bit back a moan at the erotic sight.

Their gazes locked, yearning rising between them, making her forget her breakfast. Her heart pounded in her chest, throat constricting, making it impossible to speak. Finally, Nico cleared his throat.

"It's a shame you have to go in to work today. I have a rare day off and I'm not sure I'm ready for this to end."

Alex's breath caught at his admission. She wanted him to stay, to spend more time with her and continue this fantasy beyond one night. But it was time for reality to rear its head. This couldn't be more than a one-night stand. As wonderful as Nico was, Alex didn't have room in her life for a relationship and definitely not with a guy like him. She was being honest when she said she was never in her house. Every moment of every day was spent at work, thinking about work, or with her family, usually at one of their charity events.

It was exhausting spending her every waking moment as a glorified dancing monkey—keeping up the show and making it look good. She had an image to portray, one her brother and sister had chosen to ignore, and Nico didn't fit the perception people had for a Radcliffe.

Sadness flooded her, nearly choking her as she rose from the table. "Thank you for breakfast." Alex's voice caught. "And for last night, but I have to get ready to go to work. I have meetings this afternoon."

Disappointment flashed across Nico's handsome face as he rose and took both plates to the sink. "I understand. Maybe another time."

She stared at his back as he loaded the dishes into the washer and wiped down her granite counters. She reminded herself of all the things she needed to accomplish today, of the meeting she needed to have with Barker about the new investors and the plan for Eco-Tech.

But her heart ached at the thought of Nico walking out of her house. Last night had been something she'd never done before, and it had been amazing.

Fallon had been right. She'd spent too much time concentrating on business, and had let the joy in life—the relationships and bonds she'd formed—slip through her fingers in her pursuit to reach the top of the ladder. She might arrive there first, but she would be sitting at the top alone.

Nico turned, tucking his hands into the pockets of his jeans. "Mind if I use your shower before I go?"

"Be my guest," Alex whispered, wondering how he could still smile and look at her so tenderly in the face of her rejection.

As Nico left the room, she made a decision. Would one day really hurt anything? Crossing to the table where her phone was charging, she punched in Caitlyn's number.

"The AR Group."

"Caitlyn, it's Alex. Cancel all my appointments for today. I'm taking it off." Alex disconnected the call before she could hear Caitlyn's questions and second-guess her own decision. It was yet another foreign feeling, but since meeting Nico, she was beginning to like it.

Chapter 13

NICO WAS JUST about to turn off the shower when he felt two slim arms move around his waist. Alex pressed her cheek against the wall of his back and he felt her relax into him, her sigh reaching into his soul. Without a word, he turned, his hands instinctively reaching for her face, tipping it upward so he could taste her. Sweet like syrup and warm as the water sliding over their bodies.

It wasn't supposed to be like this. Not that he was complaining at having a beautiful woman like Alex want him. But it was supposed to be a one-night thing, not the strong connection he could feel building between them, weaving itself tighter with each moment they spent together. She was a woman who was dissatisfied with life, but he wasn't even sure she realized it yet. He'd seen the misery in her face when she'd been on the phone. He'd seen it in her face when she'd mistaken him for Doug at Eco-Tech. She wasn't happy.

And while it shouldn't, especially since he barely knew her, it made him feel empty to see her upset. He got the feeling that Alex wasn't just a "poor little rich girl not getting her way." She was complex and determined. She worked hard, harder than she should've had to, and she was still trying to prove something.

Nico liked her, and even though he knew it would never go any farther than this morning, he wanted to see her smile and wanted to *be* the one who put that smile there.

But he didn't want to make her feel like she had to carry more weight than she already was. Maybe they could just have some fun.

He slid his hands over her rear, lifting her and pressing her back against the tiled wall of the shower. Her body welcomed him as her legs wrapped around his torso. "I didn't realize you were into water conservation."

Nico licked the water trailing down one side of her neck and she shivered against him. A sweet smile curved her lips and her eyes glinted mischievously. "Oh, it's one of my favorite causes."

"Please tell me I don't have to go all the way into your bedroom to get what we need."

"First drawer on the left side of the sink." She leaned forward and bit his lower lip gently.

Nico growled, lowering her as he stepped out of the shower momentarily. "Don't get too comfortable standing." He found the condoms and slid one over himself. "I liked you in that position."

He slid back into the shower, letting the spray of water pound against his back as he lifted her against the wall again. Alex let her head fall back against the tile, sighing as he buried himself into her.

"Good, because I sort of like it, too." Dropping her chin, her face level with his, she looked into his eyes, nearly piercing his soul. "I'm not going in to work today, after all."

Nico felt an odd sense of victory. "Then maybe I should slow down a little."

"Don't you dare," she warned.

Nico withdrew before plunging into her again, eliciting a gasp. Her nails dug into his shoulders. Together, they chased their pleasure to the pinnacle before letting it crash around them in a shower of bliss.

Chapter 14

"SO, WHAT WOULD you like to do today?"

Alex laughed as she pointed at the clock, her chin resting on Nico's chest. "The day is almost over. It's nearly six."

He frowned slightly, and she understood the feeling. Soon, she would have to say good-bye to him and return to the real world, where she was a high-power executive and he worked for a caterer. Theoretically, their jobs shouldn't matter, their positions in society shouldn't come into play, but she knew better. She'd watched the struggles her siblings had faced with their significant others. She didn't have time for that while she was balancing her career. She had a plan and, as the CEO of the AR Group, she couldn't risk letting her heart go down a rabbit trail, no matter how great Nico might be.

He might be The One.

No, Alex refused to even entertain thoughts of falling that hard for a guy she'd just met. She didn't believe in love at first sight, insta-attraction, or any other fantasy nonsense. She believed in facts, numbers, and science. Now, if only she could convince her lust-overloaded brain that this was nothing more than an intense physical attraction brought on by pheromones.

Nico's dark eyes focused on her face as he played with the tendrils of hair tickling her cheek. "We could do dinner."

Alex knew she needed to put a stop to whatever this was before she got any more deeply involved with Nico. The mere thought made her heart ache, squeezing her lungs as she felt the distinctive burn of tears welling. As it was, saying good-bye to him was going to hurt for some time. And the thought of dating anyone else left her feeling hollow. She was going to be searching for a long time to find anyone who could come close to measuring up to him.

But she wanted more time. Just a few more hours wouldn't hurt anyone. "We could go to the Mast."

She felt him tense beneath her. "Seriously? You do realize that place gets booked up months in advance, right? It has a three-star Michelin rating."

"I can get us in," she assured him, shrugging her shoulder and searching his face. He frowned and she realized he must be worried about paying. "I'll take care of the bill, don't worry."

Her comment only deepened the frown lines creasing his brow. She wondered what he was thinking, but didn't ask. There was no reason to dig any deeper, to make letting go any harder. Just as quickly, his stern expression was gone.

"I'll tell you what. Come back to my place and let me make you dinner." She could see the excitement blooming in his face, his eyes practically lighting with an inner flame. He was proud of his skills in the kitchen. "I want to do something special."

Logic pounded in her brain. *Say no.*

The lust rushing through her, stronger than her own pulse, answered for her. "Okay." She rose over him. "Show me something special."

Chapter 15

NICO UNLOCKED HIS front door and held it open for Alex to enter his apartment. It was minuscule when compared to her house. The entire space could have fit in her kitchen but he wasn't about to apologize for not being as rich as she was. He was comfortable in his space and was saving for his future, and he could take pride in that. He had plans for himself and he was getting there, albeit slowly.

"Make yourself at home. Would you like a glass of pinot grigio?"

"Sure." Alex looked around the room, moving toward the back door that led out to an enclosed block of cement that served as his patio. "How long have you lived here?"

"A couple of years." He headed into the kitchen, which was only a few feet away from where she stood. "I got lucky when I first moved here from Oakland."

Nico selected the wine and slid it into the freezer, then pulled chicken breasts out of the fridge. Moving easily around his kitchen, he pulled together the ingredients for chicken piccata, his grandfather's specialty, and went to work. He finished prepping the chicken and pulled the wine out and poured a glass for each of them, stowing a second bottle into the fridge for the meal. He turned to take it to her only to find Alex standing in the doorway, watching him curiously.

"You really enjoy your work, don't you?"

"Don't *you?*"

She shrugged and walked toward him, taking the glass of wine he held out to her. "There are parts I love. The rebuilding and making something that was nothing into something viable. It's like breathing life back into something that's nearly dead. But I don't think I ever hum while I work."

"Perhaps you need to let your hair down."

"That's what my sister keeps telling me." A sardonic smile curved her lips and Nico was tempted to kiss it away. He could almost taste the citrus flavor of the wine mixed with the sweet taste that was all Alex. He turned the subject back to his cooking because it didn't cause the cynicism to light in her eyes.

"I like taking everyday items and elevating them through cutting-edge culinary techniques. The chicken, the butter, the flour...all of it is just basic entities. But together, in the right combination, with the right techniques to take the whole thing to the next level, they can create something that will make your senses soar."

He dropped the butter into a pan on the stove, melting it before adding oil and laying the chicken inside, and explained the steps as he went about them. As the chicken was browning, he threw together a salad of red onion, cucumber, and tomato. He finished preparing their meal, plated the food, and poured each of them another glass of wine.

"Grab the glasses?" He reached for the plates and silverware, setting the plates on the pub table in his dining nook before pulling a chair out for her.

She smiled up at him as she set his glass of wine in front of his plate and took her seat. "Everything smells delicious."

Nico couldn't help but think how much he liked having Alex in his apartment. He slid her chair in and bent down to kiss her neck. "Just know that if you make those sex noises while you're eating again, I can't be held liable for forgoing dinner to take you to bed."

She laughed. "No promises. But I will take your warning under consideration."

Chapter 16

THE PAST TWO days had felt like an eternity. Her lust had overridden her logic again and she'd stayed the night at Nico's after dinner. Not that they'd even made it through dinner. Watching the man cook for her had been an incredible turn-on. But even that was nothing compared to the way he'd undressed her with his eyes, the way his smile reached into her chest and melted her heart along with her reservations.

But it couldn't happen again.

She'd spent the past two days fantasizing about two nights of ecstasy she'd had with a man she needed to forget. A relationship between them simply wouldn't work around the chasm of differences in their lifestyles.

With a sigh of frustration, Alex shouldered open the door of Eco-Tech and stepped out into the haze that hadn't yet burned away. She slipped the signed contracts into her tote and pulled out her phone to call Caitlyn.

The alert for three text messages from an unknown number lit up her screen. Tapping them, Alex couldn't help but smile.

Thinking about you.

It had to be from Nico.

Breakfast crowd just cleared out. The smell of cinnamon and vanilla is making me hungry, but not for food.

Her entire body heated and her face flushed.

I really missed you today. Call me tonight.

She wanted to. She wanted to experience the joy that she felt when she was with him again. Nico made her feel most like her true self instead of this serious, strait-laced businesswoman.

Damn her sister for making her face the fact that she'd turned into an emotionless robot who only thought about work. And damn Nico for being so wonderful. He made her want to turn her back on everything she'd been working toward for most of her adult life. Now that her brother had walked away from the family shipping company and her sister had made it clear she had no interest in it, either, Alex was the only one left to either take over or build another company to keep the family legacy alive.

She looked up as her driver opened the door of her limo. She didn't want to climb into the car only to be chauffeured to her next meeting, the next investor she would woo in order to buy yet another successful company and make millions for people who didn't need more. She had never wanted to get caught on this hamster wheel, chasing money the way her family had been doing for generations before her.

She'd started her company because she'd wanted to help, to rescue failing businesses, to rebuild dreams, but that ideal had become tarnished when she'd begun focusing more on the bottom line than on the people. It had only taken a few days with Nico to realize how shallow her work had become.

"I'm going to take a walk."

"Are you sure, Miss Radcliffe?"

"Yes, I...I just need a few minutes alone. Can you please pick me up at the park in about thirty minutes?"

"Yes, ma'am."

Her heels weren't exactly made for taking strolls along the San Francisco streets, but she needed to be alone with her thoughts to reconcile her wants and needs. Normally, she enjoyed the streets of the city—the bustle of activity, the eclectic mix of old and new, the various cultures making up a melting pot—but today, she was so lost in her own thoughts that the city didn't even merit her attention.

Her phone buzzed in her hand, and she realized she'd been so preoccupied she'd never put it back into her tote. Glancing at the screen, she saw her grandmother's number. Wilhelmina Radcliffe, San Francisco's Most Influential Woman, was the last person Alex wanted to talk to right now, but she'd been ducking her grandmother's calls for almost a week and the woman obviously wasn't going to give up until she talked to Alex personally.

"Hello, Grandmother." Her overly bright cheerfulness sounded fake even to her.

"Alexandra, you've been avoiding me."

Busted.

"I've just been extremely busy with this last deal," Alex fibbed. "Didn't Fallon and Anna tell you I'd be over for dinner this weekend?"

"They did, but you should have returned one of my many calls to explain your absence this week instead of having that girl do it."

"You mean, my assistant?"

Her grandmother scoffed into Alex's ear. "*Assistant?* In my day, they were called secretaries and only a woman who...no." She stopped herself before she got distracted and went off on her usual rant about her outdated ideas of women working, although she herself ran a corporation. "Anyway, yes, that is who I mean. Calling me directly would have been the polite thing to do."

It always came back to appearances and propriety with her grandmother. "I apologize."

"You weren't too busy to go out to dinner."

How in the world did her grandmother find out about dinner with Nico? If Alex found out that Fallon or Anna spilled the beans, she'd return the favor. "He was…a business meeting."

"He? I was talking about your dinner with your sister and Anna."

Damn it!

Alex pinched her lips together, forcefully sealing them to keep from saying anything more. If her grandmother didn't know about Nico, she didn't want to be the one to break it to her. There'd be questions, probably some sort of background check, and too much condemnation to deal with. It was better to just keep quiet.

Not that there was anything to confess.

"Grandmother, I'm sorry I haven't called. It's just been an unusually busy week. You of all people understand what it's like trying to run a business."

Better to pander to her ego and change the subject. *Well played, Alex.*

"Indeed, I do. I'd really like to sit down with you to discuss the shipping company."

Alex nearly groaned at her mistake. She'd played right into her grandmother's hands. "I know, and I promise I'm working on liquidating a few assets to get you more capital."

"Darling." Alex could hear the condescension in her grandmother's voice. "You own an investment group. You're practically sitting on a mint. I'm sure you already have the money to invest in the shipping company."

"That's not exactly how it works. The investors demand ownership, stocks…"

What was the use in even explaining her position? Her investors had no desire to own any part of Radcliffe Shipping. But how could she break it to her grandmother that the family business was no longer a commodity? It wasn't cutting-edge. Radcliffe Shipping was almost as obsolete as horse-drawn carriages.

Unless her grandmother was willing to restructure and find new, innovative delivery systems, the family empire was going to crumble around her and there was nothing Alex could do to stop it. Except throw her own money into it in hopes of buying her time to convince her grandmother to let her find someone else to run it.

"I'll see what I can do. I actually need to go. I'm on my way to another meeting now."

"Hmm." Her grandmother didn't sound convinced. "I could have sworn that we just drove past you on Nineteenth Street." Alex looked up at the street sign a few feet ahead of her. Sure enough, she was standing on Nineteenth.

Shit.

"I have to go. I'll see you Saturday." Before her grandmother could say more, Alex disconnected the call, dropping her phone into her purse.

Tears of frustration burned the back of her eyes. This wasn't the life she'd wanted to build. She was nothing but a well-groomed disaster. Her grandmother wanted money she didn't have to give, she was pursuing a career that wasn't satisfying her, and she was dreaming of a man she couldn't have. She needed a sign pointing her in the right direction to follow.

Then she saw it. The building looked like an old theater, complete with a marquee and pillared entry. A few of the windows were broken but she could see past the cosmetic damage to the good bones underneath. The place was abandoned, but as she crossed the street, she wrote down the name of the agency selling the property. It was rare to find a building like this for sale. Most people wanted to keep their hands on a place like this and satisfied themselves with the guarantee of a long-term lease.

A seed of what could be began to take root. Unlike her usual ventures, where she took something already in place and built upon someone else's foundation, this new one would force her to start from the ground up. She'd have to visualize its future and calculate its profitability. She'd be creating something from nothing and Alex's heart began to race at the thought of it.

She wanted to start humming. She thought about what Nico had said about why he loved his job, and suddenly felt it. She knew exactly what she wanted to do with this building. Pulling her phone out again, she called Caitlyn.

"Call this number and arrange a showing." She recited the number to her assistant.

"Okay, but what is this?"

"It's our new venture."

After disconnecting the call, she pulled up Nico's number. If she was going to start doing things differently and do things she'd always wanted to do, she might as well go all the way. She had to see him again.

Chapter 17

AFTER THREE UNANSWERED texts, Nico had come to the realization that, while Alex hadn't actually said the words, their lovemaking at his place had been her good-bye. So he nearly dropped his phone in the minestrone he was preparing when he scanned her message.

Another day off soon?

Tony Martinelli wasn't exactly the kind of boss likely to give his employees time off, and especially not for a date, but Nico hadn't asked for any additional days off in the two years he'd worked here. Plus, Julio, the other line chef, owed him for taking three shifts back-to-back while he went to Vegas with his buddies last month.

He didn't even think twice before returning her message.

Brunch? Tomorrow?

Nico slid his phone back into his pocket and tried to concentrate on the meal preparation but every second that went by was torture. He barely heard the ticket called out and repeated it back incorrectly, causing the server to shoot him a worried glance.

"You okay?"

"Yeah, no worries." He needed to get his head on straight. He never screwed up orders. It was the one place he could shut out the rest of the world and truly focus.

But he didn't *want* to shut Alex out, and that was his problem.

His phone vibrated in his pocket as he began preparing the meals for the ticket. Now he was going to have to wait until after he finished this ticket to see Alex's answer and that might just kill him. He completed the meal and sent the order out, asking Julio to cover for him as he slipped out of the room and headed for the freezer where he could check his phone.

Your place again?

As much as he hated to admit it, Nico hadn't missed the way her eyes had scanned his apartment and its meager furnishings. He wasn't sure if she'd been uncomfortable at his place or simply unimpressed. What he had suited him: it was straightforward and practical, and completely unlike her extravagant home. He'd worked hard for everything he had and, while it wasn't much, he took pride in it. However, Alex was accustomed to so much more. So much that *he* could never offer her. A fact she hadn't even realized she'd made awkward by offering to pay for dinner.

At first glance, he and Alex had little in common. She was used to the finest things in life and he was accustomed to the leftovers. She had a driver, designer clothing, and a cliff house overlooking the ocean while he had nothing but second-hand furniture in a one-bedroom place. She was upper class and he was a mere plebe, but he was beginning to wonder if the one thing he had to offer her was the only thing she couldn't buy—a way to ground herself in reality—and it gave him an idea.

Nico knew exactly where he would take her, a place where their worlds could collide into an unforgettable date. He responded:

No, I'll pick you up at nine.

Chapter 18

NICO KNOCKED ON Alex's door, fondly remember-
ing the last time he'd been here. When she opened it, he was
struck by two thoughts. First, that she was the most beautiful woman he'd ever seen, and second, that her designer suit
and sky-high heels were not only going to make her stick
out like a peacock in a flock of pigeons, but she wouldn't last
an hour on their walk.

"Hi." Her voice was cheerful. "Come on in. I just need to
grab my purse."

She turned back toward the entry, expecting him to follow but he reached out for her hand, tugging her back
toward him. He wrapped his arms around her and covered
her mouth with his. Nico tasted her, sampling the sweetness
he remembered and letting his hunger for her build again.
Alex melted into him, sighing softly.

"Wow. That was some hello." Her voice was breathy and
seductive.

"These clothes aren't going to work," he murmured
against her lips. She sucked in a breath and he realized how
his words sounded. Nico chuckled, loving the goose bumps
that broke out on her arms. "What I mean is that you'll be
uncomfortable if you wear this where we're going."

"Oh." Alex sounded anxious as she drew back and looked into his face through her lashes. Her gray eyes were still dark with desire, but were tinged with disappointment.

"Don't get me wrong, I love the idea of getting you out of your clothes."

She pressed a quick kiss to his mouth before nipping at his lower lip. "Maybe later. I'm hungry."

Without waiting for his response, she spun gracefully on her death-trap heels and, swaying her hips as if she realized that she made every part of his body harden, she headed for her bedroom, leaving him to follow.

"So, what should I wear since you deem this inappropriate?"

When he didn't answer right away, she glanced back over her shoulder at him, a knowing smile on her lips.

Nothing. I want you in nothing.

"A…a shoe you can walk in…" he stammered. "And maybe something more casual." Her gaze slid over him, taking in his jeans and flannel shirt combo. He grinned. "You *do* own jeans, right?"

The thought of her with denim hugging her every curve was enough to send longing kicking through him again.

"I'll see what I can dig up." She smiled but her eyes gleamed and he knew he was in trouble.

Minutes later, she came out wearing knee-high leather boots, a pair of tight, dark-blue jeans, and a loose ivory-colored sweater that draped off one side, baring just a hint of the golden skin he desperately wanted to explore with his mouth again. She'd left her hair hanging loose and over her shoulders in waves, making his hands itch to bury themselves into them again.

"Better?"

Speechless, he simply stared at her, wondering if he

could convince her to forget leaving the house at all. *Maybe she'll let me fix breakfast instead, so we can make love for the rest of the day…*

He squashed the thought as quickly as it came. Today, he wanted them to get to know each other better.

Rising from the couch, Nico leaned down to kiss her gently. "You look great in both, but trust me, you'll be glad you changed."

She narrowed her eyes at him suspiciously. "Just what do you have in store for me? You're not going to take me out to some remote coastal wood to throw me off a cliff, are you?"

"Nope, but I have a feeling today is going to challenge your trust in me."

"Uh…wait a minute."

"Kidding." He smiled but wagged his brows at her impishly, reaching for her hand and leading her to the front door. "Well, maybe," he conceded. "It depends on how adventurous you feel."

Chapter 19

NICO HAD REFUSED her suggestion to take the limo, insisting he drive. When he pulled into a public parking lot, she assumed they'd be within walking distance from their location, which he still hadn't disclosed, but Alex cringed as she stared at the streetcar clanging to a stop in front of where she stood, surrounded by at least twenty San Francisco tourists. People pushed past her to get to the front of the line to pick their seats and she eyed Nico warily.

"We're riding on that?"

His dark eyes gleamed. "How long have you lived in San Francisco?"

"All my life."

"And you've never ridden the streetcar?" Incredulity colored his tone. He held out a hand. "Trust me?"

Alex took a deep breath, steeling herself for her first foray into the world of public transportation.

"I hope you know what you're doing," she muttered, trying not to touch anything other than his hand as she scanned the worn red seats, unsure whether it was more sanitary to sit or stand.

Nico leaned close, his mouth brushing against the edge of her ear. "That wasn't exactly the bold declaration of confidence I was looking for, but maybe once we get where we're going, you'll change your tune."

Alex felt something in her chest loosen as Nico pressed a quick kiss to her lips. Nico was so unlike any man she'd ever dated. He had a knack for knowing exactly what she needed to hear. Somehow he was able to silence the serious, practical side of her, making her "logical" arguments seem illogical.

Alex eyed the people inside, holding the railings, before taking in the clack and whirring as it crawled away from the stop. Butterflies took off in her stomach, twisting and twirling as the car picked up speed, the buildings whizzing by as they rolled down the street. The ocean breeze tickled her skin, blowing wisps of hair back from her face, as she tipped her chin up with a smile.

When she was with Nico, her otherwise dormant desire to be a free spirit took flight. She was able to set aside the responsibilities of running a multimillion-dollar firm for a short time and feel unfettered. Away from her business pressures and her family obligations, she was free to be Alex instead of *the* Alexandra Radcliffe. Losing herself to her thoughts, she held on to the metal railing, leaning back against Nico's chest, feeling his strong heartbeat against her shoulder. His arm circled her waist, holding her steady, and his hand splayed over her stomach, making her insides flutter.

He wasn't the kind of man her family would approve of. Well, Gabe and Fallon would love him, but her parents and grandmother would say he wasn't part of their circle of influence, that he wasn't worthy. She knew his worth shouldn't be based on his lack of inheritance. Shouldn't his kindness be taken into account? What should matter is that he was pursuing his goals and reaching for his dreams, building a legacy for himself, the same way her family had, so many years ago.

The streetcar shuddered as it came to a stop and Nico's voice rumbled against her back. "This is where we get off."

Alex looked up, surprised when she saw where they'd come to a halt. "The Ferry Building? We're having brunch here?"

"This is the most eclectic collection of stores in the entire city."

"I've been here before—"

"But not with me." He reached for her hand. "And our first stop is Boulettes for brunch."

Chapter 20

ALEX COULDN'T HELP but laugh at the way Nico dragged her from one market to another after brunch. They sampled everything from wine to fish to nuts. Nico described every product knowingly, and it boggled her mind.

When they reached the end of the market, he led her into Gott's for ice cream. On their way out, she couldn't help but feel her heart clench when he bought an extra cone and handed it to a little girl standing outside with her father.

From the dirty smudges on her face and the threadbare clothing they wore, Alex knew they were just two of San Francisco's many homeless, but Nico presented it to her as if she were a princess.

"My lady," he said with a bow, making the child giggle with delight. "Your vanilla with sprinkles." He stood and shook the father's hand before introducing Alex.

"I'm Brad. What's a lady like you doing with a reprobate like this guy?" he teased, nudging Nico with his elbow before laying a hand on his daughter's shoulder. "This is Meredith."

The little girl rolled her eyes. "Merry, I told you."

"Merry," he corrected himself at her chastisement, with a benevolent smile.

"Princess Merry," Nico offered with another slight bow before turning back to Brad. "Any news?"

"Still waiting to hear back."

"How'd that interview go?"

Brad looked sheepish. "I couldn't make it. I didn't have anyone to stay with her since…well…" Alex glanced down at Merry, too intent on her ice cream to know the adults were talking about her. "I tried to reschedule but they said they needed someone right away."

Alex noticed Nico's slight frown. "That's rough, man. Let me know if there's anything I can do to help."

She couldn't imagine Brad's dilemma, raising a child on the streets, simply trying to survive. Brad shrugged but Alex didn't miss the way his eyes misted when he glanced down at Merry.

Alex didn't miss the money Nico pressed into the man's palm, nor did she miss the way Brad's eyes grew somber as he thanked Nico.

Normally, she would have walked by, barely noticing him or Merry, but Nico wasn't like that. She moved closer to him, her hand sliding into his. She was awed by his generosity, even as her guilt gnawed at the edges of her heart. She had far more advantages than he did, yet he was the one who saw clearly. She knew San Francisco was a beautiful city but, like so many cultural meccas, it could also be brutally unforgiving.

Saying their good-byes, they wandered behind the market, onto the dock where Alex leaned over the railing, watching the harbor seals playing in the water below. Gulls circled overhead, crying out as they landed to fight over crumbs people left behind. Alex felt Nico's hands land on her hips, his chest pressed against her back.

She turned to face him, letting her fingers find the solid muscle of his forearms, feeling the tingles of pleasure at touching him. "How long have you known Brad?"

Nico cocked his head to one side, studying her. "About a year, I guess. I come to the Market a lot and he's here almost every day. As you can tell, Merry is his life, and since he lost his wife to cancer last year, she doesn't like to leave him."

"She's not in school?"

"I don't think so. I know they were at a shelter for a while."

Alex tried to imagine what it would be like to lose a parent at such a young age, as well as to be homeless. Nico took a deep breath and closed his eyes. When he opened them, she could see the sorrow there for a man he was barely acquainted with. Nico took a deep breath and let it out slowly, his eyes bleak as he shook his head. He had an artist's heart. He felt things and they affected him deeply.

She slid her hands up his arms to cup his jaw, the rasp of his whiskers rubbing against her palms. "I've never met anyone quite like you."

"We don't exactly run in similar circles."

"And yet, here we are."

He lowered his mouth to hers, his lips brushing hers gently. "Are you sure this is where you want to be?" His voice sounded strained as he asked.

She couldn't help but feel as if they were standing on a precipice, as if he was asking for more of her than she was ready to give him just yet. He knew they were from different worlds but he didn't yet realize how different—and she wasn't ready to tell him yet.

Instead she decided to focus on what they had. Her gaze met his, willing him to read the truth there. "Maybe you're exactly the kind of change I need in my life."

Chapter 21

NICO SHUT DOWN his computer and rubbed his eyes. It had been a long time since he'd tried to cram that much financial information into his brain. Measurements—liters, cups, and tablespoons—were the only numbers he had room for in his head, but trying to figure out how to write up a business plan might just be the death of him.

He knew he could have asked Alex to help him but he held back. After their afternoon at the Ferry Market, something had changed between them. And it made him want to prove to her that he had plans for success. He wasn't all talk. She wasn't the only one who could build a business and he wanted to see the look on her face when he took her to *his* restaurant.

He'd spent every free moment over the past three days putting together the information he needed for the bank. He documented his competition, forecasted his profitability, and detailed how the loan would be spent. When the last *t* was crossed, he leaned back in the chair at his kitchen table. He yawned, stretching his arms above his head and trying to work out the kinks as he waited for the papers to finish printing.

If there was one thing he'd discovered this past week

with Alex, it was that fortune favored the bold. She spoke her mind, asked questions, and got answers. She wasn't afraid to go after what she wanted and it inspired him to take forward steps instead of sitting back and waiting. He'd wasted enough time waiting for more experience, for the money to come in, for the time to be right…

She didn't know it, but she'd changed him.

Nico stared at the picture on his phone, his fingers playing with the edge of the business card in front of him. It was time to make the call and set up the appointment to sign the lease. He was that certain the money from the bank would come through this time. He could almost feel the building calling out to him, could almost see the marquee spelling out the Don, making his dream a reality. He wasn't just visualizing his future—he was willing it into existence.

He hesitated, flipping the card in his fingers. It would be difficult. Even if he quit his job at Martinelli's, could he still continue working as a personal chef, since it was, at least, a steady income stream? Opening a restaurant was a hundred-hour-a-week job—he wasn't going to have time to work anywhere else, no matter what the benefit was. He could ask Lowell if perhaps Mrs. Radcliffe might want him to do breakfast every day instead, which would allow him to open the Don every afternoon and still manage evening service. At least for the first year, and then maybe he could sleep. As long as he made the food he wanted, he would bring in enough income to stay in the black the first year.

Swiping his thumb over his phone and making the picture of the old theater disappear, he punched in the number for the property management company that oversaw the building. He was finally making his dream a reality. And he had Alex to thank for giving him that final push.

Chapter 22

ALEX STARED AT the food containers lining the counter in her kitchen. It smelled phenomenal. She couldn't wait to eat it, but she needed to get it onto a plate before Nico arrived. The knock on the door interrupted her thoughts.

So much for that idea.

Hurrying to the front door, she greeted Nico with a lingering kiss, her hands greedy to touch him again. It had been three days since she'd seen him and talking to him on the phone and by text just wasn't the same as having the living, breathing man near her.

She rocked back on her heels and Nico closed the distance between them. He captured her mouth again, wrapping his arm around her waist and pulling her close. She savored the moment, her fingers digging into the hard muscles of his back.

Nico pressed his forehead against hers. "Something smells good. You cooked me dinner?"

She gave a quick, unladylike snort. "You've seen how empty my kitchen usually is. I ordered food." She reached for his hand, pulling him back into the living room. "Come on, before it gets cold."

"Sit," he said, easing her toward one of the chairs at her dining table. "I'll dish it out." Nico pressed a quick kiss to the top of her head and made his way into the kitchen.

Alex couldn't help but smile at the sudden change her life had taken. She'd gone from hectic, overworked, and stressed-out to relaxed and light-hearted, excited about what each day brought. Nico was reawakening her every passion.

"You think you got enough food?" he called back to her.

"I wasn't sure what you would want."

Nico carried four plates of food back into the dining room. "So you decided to buy the entire menu?" He smiled and sat down next to her. "How was work the last few days?"

"Small talk?"

He grinned and winked at her. "Keeps my mind off how delicious you look. Instead of eating, I'd rather lay you out on this table right now."

A shiver of desire rolled through her, like a wave that was building, threatening to drown her. Suddenly, drowning didn't sound so bad.

His gaze slid over her, igniting the yearning for him.

"Well?" he asked again.

She fought to control her thoughts. Alex licked her lips, trying to focus while he was staring at her like she was the entree and dessert all wrapped up in one delicious package. "I...um, work is good. We've finalized the deal with Eco-Tech and now I just need to streamline some of the procedures."

He took a tentative bite of the mushroom ravioli dish. "Streamline?"

"There are a few practices they have that don't make sense financially." She took a bite of a bacon-wrapped scallop and it practically melted in her mouth. "Oh, these are good."

He shot her a patronizing smile. "You think so because you've never had mine."

"You sound a little cocky," she teased.

"I am when it comes to my cooking. It's no different than you coming in, ready to negotiate, knowing you're going to close the deal. I saw how confident you can be, firsthand."

"Don't remind me," she said with a laugh. "Anyway, we're hoping to save money by restructuring the IT department. The customer service will be transferred, for the most part, to a call center overseas."

He frowned, setting his fork on the table. "You can't do that, Alex. Eco-Tech employs a lot of people in those two departments. Doug will have a fit. His employees are family."

She bristled at his reaction. "If Mr. Kincaid was so worried about his employees, he wouldn't have given up his majority share. He knew this would happen. It's not personal; it's business. Besides, I'm not the only one making the decision. I have to think about my investors."

"I think there are other factors in the mix, Alex."

She stared at him, shocked by his objection. "Excuse me? My job is to figure out how to make the company more profitable, and that includes advising them on how to cut back on frivolous spending."

"It's a person's salary, Alex. Their livelihood. Not a 'frivolous' expense. Not everything's about profitability margins. They need to know you see them as valuable or they'll find a place that does."

"Thanks for your sage wisdom," she said, setting her fork down as she glared at him. "Especially since you've run so many big corporations. I've done this before, Nico. I know what I'm doing."

The muscle in his jaw twitched as he took a deep breath,

letting it out slowly. "I can't say that I have the same experience with investors and big company takeovers like you do. But I can say that I know regular people. If you walk into Eco-Tech and start throwing your weight around, making the employees feel more like numbers on a page than people, you're never going to earn their trust or respect."

"Regular people?" She arched a brow, unable to believe how judgmental he was being. "What's that supposed to mean?"

"It means you've lost touch, Alex. Not everyone lives with an ocean view and drivers. Some of us are just trying to survive, dreaming of a life that isn't even remotely like yours."

"I've lost..." Alex paused, looking down at her hands, trying to regain control of the emotions that had quickly spiraled out of control. This wasn't who she was. She didn't lose her temper. She didn't get angry. She was too prepared and calculating.

She inhaled slowly. "Perhaps you're right, but you don't understand the nature of my business. My job is to make money for my investors, and to make as much as possible. That means trimming what they might see as unnecessary expenses."

"Even at the risk of your empathy?"

"It's not at risk, Nico. At work, my job is to maintain a profitable company. I'm sorry if you can't understand that."

"I understand it, Alex. But that doesn't make it right."

She'd known that this was coming. She'd known that their differences would eventually create a chasm too wide to cross. She'd only hoped that they would have more time.

Alex closed her eyes, blinking back the tears threatening to fall.

"You should go, Nico."

"Alex—"

"Please." She lifted her gaze, locking it on his and squaring her shoulders, forcing herself to slip on the steely coldness that had served her so well in her business. "I think it's time we part ways. I think that this—whatever it was between us—is over."

Chapter 23

ALEX RUBBED HER fingers at her temple, trying to concentrate on her grandmother's ideas about the shipping company.

"So, you see, we need a web presence. Whatever that is." Her grandmother reached a perfectly manicured hand for the crystal goblet of water, sipping it daintily, watching Alex carefully. "Don't you agree?"

"Grandmother," Alex said carefully, "Radcliffe Shipping caters to bulk shipping—containers—not to one-off projects from small businesses. Companies ship their large items overseas by airplanes now, which is causing the trouble you're now facing. A webpage isn't going to help that."

Wilhelmina Radcliffe narrowed her icy blue eyes on Alex, who was seated at the other end of the massive dining table. Alex waited as her grandmother pursed her lips thoughtfully, tapping her finger against the cherrywood table. Few people were willing to risk her grandmother's ire enough to be honest, but Alex felt strongly about this. Somehow, she had to tell her grandmother that Radcliffe Shipping was facing several major flaws. It was going to crumble if they weren't corrected quickly. She braced herself for the scathing retort.

"Then what do you suggest? It seems you have something in mind."

Alex's brows shot up. She hadn't expected her grandmother to request her opinion and was surprised by the rare show of respect. "Well, for one, you'd need to change the way operations are run at the dock. You have more men than you need. They should be working shifts around the clock rather than ten-hour days. But the best option would be to sell."

"What? That's ludicrous."

Several staff members appeared, cutting their conversation short, carrying silver trays with their meal. Alex frowned. "We aren't waiting for the others?"

"Your parents are in Paris, and Gabe and Anna are in Sonoma this weekend." She didn't sound pleased. "And Fallon? Well, who can keep track of that girl? She said something about a mare." Her grandmother shuddered and shook her head. "I'll never understand what she sees in those *animals*."

Alex knew her sister loved her racehorses and had a talent for picking them. Her brother's winery had just been featured in a high-profile magazine. They'd both found success outside the family business, much to their grandmother's displeasure.

"So, it's just the two of us." As the trays were laid before her, Alex thanked the maid, who simply nodded, not meeting her gaze.

"Why do you do that?" Wilhelmina asked with an exasperated sigh.

"Do what?"

"Thank them. It's their job. I pay them to do it."

"Grandmother!" Alex scolded. The maid hadn't yet entered the kitchen and Alex didn't miss her disgusted expression even though she ducked her head to hide it. "There's nothing wrong with being polite. They're still people."

Her grandmother's pursed lips spoke volumes. Alex knew there was no arguing with her. She was too set in her ways.

Alex spooned her soup, and when she brought it to her lips, she was greeted with a complex burst of flavors. A hearty combination of sausage and kale with a creamy texture that soothed her.

"This is amazing. You don't have a chef, do you? Is this soup from one you're looking at bringing in? Because you should hire him on the spot. If you don't, I might have to."

A tinge of regret twisted through her. She'd had a man who wanted to cook for her and she'd let him go. Even worse, she'd ordered him to leave because he'd questioned the way she ran her business. Or maybe she'd thrown him out for another reason. Maybe she'd been looking for an excuse to run away. From the argument, from facing their differences, from the truth her sister had already tried to explain. In her business, Alex was becoming more like her grandmother with each acquisition she made. She'd begun to see the companies she snapped up as made up of faceless masses rather than real people with lives outside their job. Maybe those real people were looking at her the way the maid just looked at her grandmother.

"He's okay," her grandmother said with a shrug, waving her hand at her household manager standing inconspicuously nearby. "Lowell insisted he'd be a good fit."

Suddenly, Alex was determined that she wouldn't become callous. "I'd like to thank him, Lowell."

"What?" Her grandmother sounded outraged. "I told you. I pay them well for their service, Alexandra. There is no need for us to fraternize with the help."

Lowell, her grandmother's staff manager, stepped forward, his hands clasped behind his back. He nodded to her grandmother in deference. "There is no need for that, Miss Alexandra. I will relay your compliments to our chef."

Alex took a deep breath. She didn't need to press the situation, but suddenly, it was important to her. She wasn't royalty to be served by nameless peons. Even though she was raised in a family of means, she'd never been like that. She'd always felt most like herself when she was connecting with others.

Perhaps it was due to Nico's compassion toward Brad and Merry. Or maybe it was because he'd pointed out that she was living with her head in the clouds, forgetting the real world below. Either way, she wasn't letting this matter slide easily.

"There's no need, Lowell." She rose abruptly and crossed the room. Tugging open the kitchen door, she glanced back at them, staring after her. "I'll do it myself."

Chapter 24

NICO BARKED OUT orders to his sous chef, Dylan. The kitchen was a bustle of activity.

"Hey, if you don't grab that salmon, it's going to burn." He rushed across the kitchen to retrieve the pan Dylan seemed to have forgotten on the stove.

And then everything came to a screeching halt.

"Nico?"

Alex's voice sent a chill down his spine. Her gray gaze slid over him slowly, as if she was unable to believe what she was seeing. "Do you work here?"

"Uh…" He didn't know what to say. The salmon fillet sizzled in the pan and he could smell it burning. Rushing to remove it from the heat, he turned the stove off, trying to ignore the curious stares from the kitchen staff. "What are you doing here?"

"Having lunch with my grandmother." She stared at him like he'd grown a third eye.

"Your grand—" Realization suddenly dawned on him. "Wilhelmina Radcliffe is your grandmother? She's the family you talked about. Oh, shit," he muttered, thinking back over their last date. Had he really insinuated that she didn't know how to run a business properly? That she was out of touch? *He*—a complete nobody—had told the granddaughter of the most elite family in San Francisco how to treat people. No wonder she'd sent him packing. This woman had run in circles he couldn't begin to climb to; her entire existence had been marked by wealth and power. She hadn't been born with a silver spoon in her mouth—it was pure gold. Yet, somehow, they'd connected on an intimate level.

She'd known where he'd come from and it hadn't mattered to her. She'd accepted the fact that she was dating down—slumming, for lack of a better word—and hadn't made him feel that way. She'd opened herself up to him, opened her world to him, and he'd pushed her away with his brash judgment.

His big mouth had ruined his chances with Alex, and now, it may have also destroyed his dream of running his own restaurant. If he lost this job, there was no way he could afford the place. Alex held his future employment, or unemployment, in the palm of her hand.

She looked exactly the way she had the other night. Just before she told him good-bye.

Chapter 25

OF ALL THE chefs in the city of San Francisco, what kind of bad luck dictated that she act like an idiot with the one her grandmother hired?

Once she and Nico locked eyes, she squared her shoulders. She was embarrassed but wasn't sure why she should be. "I just came to offer my compliments," she muttered. "I should go."

Alex hurried through the kitchen, unwilling to return to the dining room where her grandmother waited. The last thing she wanted was for Wilhelmina to catch a scent of what was happening.

"Alex, wait."

Nico's footsteps squeaked on the tile floor as he followed her out the door. She didn't turn around, didn't want to see the guilty look in his eyes again. He wanted to work for her grandmother. This is what he'd been after the entire time they'd been together.

He had to have known who she was. She might not have told him who her family was, but the Radcliffes were one of the most recognized families in San Francisco. Their whole relationship had been a ploy.

"Alex, will you stop?" He reached out and grasped her elbow.

She spun on him. "You lied."

"About what?"

"You pretended not to know who I was."

"I didn't lie. How was I supposed to know you were Wilhelmina Radcliffe's granddaughter? It's not like you told me," he pointed out. "If anyone lied about anything, it was you."

"I didn't…" she began, realizing he was right. She'd kept her identity secret from him. "I didn't lie; I just wasn't completely upfront about my family."

"Why not?"

"Were you?"

"Yes, actually. I was." Nico's hands slid up to draw her closer. Alex felt her stomach take a tumble and her entire body seemed to hum with longing. "I'd never hide from you, Alex. You knew exactly who I was." His gaze crashed into hers and she could read his hungry desire there. "And what I wanted."

"You didn't use me to get a job here?"

Nico dropped his chin down and shook his head. "I've been working here for months, Alex. Before we met." He met her gaze again. "You really think I'm capable of using you like that?"

"It wouldn't be the first time it's happened. Or the second, or the third."

Nico's hand rose to cup her cheek and she looked into his eyes. "You know me better than that."

"Do I? What do either of us really know about the other?"

Nico didn't wait for any further argument from her. His mouth covered hers, gently, coaxing her desire to the surface. Her hands clung to his forearms, her fingers digging into the flesh beneath his shirt, and she sighed into him. Wanting what he offered, afraid to accept it.

"Alexandra Radcliffe, where are you?" Her grandmother's voice rang down the long hallway.

Nico took a step back. "You're being paged. Go, be *the* Alexandra Radcliffe. But have dinner with me tonight, as Alex?"

"My place?"

"Sure. I have a meeting when I'm finished here but I'll meet you there at seven." Her grandmother caught sight of her and strode toward them purposefully, her heels clicking on the tile like gunshots. "We'll figure out a way to make this work," he reassured her.

Watching him stiffen at her grandmother's approach, Alex doubted it. But she wasn't willing to give up hope just yet.

Chapter 26

"EXCUSE ME, BUT don't you have someplace else you should be?" Her grandmother cast a disparaging glance at Nico.

"Grandmother," Alex scolded.

"Yes, ma'am, I do." Nico bowed his head slightly and hurried back into the kitchen.

Her grandmother turned to her with a sigh of frustration. "Are you trying to give me even more gray hairs?" She ran a hand over the perfect blond coif, as if willing every strand into place. "Did I just see you kissing him?"

"We've been…" Alex wasn't even sure what to call what they'd been doing. "Dating?"

"Is that a question or an answer?" Her grandmother pursed her lips, her disapproval obvious. "Is that why you wanted to go 'thank the chef' for the meal?"

"No!" Her grandmother arched a brow in disbelief. "I didn't even know he worked for you."

"Well, now that you do, I hope that you'll end this ridiculous relationship." When Alex opened her mouth to argue, her grandmother held up a hand, silencing her. "You are a Radcliffe. Just because your brother and sister have ignored that fact, you need to remember it and uphold our family name. There are standards that we have set in this community. A common cook, Alex? Really?"

"Chef," Alex corrected. "He's classically trained, you know. And I don't care what he does for a living, Grandmother. Nico—"

"You may not care, but I'm sure that your investors do. What would they think about a woman of your stature dating a cook?"

"A *chef*," she repeated, knowing her grandmother was deliberately minimizing Nico's position to prove her point. "And I plan on offering him a position with my latest venture."

"Really." Instead of interest in her grandmother's eyes, Alex saw doubt.

"I'm opening a new restaurant, in an old theater."

"And you plan on stealing my chef?" Her grandmother shook her head, disappointment etched on her barely wrinkled brow. "Oh, Alexandra, didn't you learn your lesson the last time you mixed business with pleasure? I thought we groomed you better than this."

Chapter 27

NICO WALKED BACK into the kitchen to see Lowell, arms crossed and glaring, standing in front of his stove. Ignoring him, he turned toward Dylan.

"Take out more salmon. We need to start over."

"You," Lowell growled. "In here with me."

Left with no option but to follow, Nico met Lowell in his office. He'd barely entered when Lowell turned to him.

"Are you crazy? Or do you not value this position?"

"Mr. Lowell, this position means more than you can imagine."

"Then why in the world would you jeopardize it by kissing Mrs. Radcliffe's granddaughter? Do you have any idea what she would do if she found out?"

Nico had a feeling he was about to find out. There was no way she could have missed the kiss in the hallway when she walked up to them. Before he could answer, Mr. Lowell pressed on.

"Mrs. Radcliffe has a strict policy—employees are not allowed to date. She doesn't believe in mixing business with pleasure. I can't even imagine what she'd think of the help flirting with her granddaughter." Lowell slid into the chair behind his desk with a long sigh. "Look, I like you, I really do, and you're a tremendous chef, but I can't let this go on. I've fired people for far less."

Nico felt a knot tighten in his stomach, crushing his hope of opening the Don. There was no way he could do it without the income from this job.

Lowell ran a weathered hand over his eyes and down his face. His shoulders slumped and made him suddenly appear old and tired.

"I didn't know who Alex was when I met her. She didn't tell me."

"And you didn't recognize her?"

How would he? It wasn't as if he had time to read the local gossip columns. He barely had time to pay his bills between shifts at his two jobs.

Clenching his jaw, Nico shook his head.

Lowell stared at him, hopefully reading the honesty of his declaration. But the staff manager had never been overly friendly to Nico and there was no reason for him to start cutting him slack now.

"You have to stay away from Miss Radcliffe. I'll make sure that Mrs. Radcliffe doesn't fire you, but only on the condition that we never have this discussion again. Whatever is going on with the two of you ends here. Agreed?"

Nico wanted to lie and agree with the man, but he knew he would never leave Alex without an explanation. Which meant that he was thinking about giving up his dreams for a woman who was supposed to be a one-night stand.

Chapter 28

"MR. DONACELLI, I'M so sorry. I'm not sure how something like this happened. There was some sort of delay in processing. Before we could inform the property owner of your lease agreement, his agent sold the property."

"Sold it?" Nico clicked the button to switch to the speaker and slid his phone onto the table next to the open file folder of bank loan documents. He rummaged through to find the lease agreement he'd signed yesterday. "But how is that possible? I have—"

"Well, technically the sale was still pending, sir, and I apologize again. The property has been on the market for quite some time, and apparently it was an immediate, one-time transaction. We didn't receive notice until this afternoon. I'm sorry for any inconvenience this causes you. We have several other industrial properties we could show you."

Nico couldn't believe this was happening. His vision of the Don's marquee began to fade in his mind. He could see his dream slipping away.

"Do you have the name of the new owner?" he asked, grasping at straws. "Perhaps I could contact him."

"I'm afraid I can't give out that information. However,

once the sale goes through, that information would become public record," the property manager offered, trying to be helpful. "We do have a quaint place off Pier 33 on Embarcadero and another near Fisherman's Wharf, although the rent is higher on both."

Quaint? Nico knew that was real estate agent–speak for *small.* The old theater had been exactly what he'd wanted. He was looking for something with history and charm to dazzle clientele.

"Perhaps I could convince the landlords to lower the rent payments slightly for the first year," she offered. "As a way to make up for the trouble this has caused."

"Trouble," he repeated dumbly, feeling slightly numb.

This wasn't trouble. This was full-out devastation.

"When will the sale be final?"

"I could give you the number of the agent, sir. You could contact him directly if you have questions." He copied down the number she gave him. "But I urge you to take a look at these other properties. Neither of them will last long."

"Yeah, I'll call you in a couple of days." That would at least give him some time to try to convince the new owners to let him follow through with his lease.

First, he'd found out that Alex was the granddaughter of his employer, and now, he lost the building for his dream restaurant. This was turning out to be a shit day all around.

Chapter 29

PLEASE ANSWER THE *phone, Alex*.

His silent plea was unanswered when he was sent to her voice mail yet again. Nico knew she was home and expecting him to show up that evening. But he had no clue what he was going to say to her when he saw her.

That's why he'd been calling. He needed to cancel their dinner and put off their conversation for as long as possible, or at least until he figured out what he wanted to do.

His problem was that he liked her.

Yet when faced with a choice between a woman he'd only known for a week and the one thing that had given him purpose his entire life, he wasn't sure he could cast his dream restaurant aside.

The Don.

The name alone conjured up emotions he couldn't contain and memories of his grandfather. He'd promised the man he'd open a restaurant in his honor. And Nico had been working toward this goal for so long, he couldn't imagine walking away from it for a woman.

But Alex wasn't just any woman.

His phone rang, the tone blaring in the silence of the car.

"Alex, hi."

"Hey, are you on your way? I got stuck on a conference call with an international investor."

Her voice made his entire body heat, even as the smile crept to his lips, until he realized what he had to do. "I'm here, but—"

"Oh, then come in. I have some great news for you."

News?

She sounded so excited; he felt like a jerk. "I'll be right there."

Disconnecting the call, he reached for the bottle of wine he'd brought. Maybe it would help to ease the discomfort of this entire matter. Surely she would understand the predicament their relationship put him in.

Alex was waiting for him at the front door, stunning him into silence. She'd left her hair loose around her shoulders and his fingers itched to run through it. Her smile almost painfully dazzling, her eyes sparkling with excitement. He tightened his grip on the neck of the wine bottle, holding the flowers out to her.

"Oh, Nico, these are beautiful."

They don't even compare to you.

He stifled the thought as she turned and headed toward the kitchen, reaching for a vase in one of her cabinets, filling it from her sink.

"So, are you ready for my news?" she asked. Her smile beamed and Nico fought the urge to drag her against him and kiss her. Alex's enthusiasm was contagious and he couldn't help the lopsided grin that tugged his lips.

"Sure."

"I'm opening a restaurant."

The smile fell from his lips and the air shot from his lungs. He couldn't have been more shocked if she'd pulled a gun on him. "What?"

"A restaurant," she repeated, dropping the flowers into the vase and setting them on the counter with a laugh of pure glee. "It's for you. I want you to be the head chef."

She was so excited that Nico felt like he'd missed a vital part of the conversation. She'd never even mentioned a restaurant before. "What are you talking about?"

Alex moved closer, laying her palms gently against his cheeks and looking into his eyes. "I'm opening a restaurant here in San Francisco and offering you the position as head chef."

"But I want to open my own restaurant," he said slowly, still trying to grasp what she was asking him to do.

Her forehead pinched in a frown. "You'd said you want to do that eventually. This way you'd have all the freedom to do it now. And none of the headaches."

"Alex," he softened his voice, not wanting to hurt her feelings. "I want the headaches. And the joy. I want that feeling of satisfaction you get when you succeed and it's because of your own hard work. I want the trial and sacrifices to be worth the feeling of success."

Her hands fell from his face, resting against his chest. She arched a brow as she met his gaze. "I get that. But…" Alex slid into one of the barstools.

"What do you really know about running a restaurant, Alex?"

Couldn't she see this wasn't just something to do on a whim?

She narrowed her eyes. "A business is a business, Nico. Growing them is what I do for a living."

Alex stood up and crossed her arms, clearly stung by his implication that she couldn't run a restaurant.

Yet he was just as offended that she'd assumed he'd be happy to give up his pursuits to work underneath her. "A restaurant is different. You have to have a passion for it, to love it, or it's just going to wear you down."

"I thought you'd be happy about this."

"This is just like before. You're looking at the business and not the people that support it. You're not looking at me. You're looking at the bottom line. I don't want to be someone's cash cow. I don't want to be a project someone tries on a whim."

"Look," she said. "I've thought it through. I have a great location and my investors are excited about the concept."

"Which is what?"

"Well," she hemmed, suddenly sounding nervous, "you sort of inspired me. I want to open a high-end Italian restaurant near Eco-Tech. I found a great location nearby—"

Nico's pulse thudded to a stuttering stop before picking up double time. "An old theater?"

"Yes! How'd you know?"

"You're the buyer?"

This couldn't be happening.

He couldn't have pissed the universe off this badly.

"Technically, AR Group bought it. But yes, we signed the contract a few days ago. I was waiting until it was finalized to offer you the position, but you obviously don't want it."

He ran a hand through his hair, frustrated with the way this entire conversation was turning out. Not only was he being forced to choose between being with her or his lifelong pursuit, but he was being forced to face the fact that he'd lost the location for the Don to her. Mr. Lowell's words came back at him. They suddenly seemed more like a warning than a threat now.

"I already work for your grandmother."

"I see." Alex pursed her lips and arched a single brow,

backing away from him and crossing her arms. "What you mean is that working for one Radcliffe is enough."

"That's not what I said."

"You didn't have to." Alex moved across the kitchen, putting more space between them. "Look, contrary to whatever happened here, I don't usually mix business with pleasure."

If he'd wondered about their relationship, she'd just clarified it for him. She'd reduced him to a business associate who had once offered her a fun distraction on the side. His fingers gripped the bull-nosed edge of the granite counter. Nico had never felt more used.

"Is that what this is? You'll be able to get a little of both whenever you need it? Because that explains a lot."

"Excuse me?" Her eyes flashed angrily at him. "What's that supposed to mean?"

"It means that you're really good at keeping your feelings under wraps so you can compartmentalize people. Now you're trying to put me in a box."

"You're kidding, right?" She shook her head. "Here I thought I was giving you exactly what you wanted, Nico. A restaurant of your own, where you could cook what you want."

"But that's not what this is. You're offering me a job. It's the same thing that I have with your grandmother, only on a larger scale. It would be *your* place, not mine. I'd still have to answer to you."

"Damn it, can't you see that I wouldn't do this for anyone else? I'm doing it because I care about you. I wanted to do this for you and *with* you."

Nico ran his hand over his face, rubbing his eyes. "No, Alex, you're doing this for you. You see me the way you see everyone else in the world. As someone to help build your castle where you sit on the throne, high above us." He shook his head. "I hate to break it to you, but it's going to get lonely on that pedestal. If you don't believe me, just look at your grandmother."

He turned and walked out. He knew that he wasn't only leaving the woman he'd come to care about, but his last chance to make the Don a reality.

Chapter 30

"WAIT A SECOND," Alex yelled as Nico headed for the front door.

"What else do you want from me, Alex? A congratulations?"

"I am opening this restaurant. Stop being so stubborn and take the job."

A bitter laugh fell from his lips and Alex cringed at the sound. She'd never heard him sound this disgusted. "You're so used to telling people what to do that you don't even realize when you're doing it. You can't always be in charge, Alex. Not you and not your grandmother."

Her breath caught in her chest, her pulse pounding so hard she thought he might be able to hear it. Rage burned through her. She was tired of being compared to Wilhelmina Radcliffe. She wasn't trying to live up to what her grandmother had accomplished, she was trying to blaze her own trail with something bigger. Why was she being punished for that?

"Fine. Don't take the job. There are hundreds of chefs who'd love the position. I'm not going to beg you to take it."

"Good. At least now I know that I was right. You see me as expendable."

She threw her hands in the air. "Are you seriously going to walk away from this opportunity? Are you nuts?"

"This isn't the kind of help I want, Alex. I don't want anything handed to me."

"Then what *do* you want?"

"You want to help, Alex? Let me rent the property. I signed the lease the day you purchased it."

Alex sighed. There was no way her investors were going to let this go now. She'd specifically chosen this group of clients because she knew they'd be excited about the prospect. "I can't. The project has already gone too far."

Nico shrugged. "You know, I came here tonight hoping to find my way out of a no-win situation."

"It doesn't have to be."

"When you ended this the other day, maybe you had the right idea after all, Alex." He closed his eyes as he spoke, and when he opened them, she could see the saddened defeat in them.

"Just go." She forced the words through clenched teeth, trying to ignore the painful ache in her chest.

She could see it in his face. He was already pulling away and he had been from the moment she offered him the position.

She should have known better. The last time she'd dated a man she worked with, he'd used her to get ahead in his own career. This time, she picked the one man who judged her for trying to help him do just that.

Chapter 31

NICO THOUGHT HIS day couldn't get any worse. He woke up late, rushed through his morning routine, and saw that it was hailing outside. After dashing to his car, he discovered that his windshield wipers weren't working, but with no other mode of transportation, felt he had to make it work.

It hadn't gotten any better at the restaurant, either. Martinelli had somehow found out he'd taken the day off for a date and had ripped him a new one, threatening to fire him if it happened again. He probably would have given his two weeks' notice on the spot, but now, without a property to lease, there was a good chance his plans for the Don were going to fall apart. He couldn't quit. Not until something else came up for lease in the same price range as the theater.

Later that afternoon, he ran through the back door into the Radcliffe kitchen, praying Lowell was busy somewhere else in the massive house. He crashed into the man and knocked him backward.

"Mr. Donacelli, I'm going to assume that you have a good reason for being late, and for tearing through the kitchen like a wild animal."

"I'm sorry, Mr. Lowell. I had car problems and the storm has made travel slow going. I didn't want to be late."

Lowell pursed his lips. "That is hardly an excuse." He waved a hand toward the staff lockers. "Go, change. See that this doesn't happen again."

"Yes, sir," Nico muttered.

"Mr. Donacelli," Lowell called, halting Nico mid-step. "Am I correct to assume that you took care of the matter we discussed yesterday?"

"You are."

"Which means…"

"It means that there are no conflicts of interest when it comes to me working for the Radcliffe family."

Lowell twisted his mouth to one side, and his eyelids lowered. Then he gave him a quick nod and disappeared down the hall to his office.

Nico arrived back in the kitchen where Dylan was already prepping the evening meal. Dylan glanced up as he entered and gave a low whistle.

"You look like you haven't slept all week. Wanna talk about it?"

"Not really."

"Just because I like guys doesn't mean I can't understand women troubles. Relationships are the same either way, you know."

"I said I'm fine. I just have a few big decisions I have to make. Why don't you chop the vegetables for the salad while I start the veal?"

Nico could make a veal scaloppini in his sleep, which gave him the mental space to figure out what he was going to do. The rug had been pulled out from under him and he wasn't sure what to do now. He couldn't get his loan without a location, and Alex had made it clear she wouldn't lease him the property. Somehow, he'd managed to lose the restaurant and the woman of his dreams in one fell swoop.

And why was it that the thought of losing Alex, not the Don, was the one tearing him up inside?

Chapter 32

ANNA THREW HER arms around Fallon and Alex's shoulders. "I can't believe the wedding is so soon. It felt like it was months away and now it's right around the corner."

"Which is why we need to get this decision finalized soon," Fallon pointed out. "What about this one, Alex?"

"Hmm?" She wasn't even paying attention as the two women combed through the bridesmaid dresses the stylist had brought over.

"Are you even listening?"

"Not really." She slumped onto the pillowed bed, clasping her hands between her knees. "I'm sorry. I'm just…" She shrugged. "I don't know."

"Do you see anything you like?" Fallon slid closer to the couch, holding a gown out to her sister. "I'll let you take first choice of the designer dresses."

Alex waved her hand. "I don't care. Go ahead."

"Wow." Anna planted her hands on her hips and stared at Alex. "Thanks."

"Oh, I didn't mean about your wedding, Anna. I meant about having first choice of the dresses. I'm sorry."

Anna waved a hand, laughing it off, but Fallon studied her sister. "What's wrong? Spill it."

"It's stupid. Don't worry about it."

Fallon crossed her arms, glaring at her sister, looking almost as domineering as their grandmother.

"Fine," Alex huffed. "It's a guy."

Anna's eyes lit up and she drew close at the suggestion of juicy details. "A guy? What guy?"

"The one you met at the bar that night. Nico." Alex didn't want to go into details and found herself searching for the easiest way to explain their relationship. "We went out a few times."

"I knew there was something going on." Fallon dropped onto the side of the couch.

"You did not," Alex argued.

"I absolutely *did*. But dating isn't a reason for this moping. That's *good* news."

"Isn't it?" Anna asked Alex hesitantly.

"Yes. Or it would've been, if we were still dating."

"You're not? Oh, Alex, I thought…" Fallon sighed heavily. "I thought this one might work out."

"It might have, if he hadn't compared me to Grandmother."

"And what, my dear, is wrong with that?" All three women looked up to see Wilhelmina walk into the room.

Alex felt the blush heat her cheeks. She glanced at her sister and Anna, certain their expressions of guilt matched her own. "Nothing," she lied.

Wilhelmina arched a brow, casting an icy gaze over each of them in turn. "That's a nice try, Alexandra, but you have a long way to go to improve your prevarication skills. There is absolutely nothing wrong with being tenacious and hardworking."

"No, there isn't," she agreed. "But—"

"And are we discussing my chef? Because if he is speaking about me that way, there will be repercussions."

Alex felt her stomach drop. She wouldn't put it past her grandmother to fire Nico on the spot.

"We're discussing someone else, Grandmother," she lied, eyeing her sister, silently begging her to change the subject. "A man we met when we went out to dinner last week."

Her grandmother glared at them on the couch. "Well, I should hope it's not the chef. I've given him a tremendous opportunity, working for me." She sniffed haughtily before looking at the racks. "*Those* are the dresses Ella brought? Goodness, you'd think I told her this was a garden party. I'm not sure any of these will work. What do you think?"

Fallon faced Alex and rolled her eyes dramatically.

"I'm going to go call Ella and request she send another rack over. Excuse me."

For the first time, Alex was grateful for her grandmother's lack of technological advances as Wilhelmina marched out of the room.

"That was close," Anna breathed, holding her hand to her chest.

"Yeah," Fallon agreed. "Except now we just went from fancy to formal for this party." She shrugged, turning back to their original conversation. "Alex, you've been a different person ever since that night at the bar. You haven't gone to the spa once in the past few weeks."

"Caitlyn told me you bought *her* a coffee the other day."

"I was being nice," Alex said as she threw her hands into the air.

"And that you asked about hiring veterans?"

Alex shrugged, the image of Brad and Merry making her eyes water.

"What did this guy do to you?" Fallon's eyes glinted mischievously. "Maybe you should ask him to do it again."

"Stop it, Fallon. Leave her alone," Anna scolded as she slid to Alex's other side. "What happened?"

"I don't know." Alex shrugged, feeling completely unsure where she and Nico had gone wrong. Maybe their relationship was exactly what she'd expected—a wildfire that burned out too quickly. "The short version is that he's Grandmother's personal chef and I offered him a job at the new restaurant space I bought. One minute everything was great. The next, he was walking out."

"What new restaurant?" Fallon asked, shocked.

Anna sighed. "Oh…oh, no, Alex. You didn't."

"What restaurant?" her sister repeated.

"What's wrong with offering him the job?" Alex asked. "He'd have been the head chef, running the place however he wanted."

Fallon reached for her sister's face, forcing her to meet her gaze. "One, what restaurant? And two, have you ever tried dating someone who worked for you?"

Alex jerked her chin back. "Look, I found a great location for a restaurant and Nico inspired me. I got the investors involved and they are ready to put some big money into it on my recommendation. I wanted him to be the head chef. He, apparently, didn't like that idea and walked out. But he told me he wanted to start his own restaurant."

"Oh." Anna looked away sheepishly. Alex looked from her to Fallon. Her sister crossed her arms and stared at Alex.

"Well, what the hell did you think would happen, Alex?" Fallon asked.

"I thought he'd be thrilled."

"You really thought he'd be thrilled you stole his idea for your own and offered him a tiny piece of the pie?"

Alex looked at Anna for confirmation of Fallon's assessment. She shrugged. "She's right, Alex. It would be your place, not his. He would be an employee—not the owner—and that brings a certain dynamic to it that isn't exactly conducive to relationships." She glanced at Fallon. "Well, most of the time. But for Gabe and me, things went smoother once he remembered I was in charge of the floral shop and I let him take care of the vineyard."

Fallon patted Anna on the arm. "No offense taken. It's hard. Travis and I still butt heads on issues. We've agreed that when it comes to the horses, I defer to his knowledge, and when it comes to money, he defers to me. You have to find a balance."

"Did I steal Nico's idea?" Alex asked.

"Well…"

"Oh, I did." Alex slapped a hand over her eyes. "What is wrong with me?"

"Nothing," Anna assured her. "Talk to him. Apologize. You can fix this."

Chapter 33

Meet me at the old theater on 19th. Please.

Nico stared at the message. It was the first one he'd received from Alex since he'd walked out of her house. He wasn't sure how to respond. He wanted to see her. It hadn't taken him long to realize how much he missed her.

He didn't just miss her. He wanted her. Needed her. For the first time in his life, Nico realized he cared more about her than he had anyone else.

That's love, idiot.

Love? Could he possibly love Alex? As much as he didn't want to admit it, he was already at that point. But she'd made sure to avoid him when she was at the Radcliffe mansion and he wasn't about to lose his job pursuing a woman who wanted nothing to do with him.

He'd been naive to want more with her. They were too different. He'd known it from the first moment he'd seen her at Eco-Tech. But he'd let himself ignore reality and fall into the fantasy where he could have it all—the woman and his dream. Instead, he was no better off than when he'd first seen her walk into that conference room. And now, he couldn't ignore the hollow ache that filled his chest each time he saw her.

Nico?

He could almost hear the soft husky sound of her voice saying his name. His entire body hummed with desire remembering the last time she heard him say it that way.

"Shit," he muttered. What harm could it do to meet with her? To find out what she wanted? To see her one last time. His fingers moved over his screen, sending her back a message: Tomorrow morning?

Her response was immediate. Perfect.

Chapter 34

ALEX SHOOK HER hands at her side, trying to rid herself of the nervous trembling. She hadn't felt this worried since her very first deal. She mentally recited the speech she'd been rehearsing for days. It sounded so unemotional, as if she were talking about someone else. She needed something more; Nico deserved more. He needed to know the truth—that she cared about him more than any deal.

Staring at the floor, Alex paced the main lobby that would start renovations next week. Soon, the tattered burgundy carpeting would be replaced with hardwood planks shipped from Italy.

"Nico, I never meant to steal your future, your dreams," she said under her breath. "It was yours to build and never mine to offer."

She frowned as the words came out of her mouth. They didn't sound strong enough, vulnerable enough.

"You've given me so much in such a short time, you've changed me for the better, and I wanted to thank you, to give you the one thing you wanted most. I didn't realize that I was taking away one of the things I love most about you—your sense of pride from working hard to achieve your goals."

"One of the things you *love*?"

Alex froze, rooted to the ugly carpeting, afraid to look up and see anger in Nico's expression. Or worse, disinterest.

"Nico," she whispered before taking a deep breath. Her heart was pounding in her chest. Against her better judgment, she looked up at him. "I'm sorry."

"Alex." He started toward her, his eyes filled with the same regrets she was feeling.

She held up a hand. "No, wait! Let me finish. My plans went completely awry but I had the best intentions and I understand your reaction. I need to learn to express my support and appreciation for good talent better. You're the reason this place is going to be a success. It has nothing to do with me. I want to change the way I look at life and at people."

A knowing smile curved his lips, making a slight dimple appear in his cheek. "I could help you with that. Whenever I'm with you, that's the type of woman I see."

The breath she hadn't realized she'd been holding burst from her lungs in a rush. "I was hoping you'd say that."

"Can I come kiss you now?"

"Not yet." She hurried over to retrieve the file folder she'd laid on what had once been a ticket counter and set it in his hands. "This is for you."

"What is it?"

"Look at it."

Nico opened the folder and stared at the documents inside, flipping between the pages before his gaze leapt back to hers. "I thought you said you couldn't convince the investors to do this."

Alex nodded. "I can be pretty convincing when I really want to be."

"Alex?"

She could hear the doubt in his voice. The last thing she wanted to do was hide anything from him. "The deal didn't work out," she said with a shrug. "So I bought the property. The only other investors are my brother and sister, neither of whom want to be involved. All that lease needs is your signature. Any renovations you want can begin as early as next week and we'll pay for them."

"Are you serious?" The shock in his face was beginning to worry her.

She held up her hands, palms facing him. "The Don will be what you want it to be. You run it entirely on your own. It's your dream. I will be completely hands off, other than taking care of the property."

"What if I don't want your hands off?" His voice was a husky rasp as he moved closer.

A sizzle traveled through her limbs as he reached for her hand, tugging her into his arms. Her hands landed on his biceps as he wrapped his arms around her waist.

"Then you'll need to tell me where you want me to put my hands."

"We'll figure that out as we go." He leaned forward, his lips brushing against hers. Yearning swelled within her. "You really think we can do this together?"

His hand slid up to cup the back of her head and she sighed in the sheer pleasure of his touch. "I know we can. But from now on, we work as partners."

He thrust out his hand. "Put 'er there, partner."

"Screw that." She reached for his hand and yanked him forward, wrapping her arms around his neck and covering her mouth with his.

His kiss was hot and feverish with denied longing.

After he pulled back, he murmured, "I've never signed a deal that way."

Her laughter bubbled out and he pressed a kiss to her forehead with a smile he didn't bother to hide.

"I think I'm falling in love with you, Alex."

She looked up at him. "Really?"

He nodded, lifting a hand to cup her cheek. "I know it's fast, but—"

"Thank goodness I'm not the only one."

He laughed. "So, where does this leave us?"

"Partners," she suggested.

"Partners," he promised. "In everything."

Chapter 35

"NICO, WHERE ARE we going? We should be at Anna and Gabe's rehearsal dinner by now." Alex tried to lift the blindfold he'd insisted she wear.

He laid his hand over hers, not allowing her to remove it. "We're not going to make it."

"What are you talking about?" She reached for the blindfold again.

"Trust me."

He'd been planning this moment for the past three months. Twelve weeks of renovations. Ninety days of working side by side, perfecting their partnership in both the business and their outside life.

He'd quit his position at Martinelli's and moved into her house, getting up early each morning to make her breakfast before she headed to the office. She'd spent most of her time restructuring Eco-Tech to increase profitability while keeping the company an employee-friendly technology firm.

As a result, stock prices had skyrocketed. Other firms approached her for funding and new investors were ready to throw their money behind her projects, includ-

ing the transition of Radcliffe Shipping to an air-sea-
and-land operation. Somehow, she'd managed to convince her grandmother to let go of the reins enough
to let Alex recruit a new CEO to take charge, proving
Alex's theories and breathing new life into the family
legacy.

Alex had found her niche and, while she credited
Nico, he knew better. He'd simply given her the push
she'd needed to open herself to being vulnerable. She'd
released her grasp on the bottom line and allowed herself to become the intuitive woman he saw each night.
And it was a beautiful sight, watching her metamor-
phosis.

He unlocked the front door of the Don, which had
transformed. Her Louboutin heels clicked on the im-
ported plank flooring as he led her to the table set in the
center of the room. After seating her, he lit the candles
in the center.

"Okay, you can take it off now."

She slid the blindfold over her head and looked
around the room, gasping slightly before smiling at the
work he'd done. This was the first time she'd seen the finished product.

"Do you like it?"

Marble pillars separated several rooms, blending with
the traditional murals on the caramel-colored walls as the
candlelight flickered. Greenery gave the entire room the
feel of dining al fresco. The room felt refined and elegant.

"I love it. It's incredible."

He ran a nervous hand through his shorter hair, still
unaccustomed to the style. He knew it gave him a more
professional appearance. As if reading his thoughts, Alex

winked at him. "I miss your curls, but it looks good on you. You'll look amazing at the opening Monday."

"I love you."

She smiled at him. "I love you, too."

Relief filled him. He had no doubts that what he was about to do was the best idea of his life. Reaching for the bottle of champagne he'd arranged on the table, he opened it with a loud *pop*. "Let's toast."

"To the opening." She reached for her glass and he felt his stomach tighten. She held it up for him to fill and frowned suddenly. "What—"

She reached into the crystal champagne flute, her fingers trembling, and withdrew a one-carat, princess-cut solitaire.

It wasn't big, but it was the best he could afford. She deserved so much more, and he would give her everything he had.

Nico reached for her hand, setting the bottle on the table, and dropped to his knee. "Alex, I had this entire speech planned for tonight but I can't remember a single word of it. But I do know that I love you so much that you take my breath away. Will you marry me?"

She stared at him, her shaking fingers raising to her mouth. "Nico."

"I know I can't give you big houses and fancy cars. I can't even give you a big ring."

"This ring is the only one I want."

"Are you really going to make me ask twice?"

She laughed before cupping his face between her fingers. "Yes."

"Yes, I have to ask twice, or yes, you'll marry me?"

"Both!" She pressed her lips against his, sharing his breath of relieved delight.

"Alex Radcliffe, you're my partner at the restaurant and in the outside world. Say you'll be my bride and my partner for the rest of our lives?"

"Why, Mr. Donacelli, are you sure you want to mix business with pleasure?"

"Every damn day, as long as I live."

ABOUT THE AUTHOR

T.J. Kline was training horses and competing in rodeos at fourteen, but writing romance has always been her first love. She is the author of the Rodeo series and the Healing Harts series.

JAMES
PATTERSON
RECOMMENDS

#1 *New York Times* Bestseller

JAMES PATTERSON

Suzanne's Diary for Nicholas

SUZANNE'S DIARY FOR NICHOLAS

This is one of my favorite romance novels I've written, perhaps because it hits so close to home. When my son was younger, my wife kept a diary for him as a keepsake of our memories as a family. This became the inspiration for *Suzanne's Diary for Nicholas,* in which a new mother named Suzanne writes a love letter to her baby son, Nicholas. In it, Suzanne pours out her heart about how she and Nicholas's father met and about her hopes for marriage and family. But she could never have predicted that her diary would be read by a woman named Katie Wilkinson, who realizes that the perfect man she so desperately loves may also be the same husband and father described in the diary....

JAMES PATTERSON

Sundays at Tiffany's

and GABRIELLE CHARBONNET

SUNDAYS AT TIFFANY'S

Love stories are harder to write for me because you can't rely on suspense and adventure to make them fast-paced, engaging reads. But I always want my readers to have a good time, so if I'm going to write a love story then you can be sure it'll be a page-turning love story. That's exactly what I hope readers will get from *Sundays at Tiffany's*. In it, Jane Margaux is in love with the perfect man. Michael is handsome, comforting, and funny. There's only one catch—only she can see him. An invisible friend who left Jane on her eighth birthday, Michael is back over twenty years later for reasons neither of them knows…yet.

I'd like to recommend a new reading experience to you. It's called BookShots.

BookShots are a whole new format of books—they're 100 percent story-driven, no filler, no fluff, and always under $5.00.

And, at 150 pages, they can make reading more convenient. They can be read in an evening, on a commute, while exercising, even during breaks at work on a cell phone.

So welcome to BookShots and the reading revolution.

JAMES PATTERSON PRESENTS

The
Weekend
Wife

They've got 48 hours for love....

BETH CIOTTA

BOOKSHOTS
Flames

THE WEEKEND WIFE

The Tuscan Hills. An olive grove. Dinner, outside on a terra cotta terrace. In my mind, these are perfect ingredients for a budding romance. So when Megan Rooney agrees to vacation to Italy with Nick Walker—as his fake wife—in order to fulfill his dying grandmother's wish, it's no surprise that she finds herself falling in love. But it's too bad they only agreed to play pretend for the weekend....

James Patterson's
BOOKSHOTS
Flames

The
McCullagh Inn
in Maine

New York Times Bestseller
Jen McLaughlin

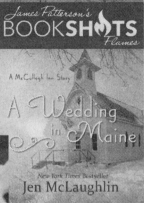

James Patterson's
BOOKSHOTS
Flames

A McCullagh Inn Story

A Wedding in Maine

New York Times Bestseller
Jen McLaughlin

JAMES PATTERSON PRESENTS

A McCullagh Inn Story

A Princess in Maine

New York Times Bestseller
Jen McLaughlin

BOOKSHOTS
Flames

THE McCULLAGH INN SERIES

Picture this: A quiet country inn in Maine, complete with a roaring fire and warm home-cooked dishes at every meal. Sounds like a typical Patterson, right? Wrong. Except once you settle into Jen McLaughlin's sweet town of Hudson, Maine, you'll be thrown into a riveting, twisty mystery in each book. Because that kind-faced innkeeper? She's got a dark past. And it lurks at every corner, ready to attack....

50

*She's got a sexy
little lust list. . . .*

Hidden
Desires

Including a
BONUS
Forever title!

JESSICA LEMMON

BOOKSHOTS
Flames

50 HIDDEN DESIRES

It may seem like Holly Larsen has it all—the lavish lifestyle, the lucrative dream job, the supportive family—but she doesn't. Personally, I know that none of those things can amount to anything when you don't have someone to love. And finding a soul mate is hard for Holly, whose heart is set on Dalton Thomas, even though he's completely off limits because he's her brother's best friend. At her wits' end, Holly does something remarkably daring by propositioning Dalton with a sexy little lust list.

K